BINDI

Samantha was waiting for Harold to collect her. She had been waiting for nearly two hours, unable to do any more work, anticipating his arrival and the things they would do.

She rose to meet him as he came in, turning up her face to be kissed, for all the world like any suburban housewife welcoming her husband back from a hard day at work. When the kiss ended, Harold produced a key to her leg-irons from his pocket. 'Freedom at last!' Samantha exclaimed.

BINDING
PROMISES

G C Scott

This book is a work of fiction.
In real life, make sure you practise safe, sane
and consensual sex.

First published in 2006 by
Nexus
Thames Wharf Studios
Rainville Rd
London W6 9HA

www.nexus-books.co.uk

Typeset by TW Typesetting, Plymouth, Devon
Printed and bound by Clays Ltd, St Ives PLC

A catalogue record for this book is available from the
British Library.

ISBN 0 352 34014 2

The paper used in this book is a natural recyclable product made
from wood grown in sustainable forests. The manufacturing
process conforms to the regulations of the country of origin.

Contents

You'll notice that we have introduced a set of symbols onto our book jackets, so that you can tell at a glance what fetishes each of our brand new novels contains. Here's the key – enjoy!

cp (traditional)

cp (modern)

spanking

restraint/bondage

rope bondage/hojojutsu

latex/rubber/leather/enclosure

fem dom

willing captivity

medical

period setting

uniforms

sex rituals

1

Selling a Flat

'I want you to tie me up,' said the attractive woman who was buying his flat. She spoke in a steady voice, but there was an underlying tension in her, as if she had finally screwed up the courage to make her unorthodox request to the stranger who was selling the flat. She awaited his reply with agitated breathing and a certain defiance.

And so Harold Woods (vendor) found himself unrolling the ball of twine he carried among his tools while Samantha Waters (buyer) undressed down to her stockings and suspenders. On the way she paused several times for effect. At the dress-unzipping stage, for example, she reached around behind her to undo the long back zip of her green dress. Harold admired her skill, and blessed whatever gods there might be that there were attractive women graceful enough to manage this manoeuvre, and that he didn't have to master it himself. And then there was the taking-off-the-pants stage. Samantha's dark-brown hair was short and crisply curled. Her pubic hair was even darker and curlier. And there was quite a lot of it, hiding the pink labia between her thighs while promising much more. The effect on Harold was . . . bracing. Samantha eyed his erection with a certain satisfaction at still being able to produce that effect at the age of 38.

When the pants had joined her dress on the carpet, Harold admired her long, full legs sheathed in sheer nylon. A leg-man, he was glad that his unexpected companion had the kind of legs he liked: not like those found on most girls – and all fashion models. He appreciated the touch of stockings and suspenders. Most women would have worn tights. Stockings spoke of a certain . . . availability. Or willingness. Or both.

Samantha looked at the length of cord already unwound and caught her breath in anticipation. 'Tie me really tightly,' she told Harold as she unsnapped her bra to reveal healthy, firm breasts with erect nipples and dark areolae, crinkly with arousal. She let the bra fall to the carpet and turned her back, bringing her hands together behind her.

'Tie my hands,' she ordered, needlessly. Her gesture spoke louder than words ever could have.

'You do this often?' Harold asked as he cut a length from the ball. 'I mean,' he faltered, 'it's not every woman who wants to be tied up, is it?'

'I suppose not,' Samantha replied. 'But I do. Have you ever done this before?'

'No,' Harold said.

'Then follow my directions, and next time you'll know what to do. Tie my wrists together,' she ordered. 'Tightly.' She held her wrists together, hands palm to palm while Harold wrapped several turns of cord around them. 'Tighter. Pull it tighter,' Samantha ordered.

He pulled until the cords bit into the flesh of her wrists. 'All right?' he asked.

'Yes. Now tie a knot where I can't get at it with my fingers.' She lifted her bound wrists away from her bottom. 'Between my wrists and my bottom,' she directed him. 'That way I won't be able to reach it with my thumbs and forefingers. Don't let the cord go slack.'

Harold did as she directed, tying in fact two knots, one on top of the other.

'Now wrap it around several more times,' Samantha directed. 'Keep it tight. Tie another knot now.'

He did.

'Now take the cord around between my wrists a few times and cinch it tight.' The cords tightened even more, biting deeper into her flesh.

'Sure you're all right?' he asked. 'I don't want to hurt you.'

'I'm fine,' she replied. 'As long as I keep the insides of my wrists out of the way of the cord I'll be okay for hours. Days, even.'

'You've been tied up for days?' Harold asked in surprise.

'Not yet. It's one of my enduring fantasies. It would be wonderful. Wonderfully exciting, I mean. I would love every minute of it.'

Harold gave a final tug to the cord and tied another double knot above the cord and between her wrists. He was reasonably sure she could not reach the final knot.

'Good,' Samantha told him, trying – and failing – to find any slack in her bonds. 'I can't reach any of the knots, either,' she said approvingly. 'The excitement lies in knowing that I can't get free on my own,' she told him by way of explanation. 'It's no fun if I can free myself. It's one of the disadvantages of human anatomy – for me, I mean – that a person can't tie herself up effectively.'

'You do this yourself?' he asked in surprise.

'It's not easy to find someone to do it for me,' Samantha replied. 'I can manage to tie my feet and legs together, but with the hands I have to have help. When I'm alone I sometimes use handcuffs, but that means having the key handy so I can free myself. It's not the same as being completely helpless.'

3

Harold took in her explanations with a certain doubt. But there was no denying that she was excited, or that the sight of her excited him as well. 'Have you ever thought of leaving the key where you can't get at it? With a friend, or hanging out of reach?'

'No, I've never had the nerve. Or the friend. But if I did, I'd need to know that someone was going to come to check on me even if they didn't let me go. I'll do it when I find someone I can trust not to flap and not to gossip.'

'Do you carry the handcuffs around with you?'

'Not always. Not today. Finding you here with the cord was a bit of luck.'

Harold thought so too.

Samantha spoke again, 'Now use some more of that lovely cord to tie my arms together. There, just above my elbows. Pull it tight.'

Harold pulled.

'Tighter. Make my elbows touch.'

'Isn't that too tight?' Harold asked.

'No. I mean it. Try to make them touch. It will make my breasts stand out nicely when they do. I've seen . . . pictures,' Samantha said vaguely.

Harold pulled, and Samantha's elbows nearly touched behind her back. She grunted as he tried to make them touch, but he had to give up when there were still some five or six inches between them. 'Maybe next time,' she said. 'It will take some practice and exercise.' Harold thought about the 'next time.' Did she intend to see him again? Her full breasts did indeed stand out very nicely indeed. He had never seen a mature woman with her hands and arms bound, or her breasts standing out quite so far as a result. He liked the effect.

Samantha turned to face him, her breasts jutting out and her shoulders pulled back by the cords around her elbows.

4

'See?' she asked. Harold saw.

'It's usually at this stage that my imaginary companion wants to slip his cock into me and fuck me stupid.'

Harold could understand that.

'Your cock looks ready,' Samantha remarked, 'but if that's what you intend, I'd like you to have a bit more patience. Use some more of that cord to bind my breasts, and then you can do whatever you like with me.'

Extraordinarily, she seemed to mean what she said – something not many women did, in his experience. More usually they meant 'do something exciting but not too startling to me'. 'How?' he asked. 'I mean, do you want me to tie them together, or what?'

The idea clearly baffled him, and so Samantha instructed him in the art of breast-binding. 'Tie some of the cord around the base of each of my breasts, against my chest. Pull it tight and make it bite into me so that it won't slip off.'

Following her instructions and nods of encouragement, he knotted the thin cord around each of her breasts and pulled it tight. Samantha's breasts, already forced out and upward by the cords around her elbows, jutted even more aggressively, if that were possible. And they looked so much more erotic with the cords biting into the sensitive flesh. Harold leaned forward on impulse and took one of her engorged nipples between his teeth. He nipped gently, and Samantha moaned in pleasure.

'Use your hands on the other one,' she commanded in a harsh whisper as he bit her again.

Harold cupped her breast in one hand as he teased the nipple between the thumb and forefinger of the other. The effect on Samantha was electric. She moaned deeply, drawing in the next breath on a gasp as he toyed with her.

'Ohhhhhhh' she said. 'Oh god, ohgoddddd!'

Thus encouraged, Harold continued to arouse the woman he had made captive, excited by the idea that she was indeed helpless to stop him from having his way with her. That 'his way' was not clear to him did not diminish his excitement at finding a mature and attractive woman, a complete stranger, so completely in his power.

Samantha appeared to be having an orgasm, merely from being bound and aroused by his hands and mouth. Her knees quivered and she made all the sounds Harold recognised from his encounters with other women at the 'moment of truth', as he called it: the moment when the woman lost all control and went shrieking or moaning or shuddering over the edge into sexual release. Some of the women he had known had been capable of only one orgasm, after which they wanted to stop. Others had managed several. Samantha appeared to belong to the latter class. Harold hoped that she would last long enough to let him slip his aching cock into her.

Abruptly the bound woman lost all control. Shuddering and gasping, she came again and again. Just when Harold thought it impossible for her to continue at that rate, she proved him right by suddenly falling to the floor. The carpet acted as a cushion, but she fell heavily anyway. Alarmed, Harold stooped to examine her. Samantha was breathing. Her body jerked and quivered in the aftermath of orgasm. Behind her back her bound hands clenched and relaxed several times. He felt the pulse in her carotid artery, strong and steady if very rapid. Her perfume was intoxicating. He concluded with relief that she had not suffered a heart attack. Explaining to the police how he had come to be with a naked and bound stranger when she had a heart attack was not an appealing idea. 'Yes, sir, and was she bound when you came upon her? And who do you think tied her up?'

In amazement he concluded that Samantha had fainted from her climaxes – the first time that had ever happened to him. Even so, he could hardly credit that to his sexual prowess. He hadn't even got to the point of intromission when she had declared an involuntary intermission.

The check of Samantha's pulse turned to a caress as he gazed at her. He sat on the floor next to her and lifted her head until it was cradled in his lap. Samantha sighed and lay still as his fingers caressed her: her face and neck and bound breasts, her ears and hair. One hand stroked her belly and her nylon-sheathed thighs. The smooth, taut skin and the sheer nylon set up counter-currents in his own excitement. He wished she were awake to allow him to arouse her again – and incidentally to satisfy his own pressing need. Harold slipped a finger into her and felt her warmth and wetness. Just from a few caresses and a bit of gentle nipping, he thought in wonder. What must she be like when she's had the full treatment? Samantha's short dark hair was dampened with sweat. Her pubic hair too was damp, and not only with her perspiration.

They sat like that for what seemed ages while Samantha's breathing slowed and became more regular. Her tense body relaxed and her fingers stopped clenching and relaxing. Apparently she slept, this strange woman who had commanded him to make her captive and who now lay completely at his mercy. Not only bound but unconscious in sleep. Harold did not know how long they lay like that, but he found every moment bewitching.

When she woke, Samantha did so at once. She seemed completely aware of herself, her surroundings and her condition. She smiled at Harold. 'That was nice,' she said huskily. 'Thank you.'

Not many women, in Harold's rather limited experience, had said 'thank you' after sex. It was a new and rewarding situation.

7

'And thank you for holding me while I slept,' Samantha said. 'I don't usually faint, but it's been a long time since the last one. You could have just left me lying on the floor.'

'No, I couldn't. You looked too beautiful and helpless. I wanted to hold you.' The warmth of his words startled Harold. They had come unbidden. He couldn't remember ever saying anything like that to any of his other sexual partners, nor even to his ex-wife before the rancour had set in. Yet even as he spoke he realised he was speaking the simple truth. He *had* wanted to hold this stranger in his arms – well, actually his lap – while she slept. Her helplessness and her complete surrender had awakened a great tenderness in him. Marvellous what can happen between two people, he thought. Tenderly he lifted Samantha's head and kissed her on the lips. He would have drawn back then, but she made it clear that she didn't want him to. Bound as she was, Samantha nevertheless managed to kiss him back ardently.

When they finally broke apart, she whispered another thank you.

Now Harold was in a dilemma. 'Shall I untie you now?' he blurted out, his first, conventional thought; conscious even as he spoke that he didn't want to untie her and lose this moment, break this spell.

'Oh, no. Please don't. Unless you have to go somewhere.'

Samantha's response simultaneously surprised and pleased him. Her next utterance mostly surprised him.

'If you have the time and the patience, I want you to tie my legs and leave me here while you do your work. If you need to go out to get something to finish the job, gag me and leave me here until you get back. I guarantee you won't regret it. And neither will I.'

Harold nodded silently. He would have sat longer holding Samantha but his own legs were cramped from being immobile for so long. How she would cope with even more prolonged immobility he didn't know. 'Are your arms and hands all right?' he asked her.

Samantha nodded, stretching her arms as far as the bindings allowed. 'See? I can still move them. But now please help me to stand. I have to go to the toilet. Sex always makes me want to pee.'

Harold understood that. Most of his former partners had the same urge after sex. So did he, now that he thought of it. He slid out from beneath this strange woman and got to his feet. Grasping Samantha under the arms, he helped her to her feet. She swayed for a moment and he thought she would fall. He steadied her with a hand on each of her elbows. It was an intimate stance. He bent to kiss her lips again, and once again the kiss was returned with ardour. This time he sensed Samantha's eagerness.

'Please lead me to the toilet,' she breathed when they kiss ended. 'I'm about to wet myself. I don't mind, but the carpet is too nice to spoil.'

Wordlessly, Harold steered his captive toward the bathroom, reflecting how Mary, his ex, had made a beeline for the same place after they had had sex. This was more fun, he reflected as he helped Samantha sit. He would have gone away then, allowed her her privacy, but she stopped him.

'Stay, please,' Samantha said. 'I won't be able to wipe myself while I'm tied up.'

So Harold stayed to watch this stranger relieve herself. It was another moment of curious intimacy. Tenderness even. She was helpless without him. He knelt before the toilet and gently wiped her dry when she had finished. By way of reciprocal tenderness, Samantha let her chin rest on the top of his head as he bent to her crotch. Harold knew that she would have embraced him but for the cords that bound her.

Impulsively he bent forward and planted a kiss on her faintly urine-smelling pubic hair.

'Thank you,' Samantha said again as he rose; whether for the kiss or the wipe he could not say.

He helped her to her feet. 'What now?'

'Back to the front room,' Samantha told him. There, she directed him to sit her on the floor with her back against the wall and her legs stretched out before her. 'Cut more of the cord to bind my feet and legs. Tie my ankles and knees just as you tied my hands,' she commanded. 'Make it tight. Then tie my thighs together about where my stockings end. I don't want to be able to move my legs at all.'

Harold did as she asked, watching in fascination as the cords bit into the flesh of her full legs. 'Tighter,' Samantha commanded, and he obeyed. When he had done, Samantha was completely helpless, unable to stand or to use her hands or arms at all. But not helpless enough to suit her.

'Now I want you to lay me on my side and hogtie me,' she said calmly.

Once again Harold looked blank.

'Bend my legs and tie my wrists and ankles together,' Samantha explained. 'That way I won't be able to move at all. If you pull it really tight, you can make my back arch, too. Try it.'

It all sounded rather painful to Harold, but if that was what she wanted, he would try to do as she asked. He dragged her to the wall furthest from the window, thinking she would appreciate not being seen by the neighbours.

'I don't mind if you leave me by the window,' Samantha told him as he helped her to sit against the wall. 'The chance of being seen adds a certain piquancy to the exercise.'

'It also adds a certain danger of being visited by the coppers,' Harold retorted as she stretched her legs out along the floor.

10

Samantha shrugged. 'That could be awkward,' she agreed. 'What would you say if I told them you had abducted me and were getting ready to have your wicked way with me?' She spoke in a teasing tone of voice, but Harold knew that there would be embarrassing moments even if Samantha told them the truth.

'Do you like your women in stockings and suspenders. Or do you prefer tights? I rather think of tights as passion killers – unless you go for the crotchless kind. *That* could be construed as an open invitation, don't you think?'

Her question presumed that there would be a next time, and perhaps others as well. Harold rather liked the idea of a rematch with this strange woman. But he shrugged at the question. 'Your legs look marvellous like this,' he answered diplomatically – and truthfully. He found her long legs in the dark beige stockings exciting. He paused to stroke them from ankle to stocking-top before passing the cord through between her ankles.

'Which do you prefer?' Samantha persisted.

'Next time,' Harold said, accepting that they would meet again, 'wear the same thing. I like what I see.'

Samantha smiled at the compliment. 'That's why I asked you to tie my legs tightly,' she said. 'I like that effect, don't you?'

'Yes, I do,' Harold replied. In truth he found the spectacle exciting. The minor matter of her cunt's inaccessibility he ignored. He could always cut her legs free and expose it. That thought excited him too.

Samantha noticed his excitement. 'Too bad my hands are tied,' she told him. 'Otherwise I'd like to squeeze your prick.'

Harold acknowledged the problem and said, 'I'd like that too, but it can wait if this is what you want now. Unless you have to go by a certain time. Do you?' His voice sounded thick and croaky to him, evidence of his own arousal.

'I'm not meeting anyone, and no one knows where I am except you. So you see I am completely at your mercy. How long will you keep me tied up?' Samantha asked. 'Overnight? Over the weekend?' She sounded willing to do either.

Entering into the spirit of the game, Harold told her that he would decide how long to keep her. She had no say in the matter. Samantha wriggled in excitement at the prospect of being tied up indefinitely. She made a pretty picture, considered aesthetically. A helpless woman. At his mercy. All the melodramatic cliches ran through his mind as he contemplated Samantha in bondage.

But Samantha wasn't satisfied yet. 'Now roll me over onto my side and hogtie me as I described,' she commanded.

Harold pulled her away from the wall by her ankles and she rolled onto her side. He used yet more of the cord to tie her ankles to her wrists, bending Samantha's legs at the knees and pulling the rope tight between her wrist and ankle ties.

'Tighter,' Samantha ordered. 'Make my back bend.'

He pulled until her back arched and then tied the last knots.

Samantha sighed in satisfaction. 'It feels wonderful,' she said, wriggling as she tested the knots and cords that bound her. 'I've never been able to do this, even though I've dreamed about it for years. Could you drag me over nearer the window so I can lie in the sunlight? It's a bit chilly here.'

Instead of dragging Samantha, Harold lifted her in his arms, supporting her helpless body at shoulders and thighs. He carried Samantha over to the patch of sunlight coming through the window and laid her on the floor.

'Leave me on my side and get on with your work. Don't mind me. I'll watch. I expect the repairs to be done well before I move in.'

Harold got on with the repairs to the skirting boards and the painting but had very little success in ignoring the woman who lay bound only a few feet away. Each time his gaze strayed to her, Samantha caught his glance, wriggled in her bonds and gave him a smile of encouragement.

'Keep it up. You're doing well, and I feel wonderful.'

It was hardly the orthodox chat between worker and customer, but Harold found it fulfilling. Working for a woman who lay helplessly bound across the room from him had its compensations. An almost perpetual state of sexual arousal was one of them. He reflected on the maxim about travelling in hope. Or working in anticipation.

Toward mid-afternoon he had to go for some more paint and nails. Harold announced his decision to Samantha.

'Oh, good. I'd like being left on my own for a while. Gag me before you go. Stuff my pants into my mouth and stick lots of that duct tape over my face and mouth to hold them in. And tape my eyes shut before you go as well.'

Harold did as ordered. Gagged and blindfolded Samantha looked even more helpless. Her nipples were erect and crinkly with excitement. He slid a finger between her thighs and felt her cunt. It was warm and wet. Samantha jerked at the touch. When he pinched her erect nipples, she moaned with pleasure. Harold spent a few minutes arousing his captive, enjoying the novel sensation of making her gasp and moan and thrash about as far as her bonds allowed. When he judged that Samantha was on the verge of coming, he stopped and stood up. It took a real effort.

Samantha moaned. He guessed that she was frustrated, but with the gag it was hard to be certain. Good for her, he thought. I've been frustrated all morning while she's enjoyed being tied up. With one last glance at the helpless woman by the window, Harold left the flat, locking the door and taking the key away with him. Even if Samantha could get free, which was doubtful, she was locked in.

The knowledge that Samantha was waiting helplessly at the flat lent a certain piquancy to the mundane task of buying nails and paint. Harold found himself prolonging the job, looking at the selection of rope for sale at Weybridge's only ironmonger's shop and imagining how Samantha would look tied up with it. He bought another ball of cord. Tying up Samantha had used almost his entire supply. Giving in to his urge, he also bought some stouter cord, braided nylon about an eighth of an inch in diameter. Samantha, he thought, might conceivably break the grocer's cord, but she would never break this stuff.

A display of cable ties caused Harold to imagine Samantha bound with some of them. He bought a packet of the longest he could find, telling himself that he could always use them for more legitimate purposes as well. Even the display of chains and padlocks took on a different aspect in light of this morning's experience, though he refrained from buying any. He did, however, buy a half dozen brass screw-eyes. They would be handy for spread-eagling Samantha later. The holes would not show in the carpet.

Harold paused for lunch, prolonging still further Samantha's period of anticipation (as well as his own). Finally he had no more reasons for delay. He drove back to the flat and let himself in as quietly as he could.

He half expected that Samantha had somehow freed herself and was lying in wait for him with a blunt instrument in her hands, but she hadn't, and wasn't. Samantha lay trussed securely still, but not in the place where he had left her. She lay in the centre of the room, on her side, still gagged and blindfolded, but curiously limp, as though unconscious. Harold remembered her fainting after the first orgasms, and guessed that she had somehow made herself come until she fainted again. The dampness of her pubic hair, and the smell of rut from between Samantha's tightly bound thighs, confirmed his guess. Here (he marvelled) was a woman who could arouse and satisfy herself while helplessly bound and alone. The thought brought a certain sense of useless- ness to Harold. Samantha didn't need him for anything more than tying her up. She could do all the rest, all the foreplay and all of the arousal, by herself. She would only need him to untie her at the end of the exercise.

Still, it must have been quite an exercise. Samantha had managed to wriggle nearly across the room in her tight bondage. She had not bumped into his toolbox with its assortment of sharp tools. That lay in the opposite direction to her progress. Perhaps she had been seeking the toolbox in order to free herself but had lost her way, disorientated by the blindfold and distracted by her orgasms. And maybe she had merely been wriggling about to bring herself off. He reminded himself to ask her later. In the meantime Samantha was still his captive.

Once more he knelt to feel her carotid pulse, allowing his hand to stroke her face and neck as he did so. Samantha moaned softly through the gag but didn't wake up. Her pulse was fine, her breathing steady. She seemed to have come to no harm.

Harold stood up, gazing down at her. He looked at her for a long time, then resumed his work.

In mid afternoon a muffled groan caused him to look once more at Samantha. She was undoubtedly awake.

15

Her body no longer lay limply. She was struggling against her bonds, heaving and jerking and making small movements on the floor. Harold could now see that it must have taken a great deal of struggle and heaving for Samantha to have moved as far as she had while he was away. As he watched her now he saw that she could move inches at a time. She repeated the sound that had attracted his attention. It sounded like 'Ahh-uhh,' as if she were trying to call his name.

Harold went over to stand silently beside the struggling woman. The sight of her futile attempts to move excited him, and so he did not reply at once to her muffled cries. He imagined that she was wondering frantically who had come and found her helpless. When she received no answer from him Samantha seemed to go into a frenzy, heaving and jerking at the cord that joined her ankles and wrists, and trying to free her bound hands by moving one against the other behind her back. But there was no slack in the cords. They held her despite her frantic efforts to escape. Harold, under her direction, had tied her too well to allow her to free herself. He recognised the irony of her attempt to escape her own expertise in bondage. And he grew more excited as he watched her struggle. He had never before experienced this particular sort of excitement, and he found it almost overpowering now.

Silently he stooped to touch her breast. Samantha froze at the touch, her body a taut bow against the cords. She turned her blind gaze in his direction as if trying to see through the tape that sealed her eyes shut. 'Ooooooo?' she grunted.

Still silently he knelt beside the tense woman and planted a kiss over the tape that covered her mouth. Harold continued to manipulate her breast, his finger and thumb pinching the stiffening nipple. Even in her doubt and fear Samantha responded to the arousal,

16

moaning deep in her throat. The kiss quieted Samantha's fears. Nothing bad could happen to her, she hoped, when her unknown captor kissed her before doing anything else.

Harold placed his other hand over Samantha's pubic mound. She was warm under his touch, and she thrust her mons veneris blindly against the unseen hand. He slid his fingers between her thighs, and Samantha moaned again.

This was finally too much for Harold. He rose and took off his clothes. His cock was fully erect, and nothing was going to prevent him from burying it in Samantha. Going to his tool box, he found the Stanley knife. 'Hold still,' he told Samantha. His voice was nearly a growl. Carefully he cut the cords that bound her legs at ankles, knees and thighs. In her struggles Samantha had pulled the knots in the thin cords so tight that they could not be untied. When her nylon-sheathed legs parted, he lay down beside her on the floor and roughly pulled her atop him.

'Kneel,' he commanded, helping Samantha to rise and straddle him. She must have known who was with her by then, and she clearly realised what was going to happen next. As he guided his cock into her Samantha lowered herself onto it with a moan of pleasure. She was thoroughly wet and parted, and he slid into her with a long glide. It was like immersing himself in a hot bath. Samantha clamped down at once on the spear inside her.

Harold reached up to encircle her bound breasts, taking both nipples between thumb and fingers and pinching them sharply. The cry from Samantha would have alarmed the neighbours for streets around if she had not been gagged. Harold had never heard a woman react this strongly to his lovemaking. He wondered how loudly she would cry without the gag, but he didn't dare

17

remove it. The sight of her face above him, blind, speechless, contorted in pleasure, gave him a sense of power that was instantly addictive. He could do anything he wanted to this woman. She could do nothing to stop him. He imagined what her body would do if he reached up and grasped her throat instead of her breasts. In such moments of heady power, he imagined, murders were committed. With an effort he kept his hands on her engorged breasts and nipples, while he worked his hips to drive his cock more deeply into her cunt.

Samantha cooperated wholeheartedly, her hips rising and falling in rhythm with his, causing him to slide in and then nearly out of her before the next downstroke brought its delicious sense of penetration. Even with her hands tied behind her back Samantha was doing her best to fuck him. Her muffled cries drove him nearly wild.

Harold nearly came when he felt Samantha clench herself around his cock in her own orgasm. Her throat was working as she moaned in pleasure. With great effort Harold managed to ride out her first orgasm without coming himself, but her second broke through his control.

When she felt him flooding inside her Samantha bore down on him with another muffled cry. The sounds of her release went on for a long time after Harold had spent himself. When at last she grew silent and still he allowed his stiff arms to relax. Samantha sank down onto his chest, his hands still cupping her breasts as she lay against him, sweaty and warm and fragrant.

For the first time since his divorce, Harold held a strange woman to him and allowed sleep to claim him. He never knew whether Samantha slept. When he awoke, the sun was getting low in the sky. Samantha was obviously awake, for he felt her clamping down on his stiffening cock, encouraging another erection and, not too long afterwards, another frantic fuck that seemed to make her frantic – if he were to judge by her wild heavings and from the cries that found their way past the gag. Harold was better able to control himself after the first wild release, and so he rode Samantha until she was drenched in sweat and was panting for breath before he came a second time.

This time he was sure that Samantha slept, for he could hear the soft snoring sounds she made. Her head lay in the hollow of his throat and she seemed utterly relaxed. Harold gently put his arms around her at waist and shoulders, holding her atop him while he too slept the sleep of the just-thoroughly-fucked.

It was nearly dark when he awoke. Samantha slept still. He imagined that her earlier orgasms while he was away, combined with the two shattering fucks since his return, had tired her thoroughly. Gently he began to allow her to slide to the floor beside him, reluctant to withdraw from her body but feeling the need for the toilet.

Samantha woke with a soft growl in her throat, and her full bladder cut loose, drenching them both in warm urine. Samantha seemed contrite, for she uttered a sound of apology. 'Not to worry,' Harold told her. 'But if you don't want a second flood you'd better let me get up. Samantha shook her head sharply and clamped down on his cock. At the pressure he too cut loose, releasing a second flood that flowed from inside her and drenched them both anew.

That seemed to satisfy Samantha. She rolled off him and lay in a sweaty soiled heap on the carpet. There was a dark stain on her stockings where the urine had soaked them, and a big wet spot on the carpet beneath their bodies. The strength of his relief surprised Harold. He had heard about golden showers, but never imagined he would ever share one.

It was now imperative that they get up. Slowly he rose, surprised at the amount of urine two people could contain. He helped Samantha to her feet and steered her towards the bathroom. There he gently pulled the tape from her eyes and waited until they had become accustomed to the light. 'Shall I untie you?' he asked when Samantha was able to look at him. Without hesitation she shook her head. When he reached to peel the tape off her mouth Samantha shook her head again.

'We both need a shower,' he told her.

Samantha nodded, indicating with a jerk of her head that he should remove her wet stockings and suspenders beforehand.

It was strangely erotic to remove a woman's stockings after such a wild fuck. Something prompted him to rinse the urine out of them. He rinsed her suspenders too and hung everything over the top of the door to dry. Harold enjoyed the odd experience of washing out the underwear of his captive. In the shower together, he soaped her body and then his own, glad that he hadn't ordered the electricity and water to be shut off yet. He dried them both with a clean corner of the painter's drop cloth. Samantha's curls hung lank on her face above the gag, lending her an air of careless déshabillé that appealed to Harold. Gently he pushed her hair off her face and planted another kiss on her mouth over the gag. He could feel her lips working under the tape as she tried to return it.

Now Samantha was completely naked save for the cords and the tape. She looked wonderful. Harold wondered what they would do next. This day's experience had taken him far from customary shores. What did one do with one's captive when the captive wanted to remain so?

'Hungry?' he asked her.

Samantha nodded, but when he attempted to untie her she again shook her head. 'O. Eeeeve eee,' she said.

Harold took that to mean he was to fetch food but leave Samantha tied and gagged once more. 'Do you want me to tie your legs again?'

Samantha nodded.

'Blindfold too?' he asked, knowing the answer already.

When Samantha was once more bound hand and foot he hogtied her and got dressed, wondering how she stood such lengthy confinement. He would ask her about it when he returned with the food. The gag at least would have to come off then. Once again Harold drove through the familiar town in an unfamiliar state of excitement, knowing that Samantha was waiting for him back at the flat in her helpless state.

The line at the Chinese takeaway he usually patronised was longer than usual. Some time passed before he could place his order, and so he had time to think about Samantha waiting for him back at the flat. Since he was moving, he had thought he would have to find a Chinese restaurant nearer to his new home. But maybe Samantha would ask him over to tie her up now and then. He would not be totally dependent on a new restaurant, he reflected with some amusement.

Harold looked over the other customers. They looked quite ordinary. He guessed that he was the only one with a woman tied up at home waiting for him to return. But there were other secrets in the world. Perhaps some of the customers had their own delights waiting for them at home. Or their torments, he thought, remembering stormy evenings with his ex-wife.

With the food in hand Harold made a detour to his new house to pick up some bedding for what looked like being an all-nighter. Sleeping with a bound woman would be another novel experience. The new house was a two-bedroom affair, fairly modern but different from the flat he had shared with Mary – and now with

21

Samantha. He had had neither the time nor the inclination to put things away. Most of what he had salvaged from the marriage was still in boxes and bundles, waiting for him to get around to making a home of the house. It was relatively easy to stuff several duvets into a plastic bag, grab some pillows and towels and load the lot into the van. No sense in sleeping on the carpet, he thought with a flutter of anticipation.

This time when Harold got back Samantha was lying where he had left her. Perhaps she was too worn out from their previous sexual exercises to wriggle around the room. He felt a glow of pride: he had never managed to wear a woman out before. But in a moment more sober thoughts intruded. Samantha had expended much more energy than he. If she had not struggled while he was at the ironmonger's she might not be so tired now. Their lovemaking had simply been the climax to a day of sexual calisthenics for the strange woman who had made him her warden.

This time, despite Samantha's reluctance, he undid the hogtie and sat her up against the wall with her bound legs stretched out. He removed the gag and blindfold too. 'I have to feed you,' he explained in response to her protests at even this limited amount of freedom. 'And I like to look at your face once in a while as well, not just your body – lovely as that is.'

The explanation pleased her, and it was true as far as it went. Samantha had a lovely face, he thought, setting their dinner on the carpet nearby. There were laughter lines around her nose and mouth. There were tiny crinkles around her dark brown eyes. They gave a character to her face that younger women usually lacked. Her mouth was wide and her lips full. Her face was heart-shaped, symmetrical, framed now by her disordered hair. A lovely woman, he decided, wondering how she had come to be alone like him.

22

'Time to eat,' he said to break the awkward silence. They knew nothing about each other and so had no basis for small talk.

The meal was mostly silent but not terribly awkward. They had shared a remarkable day and would no doubt have a similar one tomorrow. And there was still the night before them. There was a shared intimacy and the beginnings of warmth between them. A trust too, inevitably. No one asked someone else to tie them up and leave them helpless without some of that. Harold wondered how she had decided on him.

They ate in companionable silence, Harold feeding Samantha between bites of his own food. The meal took a long time by normal standards, but by the end of it Samantha knew that he was looking out for her welfare, and Harold knew that Samantha was enjoying herself and his company. 'Miles better than being tied up all alone,' was how she expressed it.

'Although,' she continued, 'there is a lot to be said for being tied up and left in an abandoned house, or a barn.'

'Has that happened to you often?' Harold asked.

'Not yet, but I'm hoping,' Samantha replied. 'But today was special too. I loved having you around looking at me, and I loved it when you left me alone. Most of all I loved it when you came back and fucked me stupid. Thank you again.'

Harold once more remembered that Samantha was the only woman ever to thank him for making love to her. For making her come, he reminded himself with a certain pride. For unreservedly giving her what she so clearly wanted. Looking after Samantha's needs was a first for him too. With his other partners there was always the element of 'me first'. That had been signally lacking today. It had been Samantha first from the moment she was tied up.

'What about tonight?' Samantha asked. 'Will you leave me tied up? Please?' She sounded as if that was her dearest wish. 'And fuck me again like before?' Her last question resolved the matter of whether she wanted to stay or leave.

Harold nodded. 'I've never slept with a woman like you.' The compliment came unconsciously; he had intended to ask how she managed to sleep in bondage, but it had come out instead.

Samantha smiled at the compliment.

Harold leaned forward to kiss her generous mouth, and she returned the kiss with an eagerness that promised much more than a night spent side by side.

'It's a long time before bedtime,' Harold said as he drew back. 'Let's at least get better acquainted. Life story please.'

'To hear is to obey, master,' Samantha replied with mock seriousness. 'But I want to hear yours too.'

'Mine's nothing special,' Harold said.

'I imagine most people believe that,' Samantha replied, 'but often the reverse is true. Telling the story to a willing listener, like me, is a wonderful experience. And I could say much the same thing about my life. Aside from my love of bondage, I'm like most women of my age: divorced, with a daughter to look after, trying to connect with other people and to make something of the wreckage of my former life.' She smiled to indicate that 'wreckage' might be a small exaggeration. 'And you?'

'Divorced too,' Harold admitted. 'Recently. No kids, so that's a relief. Looking for connections too, but not all day every day. Reasonably well-adjusted.' He smiled. 'Until today, that is. You've given me a lot to think about in a short time.'

'You mean today was a life-changing experience?' Samantha smiled as she spoke.

'It's too soon to say, but it's definitely been a day of firsts for me. How did you get into bondage?'

24

'I'm supposed to say that my father – or mother – tied me up when I misbehaved, or that one or both of them abused me sexually. That's the most common story nowadays. But it didn't happen that way. I grew up with two younger brothers and an older sister in a middle-class house in Weybridge. My brothers occasionally played Wild-West games that involved capturing womenfolk – my sister and me, mostly – and tying them up. I was surprised when it became exciting. To the others, it was just a game we sometimes played, and they all grew out of it. Only I didn't. I missed it terribly but I couldn't say anything. I only found one other person who shared my interests: my first boss, who later became my husband. When you look at me you see an object lesson illustrating the folly of a secretary getting involved with the boss. It almost never works. Or not for very long, at any rate.'

Samantha grimaced with distaste at the memory. 'But,' she continued, 'it was him who got me started into bondage and sex games again. It's an ill wind . . . the old joke about a secretary only becoming permanent after she is screwed on the desk is very nearly a lie. Most secretaries get the sack afterwards because they become demanding, or threatening, or the wife finds out. Only a few survive for any length of time. I was one of the exceptions because the boss had a kink: he liked to have his women tied up before and during sex. Of course he had to be extra careful. So imagine my surprise when one day he called me in to take dictation and I found him prepared to initiate me. He closed and locked the door behind me, an unusual act that set the alarm bells ringing at once. But he was an attractive man, and I realised I didn't really mind becoming his mistress. More ominously, there were several lengths of rope tied to the legs of the desk – and the desk top was clear. It didn't take a genius to figure out what he had in mind.

25

The old instincts made my heart race. And at least this wasn't going to be one of the usual quickies. It would take some time to secure me in position, for one thing, and the preparations showed that he had planned my seduction. It seemed thoughtful at the time. How he knew, or guessed, that I would acquiesce is a mystery to me.

'I had several alternatives. I could try to unlock the door before he grabbed me. I could fight him, or try to. He was a strong man. I could scream for help. Instead I found myself doing the least likely thing. I walked over to the desk and laid myself over it on my back. I stretched out my arms and legs and waited for him to take the next step. To his credit, he was neither slow nor ashamed. He arranged me artistically with my bottom near one edge of the desk and tied my ankles to the opposite legs of the desk, carefully raising my skirt to allow me to spread my legs for tying. Then he tied my wrists to the other two legs and I was spread like a starfish awaiting him. I was wearing pants and tights that day, not expecting anything out of the ordinary. But he was prepared for that as well. I suppose he had learned from experience. He carefully cut my pants away with a pair of shears. Then he cut a hole in my tights in the crotch area. And then he took down his trousers and had me without any further ado. To my own surprise, I came like a bomb at least once. There were several smaller seismic disturbances along the way. When he came I almost blacked out. It was a wonderful new experience for me.'

Samantha paused in her narrative to settle herself more comfortably against the wall. She wriggled her shoulders and stretched out her legs. Harold admired the view. Naked bound females were a new experience for him.

'In nothing flat I got addicted to being tied up before sex. He did it every time, and I loved it. Eventually we got married, and Amanda came along, and our sex sessions became fewer. I guessed that he was doing the new secretary, but I never asked. I didn't really want to know, and our sex life was mainly satisfactory whenever we could count on enough time for him to tie me up without being interrupted by Amanda.

'But in the end something changed. He became more violent – brutal even. It started with him wanting to spank me while I was bound. This involved him tying my hands behind my back and tying my ankles together. I suppose he enjoyed it, but I didn't. He would come all over my flaming bottom and then leave me tied up and frustrated while he watched the telly.

'He took to leaving me tied and gagged while he went out. That was all right because I could bring myself off by trying to get free. I never managed it. Get loose, that is. He was too good with his knots, but I had a lot of fun trying.

'Eventually it got out of hand. I remember one night he came home slightly drunk. He took me down to the basement, tied my hands behind my back and stood me on a low stool. He tied my ankles together. When he put a rope around my neck I began to be frightened. He tied the other end to a hook in the ceiling and left me balancing on the stool. I couldn't move for fear of falling off and strangling myself. He turned off the lights and left me alone like that for hours. I was disorientated in the dark, and several times I nearly fell. When he came back he pushed me off the stool. I panicked. The rope was strangling me. I thought he wanted to kill me. I jerked and twisted while he watched me hanging myself. I was terrified, but I had a monster orgasm just before I blacked out.

'I came to still tied up and with a sore neck. I was in our bed and he was looking at me really strangely. He gave me the shivers.

'He asked me if I had come while hanging. I was frightened, but I told him that I had. A good one? he asked. I nodded. He said we'd have to try it again sometime. Then he left me alone again. I struggled all night, I guess, but I couldn't get free. He came in the morning and untied me before going to work. I gathered up a few things and left the house with Amanda. I made a quick trip to get some cash and left town. He never tried to find me.

'But he left me with a permanent liking for bondage and sex. Just being tied up can make me come if I struggle. Add a cock and it's indescribable – as you saw a few hours ago. Right now I'm charging my batteries for the next one. Leaving me tied up turns me on and gets me ready for a good fucking. Other than that I'm fairly conventional. I get along well with people and dogs. I respect cats, and I go to work every day. The difference only shows in the bedroom. Or in the deserted flat, as the case may be.'

Harold thought his life story was fairly tame when compared to hers, but as he thought about it he found that their lives differed in only minor ways. Aside from her introduction to bondage and her continued liking for it, Samantha's life was like anyone else's. Like his own. He suddenly realised that he had been drifting, taking things automatically, not seeking anything out of the ordinary. He said so.

Samantha asked him, 'Until now?'

'Yes,' he said. 'Until now.' He leaned over to kiss her again. 'Thanks for waking me up.'

'Oh, that's all right. Thanks for tying me up.'

Harold thought the time was right to ask the really interesting question. 'How do you stand being tied up for so long and left alone with your thoughts?'

'It's the thoughts – fantasies, really – that make it interesting. I often fantasise that I have been abducted by a brute who will show me no mercy. He'll make me his sex slave, and the emblem of my slavery is the physical bondage in which he leaves me. A bit like you did this afternoon. While you were away I struggled against the ropes and had fantasies of you coming back and fucking me stupid. Which you did. And those fantasies let me bring myself to orgasm many times while I waited. Also, I like to know that I am helpless and in someone else's control. When I can do nothing for myself I am not responsible for what I do or for what is done to me. No sin, you see. No remorse. Freedom, in a paradoxical way.

'I suspect there's more to it than that, but that's enough to be going on with. And as to the duration – that's largely a matter of training myself. Of course I have to be tied in a certain way if I am to remain tied for a long time. Like you did today, under my instruction. Now that you know how to do it, I won't have to tell you next time. You can take charge of me and do what you like. That will be more fun.

'I can endure more extreme bondage if it's going to be for a relatively short period. For example, I can hang upside down by my ankles for about an hour or so. Or I can stand being strung up by my wrists to the ceiling for an hour or two. As I am now, I can easily endure all night and all day tomorrow. I hope at least that you will let me sleep this way.'

'I thought you might ask that,' Harold said. 'I suppose you may as well have your wish as long as you can stand it. But suppose I get the urge to have you during the night?'

'You solved that problem this afternoon. You still have the knife handy, and I don't suppose it will cost much to replace any of this cord you cut away. I like it, by the way. When I struggle the knots just get tighter. The idea of having to be cut free at the end of the

29

session is exciting. If you have to cut me loose, then I know that I am completely helpless – always a nice feeling for perverts like me.' Samantha's ironic smile lightened her face.

'I suppose I understand some of that,' said Harold. 'Is there anything I can do to make it better for you? If we are going to do this again, maybe you should take the time now to tell me what you especially like. Then I can do what you like without having to be instructed each time. It isn't as if either of us is going anywhere this evening. There are no television programmes we have to watch. All we can do is talk and fuck. So talk now.'

'And fuck later?' Samantha said with a smile.

He nodded.

'All right then,' she agreed. 'Tonight I want to sleep tied up as I am. A hogtie has its uses but is not very comfortable for that. You should gag me again, but before you use my pants rinse them out in cold water and leave them damp before you stuff them into my mouth. They get rather stale after a long time, and I could suck some of the water from them if I get thirsty while you're asleep.'

'What makes you think I will sleep with you tied up beside me?'

'You'll sleep,' Samantha assured him. 'So will I, though not as soundly as you. I will wake up in the night struggling against these cords, and I will probably come again. Many times, in fact. It's been known to happen. If I wake you with my struggles, and if you happen to have an erection and an urge, you can cut my legs free and have me. I won't be able to object. Not that I would in any case.'

'Anything else?'

'The blindfold, of course. I like to be blind when I'm tied up. You don't happen to have any ear plugs among your tools, do you? Not being able to hear properly adds to the sense of helplessness.'

30

'I'll put them on my shopping list,' Harold promised. 'For next time. Shall I buy a whip as well?'

'No. I have one already.'

'You like being beaten too?'

'Well, sometimes. And in moderation. I have no desire to be flayed alive, for instance, but a little pain helps make the orgasms more . . . explosive. I said I was a pervert, didn't I?' Samantha's ironic smile came again.

'No hanging, though?'

'No. I'm not a *complete* pervert. That's too dangerous.'

'What would you like now?'

'Well, a bit more of the spring roll and a taste of wine would be good. Then you might try kissing me and stroking me in strategic places. That might be fun for both of us provided we don't get carried away. Oh, and you might roll me over and inspect my bonds from time to time to make sure I can't escape. And handle me in general as if I were an object rather than a woman. Be gently rough with me.' Samantha smiled at the oxymoron. 'That helps me to imagine that I am the captive of an insensitive brute who cares nothing for me. Even if he does.'

Harold knelt astride her bound legs and bent to kiss her. 'The spring roll can wait. This can't.' For the first time he kissed Samantha fully, on her open mouth, without the gag between them. Samantha made it clear that she wanted to be kissed, and even though she could not take him in her arms, she nevertheless enjoyed the closeness.

The kiss lasted for a long time. When Harold drew back Samantha smiled up at him. 'That was ever so much better than the spring roll,' she told him.

Harold smiled too. He was enjoying himself more than he could remember since the divorce. Older women beat younger ones, he thought. Samantha knew what

31

she wanted and was clear about what she expected of a man. She was decisive too. Once she had announced her desire to be made captive she stuck by it.

Obeying her earlier instruction, Harold shifted his position so that he could grasp Samantha's ankles. Without warning he jerked at them, pulling her away from the wall that propped her up. The top part of her body fell to the floor, and he quickly, roughly rolled her over onto her stomach. He probed at the cords binding her wrists, feeling the knots. Like the others, they had pulled themselves tight as she struggled. They would have to be cut loose. The same was true of the bindings on her elbows and her legs. Samantha was not going to be able to free herself. The knowledge gave him a certain glow of satisfaction from having someone else in his power.

Samantha seemed to enjoy being handled. She smiled at him when he rolled her onto her side and took her bound breasts in his hands. The cords bit deeply into her flesh but Samantha didn't seem to mind. Certainly she was in no pain. Or maybe she was, but was treating it as part of her fantasy. Her nipples erected very quickly as he squeezed them, and Samantha moaned in pleasure as he continued to caress and pinch her breasts and nipples.

Harold remembered her injunction about not getting carried away, and concluded that it was meant to apply mostly to him. Samantha wanted him to arouse her – perhaps even make her come – while remaining chaste himself. Though one-sided, the arrangement allowed him a certain satisfaction as she moaned and trembled under his hands. Power over her, the ability to control her pleasure and pain: that was his reward. He had not thought of it in those terms before this morning.

Samantha, meanwhile, was getting carried pretty far. When Harold slid his hand between her tightly bound thighs, his fingers brushing her labia, she shuddered and arched her back, thrusting her hips forward to meet his fingers. He managed to slide a finger into her cunt. Samantha cried out when he touched her clitoris. Harold concentrated on that, rubbing and teasing it between his fingers. Ideally he would have liked to use his cock. A bit of mutual pleasure would have been very nice. But he knew that Samantha didn't want her legs untied now that she was all trussed up for the night.

Samantha was having no trouble in the pleasure department. Her body arched. Her hips thrusting backward and forward against his fingers, she had her first orgasm of the evening. Harold wondered how often she could manage it in one day. Perhaps one day he would find out. He could always ask her, but he doubted if she had ever counted. He doubted very much if she was counting now. Neither was he, of course. The important thing was taking place between her straining thighs and inside her belly. And in her head. This was her fantasy. Samantha came again with a loud cry. The neighbours would be alert now to their activity. Samantha was past caring. Harold wondered if he should stop and gag her, but then, they would not be his neighbours for much longer. And Samantha would probably not appreciate the pause. So he continued. And so did she, moaning and shuddering and tugging against the cords that bound her.

At some indeterminate point Samantha gasped, 'No more, please. I can't go on any longer,' before giving the lie to her own words by beginning another moaning orgasm.

But Harold had got the message. He withdrew his fingers when Samantha grew still, watching her as she gradually recovered.

She looked at him contritely. 'It was great for me. I'm sorry you couldn't join in.'

'I'll live,' Harold said manfully, acutely aware of his erect cock. It didn't look as if it was going to get any relief soon. But then he remembered the afternoon and early evening. It might not be too bad if he waited for a bit longer. It might make things better.

Samantha too looked as if she would benefit from a rest.

Harold rose from the floor and went to make their bed for the night. He spread two of the duvets on the floor near the window out of habit. Normally he liked to sleep near an open window – but he had never slept near an open window and beside a bound woman. There were no curtains to keep out curious eyes. He remembered that Samantha didn't seem worried by being seen. If she can take, so can I he thought. He just hoped that no one called the cops.

He had taken four pillows from his new house. These he arranged against the wall, using it as a headboard. He pulled the duvets into position and laid the last one ready to cover them. On a sudden impulse he got his cordless drill from the toolbox that had stood neglected since they had discovered the joys of sex. He drilled a hole in the floor near the 'foot' of their temporary bed. The carpet would conceal it later, he knew. He screwed one of the brass eyes he had bought earlier into the hole.

'And so to bed,' he told Samantha. He grasped her under the arms and dragged her across to the bed. He hoped she would construe this rather cavalier treatment as 'handling.' He laid her on the duvets and arranged pillows for her head. Then he rinsed her pants out and stuffed them into her mouth. Duct tape again held them in place. He wanted Samantha to see the next part of his preparations, so he didn't blindfold her yet. With more of the cord he tethered her to the screw-eye by her ankles. 'No more a-roving tonight,' he told her.

Samantha smiled above her gag.

'Shut your eyes,' he commanded. As he applied the tape he could feel the tiny movements of her eyes and eyelids under his hands. He pressed the tape against her eyelids all round. 'Can you see any light?'

Samantha shook her head and made a contented noise as she settled into the makeshift bed.

Harold gathered the remains of their impromptu supper and took them into the kitchen. He got into bed beside Samantha and pulled the duvet over them before he turned to take her in his arms. One arm went beneath her head and the other around her waist. He laid his hand lightly over her bound wrists, to let her know he was keeping check on her. As he settled against her, Harold discovered that sleeping beside a bound woman had its compensations. He kissed Samantha over the gag, and once again felt her lips working beneath the tape as she tried to return the kiss.

2

Sounds in the Night

In the night Harold woke when he felt Samantha struggling beside him. He watched her as she heaved and jerked and tugged at the cords, and eventually came. He could tell by the shudder that passed through her, and by the sharp thrusts she made with her hips as she ground them against the duvet beneath her. The gag stifled most of her moans of pleasure, but Harold heard a steady humming sound as she aroused herself. As he watched and listened to Samantha arousing and satisfying herself Harold felt curiously left out again. She didn't need him to pleasure her – only to tie her up. Samantha seemed to take particular pleasure in being tethered by her ankles. Several times Harold felt her straining or jerking against her tether, and each time it brought her up short she went off into a series of orgasms. There was some small consolation in having thought of it himself.

Eventually Samantha lay quietly. Charging her batteries for the next bout, Harold thought, a little sourly. But as he lay he thought of the Stanley knife, and of their wild fuck that afternoon. He rose from the bed, got the knife and laid it ready. Back in bed, he once more held Samantha's trussed body against his own, so that he would have a warning when she felt sufficiently revived to begin again. The night wore away without any more activity from Samantha. Harold thought that he had missed the best of it, that she would be all worn out and would ask to be untied so that she could dress and go her way. But as the first rays of the sun shone through the window Samantha stirred and moaned beside him. The tether once more tightened as she tried to jerk her ankles free. Harold woke at once and groped for the knife. He flung back the covers and slashed at the tether. Then he cut her legs free and lay down beside her. The cords had left angry marks at her ankles, knees and thighs. They were curiously erotic, the marks of her slavery to pleasure. But Harold only looked at them in passing. He hauled Samantha on top of him and arranged her again astraddle him. As before, Samantha realised what he wanted and did her best to cooperate. She held still while he guided his cock into her, and then set off on the most amazing series of thrusts and heaves and internal clampings, as if to compensate him for having had to watch her go it alone during the night. And Harold found himself amply compensated as she squeezed his cock and thrust at him with her hips. He came almost at once, but Samantha didn't seem to notice. She continued fucking him, coming again and again. Her frenzy was contagious. Harold felt himself growing erect again in what was nearly record time. He put his arms around her and held her hips against him. Samantha bucked and heaved, but he held her firmly. She was moaning almost continuously as she came. When Harold came for the second time she moaned loudly through her gag, and then went limp against him.

They lay joined for a long time. Then Harold, remembering the golden shower that had accompanied their coupling the previous afternoon, disengaged himself carefully and got to his feet. He lifted Samantha's limp body and staggered to the bathroom with her. He laid her carefully in the bathtub before using the toilet himself. When he was done he stood looking down at this seemingly inexhaustible woman. As he gazed at her she stirred. Her eyes fluttered under the duct tape as she strove to open them. 'Mmmmmmff!' she said loudly through the gag. When Samantha realised that she was lying in the bathtub, she parted her thighs and opened her bladder. Harold watched as the stream rose in a shallow arch from her vulva and ran away towards the drain.

'I never knew a woman could pee so strongly,' he said. Unable to speak or see, Samantha nevertheless seemed to smile again. Later she explained that it all came from practice in holding it in for long periods. 'A matter of training. I needed it when I my ex left me tied up all day – or night,' Samantha told him. Harold put the plug in and filled the tub with warm water. Samantha sighed in contentment as she felt the water rise around her. She braced her feet so that she would not slip under the water. Tied as she still was, she knew the danger of that. She seemed accustomed to bathing while tied up.

Satisfied that she would be all right for a while, Harold left her to soak. He had nothing special to do, but he liked the idea of Samantha lying bound in his – now her – bathroom waiting for him to fish her out and deal with her. To handle her, as she put it. He gathered up his tools and tidied the scene of the last repairs while Samantha soaked. Nearly thirty minutes later he went back for her. He pulled the plug and let the water drain away before helping his slippery captive to her feet. Once again a corner of the drop cloth served as a towel. Samantha made contented noises as he patted her dry.

Roughly he turned her around and inspected the cords holding her wrists and elbows. They appeared to be tighter than before, swollen with the water. Samantha shivered excitedly. She did not indicate that they were too tight, but Harold thought that they were. The cords around her breasts seemed tighter as well. He led her into the bedroom and removed the tape over her eyes.

Once again Samantha blinked at the sudden light and closed her eyes. While she accustomed herself to seeing again, Harold peeled off the tape over her face and mouth and pulled the wadded-up pants out. She worked her jaws. They were doubtless cramped from being held open all night.

Harold got his Stanley knife and began to cut her free despite her protests. Her wrists were deeply marked by the cords.

'At least leave my elbows tied,' she asked him. 'I won't be able to get free, and later you can tie my hands again.'

'You've been in this one position for too long. Time you had a chance to move about.' He cut the cords on her elbows too, finding them deeply marked as well. As the cords fell away Samantha let out an involuntary sigh of relief. He saw that she could barely move her arms after nearly twenty hours of being tied up. Harold carefully cut away the cords around her breasts, regretting the loss of fullness and jutting aggressiveness, but recognising the necessity. There were deep grooves around the base of her breasts, red and angry. He wondered how she had endured it for so long.

'Training and practice,' she told him later when he asked. 'All masochists have to learn to endure pain before they can begin to enjoy it.'

'And you enjoy it?'

'Well, some of it. Being tied up is worth the aches and pains. And the extra kick it gives to sex is a minor compensation, too.' Her ironic smile made its first appearance of the day.

Harold shook his head. 'I'm glad you like it, then. I've enjoyed what we've done.'

'Me too,' Samantha told him, 'but I don't have to be home until later this evening, when Amanda gets back. Do you have anywhere you have to go?'

'Only to get us something to eat,' he said. 'You want more?'

'Oh, yes, if it's possible. I don't often get this sort of opportunity. I have to make the most of it. Tomorrow will be dull indeed after this weekend. Work is the curse of the fucking classes.'

Samantha surveyed the cut pieces of cord lying all over the floor. 'It's too bad you had to cut all those cords off me. Couldn't you have saved some of them? Untied the knots?'

Harold shook his head. 'Too tight,' he said.

'What will you do about tying me again?' Samantha asked him.

'I thought of that yesterday,' he replied, nodding toward the carrier bag that contained his purchases from the ironmonger. 'More cord in there. A bit better for what you have in mind.'

Samantha brightened up at once and leaned forward to kiss him on the mouth. Much later she would praise his resourcefulness verbally. 'Do me now,' she urged him. 'I don't want to lose a minute.'

'All in good time,' Harold replied. 'I need to make some preparations, and so do you. I believe you'll find your stockings and suspenders have dried out overnight while you – we, I suppose – were entwined in the throes of lust. Go put them on. I like the effect. I will be ready when you come back. Be sure to have a long pee, and rinse out your pants again if you want me to gag you.'

40

Samantha went back into the bathroom and Harold rearranged their bed, moving it away from the wall and toward the centre of the room. At the head end he installed another screw-eye in the flooring. Removing the one to which he had tied Samantha's ankles the previous night, he moved it to one of the bottom corners of the 'bed.' He installed the third at the other bottom corner and was ready when Samantha came back from her trip to the bathroom.

She wore the plain dark beige stockings and suspenders and carried her pants. She paused for effect, posing with her weight on one leg and the other thrust forward. She had marvellous legs, Harold decided again. The stockings lent an erotic touch he liked very much. The marks left by the cords still showed beneath the sheer nylon, and around her wrists and elbows and breasts.

'Like what you see? Is there anything else you'd like?'

Harold smiled and shook his head. Samantha brightened too.

He beckoned her nearer. She came at once, dropping the model's pose and looking like the eager wanton he had met the day before. Her nipples were erect and she was breathing rapidly. Harold wondered how much of Samantha's eagerness came from being with him, and how much from the prospect of being tied up again. Mostly the latter, he thought glumly. But when he turned the proposition around, he had to admit that much of his enjoyment of Samantha came from the novelty of bedding a woman who was into bondage in a big way. He liked her very much, unusual after such a short acquaintance. She looked beautiful still. Meeting someone for the first time, all we have to go on are appearances. It takes a long time to decide on long-term commitments, he told himself, but already he was hoping that she would stick around.

'What now?' Samantha asked when she stood before him.

Harold shook off his mood and showed her the nylon cord he had bought for her. It was thin enough to pull into every one of her curves and strong enough to be well-nigh unbreakable. Certainly she could not break it with any force at her command. He told her so.

'Oh, my. I feel wet already,' Samantha said.

Harold cut a length of cord and motioned for Samantha to hold her hands out in front of her. She seemed disappointed.

'Not behind my back?'

'Not this time,' he replied. 'But be patient and all will be revealed.' As before, he pulled the cord tight around her wrists, placing the knots out of her fingers' reach, and as before he cinched the cord between her wrists. There was still a longish piece of cord dangling when he had finished binding her hands. Using this as a lead, Harold pulled Samantha over to the impromptu bed and had her lie down on her back. He led the cord through the screw-eye and pulled her arms up above her head. When he tied the last knot Samantha was left lying on her back with the entire front of her body exposed and her arms and hands tied to the eye.

Samantha must have done something like this before, for she slid down, pulling the cord taut between her wrists and the eye screwed into the floor above her head. When Harold tied another length of cord around her left ankle, she extended her leg down toward the eye at the left corner of the duvet on which she lay. 'Stretch me tight,' Samantha told him as he tied the cord to the eye.

When her right ankle was similarly secured, Samantha looked up at him with a smile. 'This is good. You're getting the idea now,' she said.

Harold looked down at Samantha, admiring her tautly stretched body and the sheer nylon of her stockings, indented at her ankles by the tight cord. He smiled too at her complete vulnerability.

'Will you take advantage of the situation and plunge into me immediately, or will you leave me to stew in my anxiety and doubt?' Samantha gave him another of her ironic smiles, but in truth there was nothing she could do to influence him.

Harold was glad he had thought of this one himself, with no prompting from Samantha. He thought she might have a hard time making herself come in this position. Whatever it took to drive her shuddering over the edge would have to come from outside. From him. Before she could ask him to, he stuffed her pants into her mouth and taped them in place. He would need more duct tape soon, he thought with a certain satisfaction. He taped her eyes shut as before, feeling once again the tiny movements of her eyeballs and eyelids as he pressed the tape in place.

When Harold stood up to observe his captive once again, he felt a certain pride in knowing that she was once more dependent on him for everything – for her freedom as well as her pleasure. It would be interesting to see how Samantha reacted when she had to wait for another to release her passions.

Samantha wriggled and pulled at the cords, but could not free herself. Harold watched her attempts with a rising excitement. The idea of 'plunging straight in', as she had put it, seemed like a better idea all the time. Samantha was fully open to him, the pink lips of her cunt showing through the thick forest of her pubic hair, and promising even pinker and warmer depths between her outspread thighs. There was a lot to be said for having a lady-in-waiting.

Harold decided on a slightly more subtle approach. Plunging in seemed gauche after all the time they had spent together. He knelt astride Samantha's body, intending to kiss and bite her labia and clitoris. His cock, erect again, hung just above her face. A better idea appeared on his mental horizon. Harold shifted until he could take off her gag. He left her blindfolded.

Samantha would have protested at the removal of the gag if he had not quickly got into position again, offering her a gag of a different sort. When he bent to use his lips and teeth on her exposed cunt, Samantha immediately raised her head and groped with her mouth for his cock. A woman who knew what she was supposed to do was a welcome miracle, Harold thought as she took him into her mouth. A woman who took to sixty-nine without demur was even more welcome. He could never understand why so many women (in fact, nearly all of those he had known well enough) objected to the practice. Harold bit Samantha's labia and she gasped with rising excitement. He could smell the odour of her arousal as he sniffed at her cunt.

Supporting himself on his elbows and forearms, Harold couldn't use his hands on Samantha. Next time we do this, he reflected, accepting that there would be a next time, she can get on top and I can get at her cunt and arsehole with my hands. Then he concentrated on arousing Samantha with the equipment available. He forced his tongue into her and felt it brush the engorged clitoris at the apex of her labia. He knew he had found the spot by Samantha's sudden gasp, and by the way her body convulsed beneath him.

When the first shock had passed, Samantha closed her mouth around his cock and began licking and nipping it. Harold found this entirely to his satisfaction. Other lovers had, at best, approached the job as amateurs, many of them reluctant or half-hearted. Samantha showed an eagerness and an expertise that Harold admired. And enjoyed. There was no sense of half-forcing a woman to do something she didn't really like. Likewise, Samantha showed an appreciation for his efforts on her behalf – unless she was faking an orgasm. Harold rather doubted that. As far as he could judge, she had not faked the earlier ones, and this one felt like the ones he remembered from the previous day – and night. She pulled and jerked against the cords that held her spread out beneath him. The sounds that emerged from around his cock were genuine moans of pleasure as his tongue found her clitoris. And she swallowed his semen when he could hold back no longer. It was an altogether satisfactory performance for them both, if he was any judge at all.

Harold stood up to admire Samantha's long legs and full breasts. The dark beige stockings gave off highlights as she pulled restlessly against her bonds, the muscles in her legs standing out beneath the sheer nylon in a most erotic fashion. Harold was glad he had begun the repairs when he had. Otherwise he would have missed meeting this remarkable woman. He hoped that she felt the same about their meeting.

But now there was the matter of what next. Harold guessed that Samantha would like something to rinse out her mouth with. Then perhaps some coffee, or even a real breakfast. Sex was thrilling but not as filling as food and drink. On the other hand, she would probably not want to be untied, if yesterday was any indication.

When in doubt, every tyrant can put the matter to a vote. 'What would you like to do next?' he asked.

'You decide,' Samantha said, unhelpfully.

As there was nothing in the place to tie her to, Harold left her as she was. There was just enough duct tape left to gag her – he knew that she preferred that. He would have to get more tape when he went to get supplies. 'Breakfast in a bit,' he informed his naked captive.

Samantha said, 'mmmm,' which he took as assent. It didn't matter in any case. He locked the door when he left. Knowing the neighbourhood, Harold went to the nearest DIY shop to replenish his supply of duct tape. The display of rope and cord was even more lavish than at the ironmonger, but he already had enough for his purposes. It was strange, he thought, how differently he had come to regard such displays since the day before. Samantha had changed his outlook in just that time.

He parked his car near the flat and walked to the convenience store around the corner. He knew the Pakistani family who kept the store. Many times they had provided him with emergency lunch or supper when he forgot to shop at the supermarket – especially after he and Mary had separated and shopping was too much of a chore. This time they furnished half a dozen jam donuts and filled his flask with fresh hot coffee. Another emergency service.

'I understand you are moving,' the shopkeeper's wife said sadly. 'It has been a pleasure to know you. We will miss you when you are gone. Now I will have to look elsewhere for a suitable husband for my Ranee.'

Harold took the last as a mild joke. He knew that he would not be even considered a suitable match for the elder daughter. A pity in some ways, he thought, because Ranee was very pretty. 'Never mind,' he told the mother. 'Ranee is as beautiful as you are, and she will have no trouble finding a husband. You will have young men thronging the shop when the word gets around. In fact, Joe might have to work harder to keep from losing you to one of them.'

She smiled at the compliment, Harold realising he must have developed a taste for older women in the last twenty-four hours.

After the usual promises to drop in when he was in the area, he walked back to the flat where his first older

46

woman awaited him. Some experiences, he decided as he walked, weigh more heavily on our lives than others. Samantha looked like being one of them – after fewer than twenty-four hours.

The flat – and Samantha – was undisturbed. Harold guessed that she had tried the ropes while he was away. She might even have managed to make herself come, but it was unlikely. In this position she was open to all comers but protected from her own urges by her immobility. She made a noise of enquiry through her gag. This time Harold replied: 'It's only me. Coffee and doughnuts in a moment.'

He spent a moment admiring Samantha stretched out in her bonds before him. I could look at her for hours, he thought. And, yes, she *is* beautiful. To me, at any rate. The difference in their ages didn't matter to him then.

Eventually, Harold removed the gag and blindfold, before untying Samantha. To her unspoken protest he replied, 'You need to go to the toilet. So do I. And I want some time to admire you moving about in your stockings and suspenders.'

Samantha smiled at that.

Harold was relieved – and surprised at the truth in his words. Samantha moving about the flat was glorious. He knew that the effect was due to the things they had done. He would see if the effect faded when they were apart, as he knew was inevitable. But already he was making plans to see her again.

Harold took off his clothes while Samantha was in the bathroom. His cock signalled its base intentions.

Samantha was pleased by the compliment when she returned and saw his readiness. 'I'm glad to see you're interested,' she said with a genuine smile.

They talked companionably as they ate. Harold learned that Samantha worked as an editor on the local weekly paper and enjoyed the work. Also that her daughter was planning to go to university in Reading in a few weeks. So the coast would soon be clear, he thought happily. Samantha learned that Harold was a self-employed builder who worked all over the surrounding area, wherever work was available. 'Do you have access to any deserted houses – or barns?' she asked with interest. 'Somewhere you could leave someone like me tied up for days?' She was at least half-serious, Harold decided. Her question also told him that she was interested in him too. That was a good feeling.

When they had eaten most of the doughnuts and drunk all of the coffee, Samantha crossed the few feet to his side, sliding across the carpet on her bare bottom. She grasped his cock with sticky fingers and squeezed it tightly before beginning to slide her hand up and down its length. Harold liked that. In his turn he stroked her legs through the sheer nylon of her stockings, admiring the shiny material and its smoothness under his hand. Gradually they progressed to other areas, to their mutual satisfaction. At one point Harold found himself lying on his back under Samantha's cunt while she straddled him with his cock in her mouth. This time he could use his hands to explore her clitoris and arsehole. Samantha sighed with pleasure as his fingers gradually aroused her. The sensations from his cock were becoming urgent when Samantha abruptly shifted to present her cunt to his cock. It slid into her as if finding its natural home, and they fucked slowly and thoroughly for what seemed like hours. Vanilla sex was good too, after the rum-and-raisin variety. Samantha used her freedom of movement to raise and lower her hips slowly and far more than she had been able to do while bound. Her orgasms were gentler but longer. Harold bit his lips when she clenched herself around him. The rhythmic

48

tightening and loosening of her vaginal muscles nearly made him come. Samantha sighed in pleasure. Harold reached the point of no return, signalling it by a rapid series of deep thrusts. Samantha caught the mood at once, and matched his rhythm. This time, he came, and when he did Samantha went into a long orgasm that shook her whole body. And she screamed this time – a ladylike scream, but audible to anyone within a hundred yards. Afterwards they lay entwined for a long time. That felt good too – peace after the weekend's storms.

They dressed as Sunday turned to early evening. It was time to part. Staying any longer would have been pointless. Harold knew this, and yet he was reluctant to let Samantha go. There should be something to mark the end of the weekend, and to reinforce the promise of the second encounter she had mentioned. Had she been serious, or merely humouring him for the sake of present pleasure? Samantha didn't seem the kind of person to use others, but he didn't really know her.

Nor she him, he realised. They both knew only what the other had revealed. Not that much, but all relationships (he told himself hopefully) had to begin this way. There could be no rushing things. But it would be nice to know he would see her again.

'Would you like to meet next weekend?' he asked.

'I can't. Amanda and I are moving then. We'll be busy the whole time packing and loading and unpacking and unloading.' Samantha smiled regretfully.

Harold was not to be dissuaded so easily. 'Have you arranged for the removal company yet?'

'Not yet. I'm having trouble finding one, to tell you the truth.'

'I can get a Transit van for next weekend. If you like, I can come and help you move.'

Samantha smiled more widely this time. Gratefully, even happily, he told himself.

'I don't like to impose. You must have other things to do next weekend.'

Harold almost said there was nothing more important than seeing her again, but at the last moment he only shook his head. 'I don't, unless you count doing the unpacking and sorting at my new place. Don't spoil my record. I've been evading that for nearly a fortnight.'

Samantha smiled again. 'Thanks, then. It would be a great help. And it will be good to see you again. But my daughter will be there, so be warned.'

Harold supposed that meant no repetition of yesterday and today, but even so he would gladly go. He resolved to rent a Transit if he couldn't borrow his friend's van.

Samantha gave him her soon-to-be-old address and telephone number – 'in case something else comes up.'

Harold didn't think that anything would, but he kept silent. There was such a thing as putting too much of one's desires onto another person. And besides, it would sound too much like schoolboy protestations of devotion. Not cool.

Harold made several trips, loading the bedding into his van and returning for his tools. These he stowed in the boot, making a mental note to buy more duct tape. He locked the door as they left, giving her the keys. 'The place is yours now. You might just as well have the keys now as on Friday.' Samantha put them into her handbag.

They left the flat together, subdued. All partings, even temporary ones, had the effect of making him pensive. They parted on the street with a quick cheek-to-cheek kiss and a small smile. But as she turned to her car Samantha said, 'Cheer up. It'll probably happen again.'

And he did. 'Yes. I'd like that,' he said. Then she was gone.

* * *

Harold went through the week as usual. There was no call from Samantha. Should he call her to confirm? That might seem too pushy, he thought, so he contented himself with calling a friend who ran a local light haulage business: could he borrow a Transit for next weekend? No problem, said Steve. When do you want it?

That evening he did call Samantha. The voice on the telephone was not hers. Probably it was her daughter. Amanda. Yes, that was the name. She sounded young, in some indefinable way. He asked for Samantha, giving his name and saying that he was the person whose flat they were buying.

'Mum! It's the man who owns our flat.' While he worked out the logic of that he heard footsteps coming nearer. His heart beat harder. Like a schoolboy in love, he thought scornfully – but that didn't make him any calmer.

Then came the well-remembered tones of the woman with whom he had spent the last weekend. If anything, his heart beat harder. 'I've got the van,' was all he said.

Samantha sounded pleased. 'Amanda and I really appreciate this, but you don't have to do it.' Was she being circumspect because her daughter was in earshot? Probably, but he had hoped for at least an allusion to their last encounter. As if reading his mind, Samantha asked him if they would need any cord or rope for securing their furniture. Harold thought he detected a laugh in her voice. Confused by the mixed signals, he told her that they would need a fair bit. They agreed to meet at her old house on the Saturday morning, he to bring the van and his enthusiasm, she to supply coffee and cord, as she persisted in calling it.

Friday went by at a snail's pace. Friday evening television was a bore. Going to the pub with his mates held no allure. He certainly could not tell them about

51

the marvellous older woman who wanted to be tied up and fucked. 'I met her last weekend. She's fabulous,' he imagined himself saying. If they didn't laugh at him they'd want to meet her, perhaps with an eye to trying her out themselves, with their own favourite perversions – on the assumption that a woman who liked 'that sort of thing' would be game for whatever they wanted to do to her. Harold stayed at home, unable to settle on anything. He slept restlessly, and woke groggy in the morning.

At least it looked like being a nice day, he thought as he showered. The sun shone as if in benediction on a cool morning with high blue skies and a cool north wind that hinted at winter's arrival. Harold waited impatiently for the van to arrive. He expected that the day would be spent mainly in moving. There would be the inadvertent chaperonage of the daughter as well to prevent anything more interesting from happening. Nevertheless, he would be in Samantha's company for some considerable time, and he would learn more about her life and routines. There would be plenty of opportunities to set up another rendezvous. The 'my place or yours' question was already settled. With the return of Amanda from her grandparents' home, it would have to be his. He looked around his house with a new eye as he waited for the van.

How would he tie Samantha here? Nothing startling came to mind. Most houses, his included, were not built or furnished with bondage freaks in mind. He would have to make some modifications. He would also have to put away the clutter in which he had lived since moving in.

The van arrived to break off his train of thought. Steve asked what he was going to do with it.

'Help a lady and her daughter move into my old flat,' he said laconically.

'She paying you?'

'Yes. I'll split with you if you'd like. You know, some of whatever she gives me. We didn't really set a price.'

'That's all right. I just wanted to be sure you weren't going to accept payment in kind,' Steve said with a laugh and a knowing leer. 'That's a good way to go broke, even though it's a lot of fun.'

They both got into the van and Harold drove Steve back to his office. Then at last he was on his way to Samantha's place.

3

Chez Samantha

Samantha lived in a detached house, with large gardens front and back. The house was well-maintained, the gardens likewise. It turned out to have three bedrooms and two toilets. Harold wondered why she was moving into his old flat, with its tiny patch of garden and only just enough room to park a car. As he drove up a young woman was struggling with an armchair that seemed reluctant to leave the comfortable looking house. Amanda, Harold thought at once.

Amanda proved to be an attractive younger version of her mother. Smaller, but she would end up with her mother's face and figure before she was too much older. It would not look bad on her, Harold concluded. It suited her mother well enough. Harold got out of the van as she looked up. He helped her extricate the chair from the doorway before he spoke to her.

'You must be Harold,' she told him as she brushed her longish hair away from her face. 'Mum said you'd be round to help out. I'm Amanda,' she finished unnecessarily.

They shook hands solemnly in the way that complete strangers do. Unembarrassed, Amanda looked at him steadily, assessingly. It was disconcerting to be weighed up so thoroughly by one's juniors. Later he learned that

Amanda was an intelligent young woman as well, nineteen-going-on-university.

At that point, Samantha came to the door. She was dressed more sensibly than last weekend. Inevitable, Harold thought. One doesn't dress for town when moving house. Even in slacks and a man's flannel shirt she managed to look attractive, but then Harold had already had the benefit of seeing her naked. He knew the shape of her body even under the sensible clothes.

Her wide smile pleased Harold immensely, and didn't escape Amanda, who nodded thoughtfully. 'I'm so glad you could make it,' Samantha greeted him. 'We've just begun and already it's turning into a mess. You've met Mandy, then?'

'*Amanda*, Mum. Please.' It sounded like a familiar complaint.

'Amanda, then,' Samantha corrected herself. To Harold she offered a cup of coffee – or tea if he was so inclined – before they plunged into the bedlam of the house.

Amanda invited herself to the kitchen where she continued to assess the interplay between Harold and her mother. Apparently she found nothing to complain about, for she winked at Harold when her mother's back was turned.

He nodded conspiratorially, thankful for the favourable opinion. If one has designs on the mother, it usually helps if one has the cooperation of the daughter.

'I'm going away to uni in a fortnight,' Amanda announced to Harold. 'Mum doesn't want to keep this house on just for herself, hence the abrupt tearing-up of roots. It's a pity – we both like the house. But she's right. It will be too much for her when she's alone. Unless you plan to move in with her. Then the two of you could keep the place going so I'd have a place to bring my friends for wild parties.' She ignored her mother's suddenly beet-red face and Harold's uncomfortable glance.

'Grow up, both of you,' she commanded in the uncomfortable silence that followed her remark. 'That sort of arrangement happens every day. I'll probably have a live-in lover within a fortnight of getting settled. So long as two people get on all right it's easier than coping alone. So long as the sex is good, that is.' After that show-stopper Amanda wandered away to continue packing the contents of her room.

Harold and Samantha looked at one another in silence, Samantha embarrassed by and for her daughter, Harold at a loss for anything to say.

At last Samantha said, 'They grow up so fast nowadays. I wouldn't have dared say anything like that to my mother.' Nevertheless, she seemed proud of her daughter.

Harold too gained a new respect for the young woman as the day went on.

At one point in the packing-up Amanda asked Harold, 'Do you like my mum?'

Harold nodded, taken aback once more by her straightforward approach.

'Good. She likes you.'

This time Harold had a reply. 'Why do you say that?'

'She's been talking about you off and on all week. She said you had met at the flat where you were doing repairs. She said you were very nice about doing the work, and she's been smiling secretly – or so she thinks – ever since you called up to say you'd be round. Did she make you tie her up?'

It was another show-stopper. Harold felt not unlike someone who has swallowed a wasp and wishes he had kept his mouth shut.

Without waiting for the reply that was not going to come, Amanda continued, 'I saw the marks on her wrists and ankles. She must have made you tie her up for a long time. They took ages to go away, and she kept rubbing them thoughtfully whenever she thought I wasn't looking. I've known about mum's kink for years, so I know the signs. I guess she had a good time with you. I asked her what she had been doing while I was visiting my nan, and she said that she had spent a good deal of the time at the flat talking about the repairs and learning about the place and the neighbourhood. I suppose she got you to leave her tied up while you worked. Did you get much work done?' Amanda smiled archly, but with amusement.

Harold was once more silent.

Amanda went on, 'You needn't answer. I don't mind what she does as long as it makes her happy, and she was smiling whenever I caught her unawares. She's my mum, and she deserves whatever happiness she gets. I suppose we all do. But you be sure not to hurt her – either physically or emotionally. Be as good to her as you can,' Amanda told him.

'She told me something about what she went through with your father,' Harold replied. 'I don't intend to do things like that. I don't intend to hurt her physically. As to the other . . . well, there's no guarantee about that from either of us. Nor from anyone else. We just have to go on and see.'

Amanda nodded thoughtfully. 'I guess that's good enough.' She changed the subject again in the abrupt manner Harold was beginning to associate with her. 'Anyway, there's plenty of rope and twine lying around the place today. She will fantasise about being tied up while we do the work. Watch her expression as she handles the rope. You'll see her flushing and trying to catch her breath. It's a really big thing with her. One day she'll feel free to talk to me about it.' Amanda vanished to pack more of her things.

On her next appearance she announced: 'There'll be plenty of time for you both to have fun while I'm away at uni. But be good to her. I mean it.'

This time Harold felt bold enough to ask Amanda the obvious question: 'How did you find out about . . . your mum?'

'I found her handcuffs one day while I was tidying up. I never said anything because she kept it quiet. And one day I came home early and found her tied up in her bedroom. She was asleep. I could see that she had done it to herself. The handcuffs gave the game away. The key was on the night table. The place smelled like . . . like it smells in my boyfriend's car after we've just fucked. So I knew what she'd been doing. I crept out and went to a friend's house. I called before coming home to be sure she was presentable before I got there. Adults get embarrassed so easily.'

As they gradually moved the mountain of things from the house into the van and out again at the new flat, Harold watched Samantha. As Amanda had predicted, her mother became very thoughtful whenever she was tying up a parcel. Samantha caught Harold looking at her as she ran a piece of rope through her fingers. She blushed and looked away. Whenever their paths crossed, Amanda continued to give Harold bits of advice and information about her own plans and about her mother's likes and dislikes, her needs and her habits. It was almost as if the daughter were handing over custody of her mother before going away. At one point she said, 'I kind of like you, too. You'll be good for mum.'

Towards the evening, when the mountains had become small hillocks, Amanda spoke to him again. 'We'll be sleeping at the flat tonight and trying to make some sense of all this, but tomorrow I'll slide away on some excuse and you can take my place. Tell mum now that you'll be available to help put things to rights tomorrow, so she'll be ready to accept your offer to come and help. I'll suggest she call you when I slip away. I can't guarantee she will. That's up to her. But I think she will. There'll be plenty of rope lying around the place, and I'd be surprised if she didn't make some use of it. But be careful. And be good to her,' Amanda repeated for the ninth time. 'Give her whatever pleasure you can. I'm sure she'll do the same for you.'

'She already has.'

'And she will again. Take care of her.'

'You're very tolerant.'

Amanda shrugged. 'Have to be with a pervert for a mother, don't I?' She smiled at the quip. She had obviously heard Samantha use the word around the house. 'It could be a lot worse. Dogs or horses, for instance. Then I'd have to help clean up the mess when Shergar shits in the bedroom. And don't worry about me tomorrow. I'll call before I come back. If I get no reply I'll assume the worst and stay away until I can talk to her.'

Harold left them at the flat with the last load of the day. He guessed that one more trip with the van would do the job – all except for the tidying away.

Around mid-morning of the following day, Samantha called. After the hello's and the usual pleasantries, she asked, 'Have you seen a jewellery box anywhere? I can't find it around here.'

No, he had not. 'How are you managing otherwise?'

'All right, I guess. Never realised I had so much junk. And Amanda's had to go to help a friend with her thesis.' Samantha sounded mildly annoyed, as if she had been deserted at a bad time.

'Need any help putting things to rights?'

Samantha sounded more than half willing. But still doubtful. 'Are you sure? I mean, it's Sunday. And there's such a lot . . . I know you offered yesterday, but things might have changed . . .'

'See you in an hour. Have you eaten?'

'No. Too busy.'

'Come to lunch with me and we'll get stuck in afterwards.'

This time Samantha was wearing a dress. Were there tights, or stockings and suspenders underneath, Harold wondered. She wore high heels. Dressed for an occasion. He was glad he had worn casual trousers and a blue jacket. His working clothes were in the van.

The Sunday traffic was not so bad. They made good time to the coast and Harold drove to his favourite seafood restaurant overlooking the sea. There were only a few dog-walkers on the beach. The summer crowds had long since gone, the kids back in school, their parents back at work. The sea was a light, blue-grey: autumn-coloured, Samantha called it.

They had fresh trout with green salad and baked potatoes. A speciality of the house, he told her. The awkwardness passed gradually. He asked her to choose the wine, saying he had no idea of what to order. She chose a Chablis, light and faintly sweet. The meal was delicious.

On the way back to Weybridge Samantha looked more closely at the van. She startled him again by remarking that she might like being tied up in a van and driven around the country before being fucked. It was such an outré remark; sudden, direct, like the Samantha of last Saturday. 'Oh, not necessarily today,' she said, 'but sometime in the future, when we can plan the day. Today we have to get back to the flat, I know.'

Harold did not know as certainly as she did. Her impromptu remark had set him to thinking of having her all to himself in a secluded place. And he racked his brains for the right secluded place in the crowded island that was England. She was right about one thing, he thought. It would take some planning. Outdoor sex always did. If one added bondage, the job became even trickier. But at least she had indicated her interest in yet another encounter. He felt much better than before. Easier, more certain of his ground. He too looked at the Transit with a new eye. It might become a travelling boudoir-cum-prison. It was looking battered from its career as the workhorse of Steve's haulage firm. Well, he thought, maybe not this particular van. But he could always rent one.

Samantha sat sideways on her seat, one leg drawn up beneath her and showing a fair amount of nylon-sheathed thigh. And yes, there was just the merest hint of stocking-top. Harold felt even better, believing (and why not) that she had chosen to dress this way for his pleasure. The sun shone, the skies were blue, and he was driving through some lovely country with a beautiful and interested woman.

But everything must end. The ride ended back at the flat, which looked indeed as if a bomb had hit it. Everything was everywhere. The only usable things were the beds which he had helped set up the day before for Amanda and Samantha. Even they were now piled with clothes waiting to be put away.

Much of the rope and cord and twine they had used in packing up the day before was lying about. It looked as if Samantha had painstakingly untied each knot and laid it all carefully aside for future use. With a conspira-torial grin, she called herself a string-saver.

The flat was subtly different. It was hers. No longer his. By the simple process of moving her things into his old flat she had given it a new identity. Harold was conscious of being a guest where before he had been at least half-landlord. Recognising the distinction, he was pleased that she had invited him into her space.

'I found my jewellery box,' she told him. 'It was at the bottom of a box of books.' Samantha produced an oblong wooden box and opened the lid to reveal the usual collection of rings and pendants and ornaments. At the bottom of the box lay her handcuffs. 'This is why I was so anxious about the box,' she told him. 'I was ever so self-conscious about buying these when I visited America. I screwed up my courage and went into what they call a police equipment shop that had a window display. It made my legs feel weak – all those ingenious ways to make a person helpless. I was sure my desire showed in my face, my voice, was tattooed across my forehead for all to see. But the man sold me these with the greatest of aplomb. If he guessed what I wanted to do with them, he never gave the slightest hint. He advised me on the best type. I only regret I didn't have the presence of mind – or the nerve – to buy a set of leg-irons at the same time. So I wouldn't like to lose them and have to go through it all again.'

'You can buy any sort of handcuffs or leg-irons anonymously on the Internet now,' Harold told her. 'There's very little you can't buy online. They even sell thumb and toe-cuffs for the seriously kinky,' he told Samantha with a smile. 'All sorts of whips and gags and rubber wear. You only have to fill out the order form and give them your credit card details. About a week later whatever you've ordered arrives in the proverbial plain brown wrapper.'

'Have you bought anything like this online?'

'Not handcuffs. Mostly tools. The occasional book or record. But if you tell me your birthday I'll buy something you'll like.'

'November the thirtieth,' Samantha said at once, and blushed. 'But don't ask how old I am.'

'Your age doesn't matter.'

'When is your birthday?'

'It's in January. The third of January.'

Samantha filed the information away without comment. Harold thought that the mutual exchange of details was a good sign for the future.

Samantha set about putting away clothing and personal things while Harold tackled the furniture. He rearranged the sofa and chairs and television into some semblance of a sitting room. Then he went into the kitchen to see what could be done about the jumble of pots and pans lying everywhere. He had to give up. This was Samantha's department. 'Got a moment?' he called through to her.

She came to the kitchen with an armful of dresses ready to hang.

'If you'll supervise, I'll put this stuff away. A pot of coffee would be nice, but I can't even find the coffee-pot.'

'All right. Just let me hang these up. I'll be right back.' Samantha disappeared again. Several minutes later she returned bearing her handcuffs. 'Would you mind terribly . . .?' she asked, offering them to Harold. 'It's just that this pervert is feeling a little bit perverted now, and after last weekend we're hardly strangers. It's not like you'll take advantage of my helplessness, is it?'

Harold smiled. 'The thought never crossed my mind.' He took the handcuffs from her. The key was in the lock. It was the screw type, that had to be screwed in to release the handcuff, and unscrewed again to lock it.

Samantha showed him how it worked and then turned around and brought her hands behind her back. Harold had a bit of trouble with the first lock, but the second was easy. Samantha turned to face him again, her wrists locked behind her back and looking as fetching as a woman in that position can. Harold took her into his arms and kissed her on the mouth. She had not forgotten how to kiss since their last meeting. Nor

63

how to become excited. Her breath was shallow and rapid when the kiss ended at last.

'We must practice restraint,' Samantha said breathlessly.

Harold asked why.

'So that we can enjoy it that much more when we no longer have to,' Samantha replied with an impish grin. 'Oh, I wish I'd had the courage to buy those leg-irons.'

'Never mind. We'll make do without them,' Harold told her. With a length of rope he hobbled her, leaving about a foot of slack between her ankles. He also took the opportunity to run his hands up her legs as far as her crotch. Yes, she was wearing stockings and suspenders. And yes, she was excited. Her labia were warm and parted, and he could smell her aroma as he stroked her cunt through her knickers.

'What if Amanda walks in and catches us?' Samantha asked. 'I'd die of embarrassment.'

Harold felt he did not have the right to tell her that Amanda already knew. Amanda had said that her mother would have to reveal her secret in her own time. Nor could he say that Amanda had promised to call before returning. Samantha seemed to be enjoying the tension, so he kept quiet. He picked up the key to Samantha's handcuffs and deliberately placed it inside one of the cupboards over the work top: out of her reach as long as she wore the handcuffs. Samantha looked worriedly at him. It was a decisive moment.

Then she seemed to catch fire all of a sudden. Her token protests as he raised her dress to her waist were silenced as he probed her cunt.

The dress kept falling down, so Harold took the time to remove it. Samantha protested at this. 'Amanda . . .' she said breathlessly. Under the dress she wore a slip. That joined the dress on the floor around her ankles. So did her pants. Her protests became weaker when he buried his face in her crotch and began to use his tongue and teeth on her labia and clitoris. A finger at her arsehole silenced them completely. Samantha thrust her hips forward against his face with a last, smothered, 'No, don't do this to me.' On the next breath she moaned in surrender, as his finger slid past her anal sphincter and into her back passage. With his free hand he caressed Samantha's firm, smooth buttocks

'Ohhhhhgoddddd!' Samantha moaned as he licked and bit her labia. His tongue found her engorged clitoris, and he concentrated on that, inhaling and tasting her aroma as she grew wet with the onset of her climax. The muscles in her anus clenched around his finger as she half-fought to expel it.

Harold was painfully erect, his cock straining against his trousers. It would have been good to be naked like Samantha, but he did not want to break off to shed his clothes when his mistress was on the verge of climax. He continued to arouse Samantha with his hands and mouth, and was rewarded when she came.

Samantha gasped and drew in a long shuddering breath. Harold thought she was going to scream it out, but at the last moment she closed her throat. The air in her lungs emerged as a series of whimpers as she shuddered and jerked with the strength of her release. The last of it came out as a groan. Harold tasted her juice as she ejaculated.

It was too much for him. He stood despite Samantha's protests and almost literally tore off his clothes. Kneeling once again before her, he untied the hobbles and pulled her to her knees on the kitchen floor.

Samantha, realising that he was going to penetrate her, stopped heaving and did her best to cooperate. She spread her knees and prepared to straddle him so that he could slide into her more easily. At the last minute before he entered her Samantha begged him to gag her.

'Stop my mouth. I can't stop myself. Please don't let me scream when you come inside me.'

Harold used her pants and the piece of rope from Samantha's ankles. He stuffed her mouth full and used the rope to bind the gag in place. Above the gag, Samantha's eyes were dilated with the intensity of her need. Behind her back her wrists tugged uselessly at the handcuffs. Harold sat on the floor with his back against the cabinets and arranged Samantha above his erect cock.

The cry as he slid into her proved the need for silencing her. Unmuffled, her scream would have brought the neighbours running.

Samantha heaved and bucked in his lap. Her moans of pleasure were nearly continuous, rising in pitch as she came. She never slackened from the moment he was inside her. Though she wore the handcuffs, Samantha moved more wildly than ever, oblivious to the possibility of falling off. And she came. Harold merely held himself still as she reared and plunged on his cock. Then he had to hold himself back as her excitement infected him.

'Uhh-huuuuh, uhhh-huuuuh.' Samantha signalled each rise and fall as she rode him to climax. And when he came too she moaned loudly and ground her hips against him frantically, seeking to draw out the last ounce of pleasure from them both.

Samantha looked wildly at him over her gag as she came with him, and then slowly leaned forward until her head was resting on his shoulder and her full breasts were pressing against his chest.

They half-lay and half-sat for a long time, Samantha shaken by small stirrings inside her, clenching and releasing his cock and moaning softly. Harold's arms held her steady in position. If she seemed reluctant to break their coupling, he was at least as reluctant. The violence of Samantha's response had shaken him. If this was what restraint produced in her, then he was all for it.

Samantha broke the tableau by suddenly sitting up with a cry of dismay: 'Oyyyett!'

Harold remembered last weekend's golden shower as he helped a shaken Samantha to her feet. In her stockings and suspenders and high heels, her wrists handcuffed behind her back, she fled in the direction of the bathroom. Harold got more slowly to his feet.

Samantha's muffled cry from the bathroom sounded frantic. Harold hurried. There he found her crouched before the toilet trying to lift the lid with her manacled hands. It kept slipping out of her grasp. She was trying to keep her legs closed to contain herself, but there was a dark trail down her stockings already. Harold managed to lift the lid and get her seated before the floodgates opened. Samantha sighed in relief and gave him a grateful look.

Once again, as he had the last weekend, he wiped her dry when she was finished, and then kissed her labia through her damp pubic hair. He held the pose for a long time, enjoying the intimacy. He felt Samantha's chin come to rest on the back of his head: her mute expression of thanks. He embraced her, his hands resting on the handcuffs behind her back.

Samantha lifted her head and Harold released her. He helped her to stand and then used the toilet himself. He smiled at her. Her smile in return was both grateful and tired and somehow more intimate than anything they had shared before. It seemed to say, 'Now you have seen me at my most frantic, and you're still smiling at me.'

Harold put his arm around her waist and led her into the front room. Samantha leaned comfortably against him as they walked.

She sat down on the sofa, leaning forward because of the handcuffs. Harold selected another piece of rope and hobbled her ankles once more. He sat down as well and pulled her over until she lay on her side with her head in his lap. He stroked her hair and face, her neck and lips, and she drifted off to sleep. Harold too drifted off. It was a contented and restful sleep for him.

The ringing of the phone awakened him. Samantha too woke up, looking panicky.

'Aammaa!' she said through the gag.

Harold too had guessed that it was Amanda, making her promised call. As he was the only one able to, he answered the phone while Samantha made frantic free-me motions and muffled sounds. She struggled to sit up.

It was indeed Amanda, calling as promised. Harold said that her mother was in the toilet but would be out in a moment. Could she hold on?

'That means mum is still tied up. I guess those noises are her trying to talk through her gag. Don't bother about letting her go just to talk to me. Just tell her I'll be home in two hours. That should give you both time to get decent and make it look as if you'd been tidying up the place. Or if you really don't care about appearances, you could have another fuck. Not too many people can manage longer than an hour, even if one of them is tied up. Have fun!'

'Er . . . yes, that's right. You'll be home in two hours. Are you hungry? Your mother and I were planning on getting in some fish and chips, or a pizza. Would you like to eat with us?'

Amanda said she would eat with them. 'I want to see how mum looks after a good fucking, so be sure she has a good time. See you.' She hung up. Samantha was struggling against the handcuffs and making frantic sounds through the gag. Her eyes were wild.

'Calm down,' Harold told her. 'Amanda says she'll be back in two hours. She'll eat with us.' The edited version of Amanda's conversation seemed to calm Samantha down somewhat, but she obviously wanted him to let her go. Regretfully, Harold removed the hobbles from her ankles and untied the gag.

'Oh God, what will Amanda think of us!' She sounded genuinely disturbed.

Harold wished he were at liberty to reveal the extent of Amanda's knowledge, tolerance and love for her mother, but then, he thought, that might make Samantha even more agitated.

She followed him into the kitchen when he went to get the key to her handcuffs. Her hands once more free, Samantha looked frantically for her dress and slip. Quickly, she slid into her clothes and made a beeline to the bedroom to repair her appearance. Some twenty minutes later she emerged looking less the satisfied mistress and more the mother of a teenaged daughter. She had taken the opportunity to change her damp stockings and shoes.

Harold smiled at her and got a ghost of a smile in return. 'Pizza or fish and chips? There's a place near here that does both. They're quite good.'

'Pizza,' Samantha said. 'Pepperoni.' Her voice was shaky but stronger. 'It's Amanda's favourite. Mine, too.' She fumbled for her purse to give him the money. When Harold demurred, she insisted. In the end he took the money and went to the take-away three streets away. He arrived back at the flat just as Amanda was getting out of the taxi.

'You look presentable enough,' she said when she saw him. 'And you seem to be a good provider, too. That smells like pepperoni. Yum!'

'Actually, your mother paid for this. She insisted.'

'It doesn't matter. I was just making conversation while I looked for signs of recent fucking. I hope you made Mum feel good.'

'Look, Amanda, I don't think we should talk about what your mother and I do. I have kept your secret from her. Let me keep hers from you in return.'

Amanda thought for a few moments. 'That sounds fair to me – providing you really didn't tell her what I saw.'

'Judge for yourself. If she knew that you knew, she'd be terribly embarrassed. You'd see that in a moment. Likewise, if she knew that I'd told you what we get up to, she'd be very angry.'

Amanda nodded, and they went in together. She said nothing about the virtually untouched mounds of clothes and books and personal bits still lying around the place pretty much as she had left them.

Mother and daughter embraced. Amanda carried the pizza into the kitchen and pointedly failed to comment on the absence of knives and forks and plates. Eventually she returned with paper plates and napkins. She had found the cutlery. They drank Coca-Cola from cans. Samantha kept looking for signs that Amanda suspected what they had done with the afternoon. Amanda looked for signs that Harold had told her mother about Amanda's revelations to him. Harold looked and felt uncomfortable, the man in the middle between two women whose good opinion he sought, though for different reasons.

After eating it was time for Harold to go. As he drove home he found himself smiling from time to time. He had a good feeling about Samantha, and the beginnings of one about Amanda, though he was still wary there. For all he knew, she was telling her mother now what she knew about the kinks in her sex life, and Samantha might even now be blushing furiously and vowing to give them (and him) up for good. Harold doubted whether she could keep such a vow, but knowing that her daughter knew of her 'perversion,' as Samantha half-joking called it, might inhibit her for an indefinite time. Harold was not in favour of any inhibitions.

The need to earn a crust kept Harold, though not his thoughts, away from Samantha. All he knew of her was what he had learned during their two meetings. Of the rest of her life, and in particular of any other men she might be involved with, he knew nothing. Amanda, he knew, could fill in some of the blanks, especially about other men, but he didn't want to give her the satisfaction of knowing how serious he was about her mother. Nor did he want Amanda to begin to think herself able to control his contact with Samantha by doling out information, none of it verifiable. Amanda seemed straightforward enough, though her bluntness was often an embarrassment. But his instincts were all in favour of him keeping his feelings private – even from Samantha. Besides being unwilling to put premature strains on her, he was also loath to reveal that she had got to him so soon. The latter trait was left over from his schooldays, when a boy would do almost anything to make the girls notice him, while shying away from outright avowals of affection. And his experience with his ex-wife, as well as with several former lovers, had likewise made him cautious of avowals. Not yet, at any rate. But his thoughts strayed to Samantha whenever they were left to themselves. As he drove to and from work that week, Harold kept an eye out for a suitably secluded lane or field to which to take Samantha for the tryst she had spoken of. There weren't many.

Samantha did not call that week. Harold told himself she was coping with the twin strains of sorting out the flat and Amanda's imminent departure for university. It was a natural, logical step, yet the prospect of having a truly empty nest would bother any mother. He hoped that she would turn to him for solace (and the odd bit

71

of sex and bondage – he was not wholly unselfish), but the call didn't come. He was close to calling her himself, but could think of no pretext that did not sound as if he were pressing his suit, as it would have been called in earlier times. So he too maintained telephonic silence. Amanda, he reasoned, would still be there, and he was wary of revealing anything more to her about the state of his involvement. The silence grew.

It was Amanda who broke it. On the Thursday of the next week she left a message on his answering machine. It was in typical Amanda style: 'I hate answering machines. Where are you? I'm going to Reading on Friday. Mum is driving me and will stay overnight to help me get settled. She won't admit it, but she's feeling down. I can barely conceal my excitement about beginning an independent life, so I'm no help to her. Call her, damn it! Tell her you'll meet her for lunch on Saturday. Tell her you've found a spare key to the flat and want to drop it off – unless she's already given you one. In that case you're on your own. But call her!'

Harold smiled at the idea that he was coming to depend on Amanda for excuses to call her mother. He called Samantha's number, hoping to catch her before they left for Reading. Amanda's voice on the answering machine informed him that she was away but that he could leave a message for her after the tone. Presumably one could do the same for her mother. Harold began to understand Amanda's aversion to the devices. Nevertheless, he said that he would call again on Saturday afternoon to collect the last things from her old house. He had a van, he said, hoping that the hint (and the timing) would remind her of her earlier wish.

On Friday Harold cleared out his van. He spent Friday evening and Saturday morning making it into a travelling boudoir-cum-prison – insofar as his imagination allowed him. This might be the time; he might find

72

the place. The anticipation made the preparations enjoyable. The duvets were pressed into service once again. Harold thought of the mattress from his bed, and rejected the idea. It might just fit into the van, but it would be obvious to the neighbours (and to Samantha) what he was planning to do in the van. Duvets it would have to be. He packed as many pillows as he possessed, rolled up in the duvets so as to conceal them until he was certain that Samantha was up for the game. As for cord, Samantha preferred thin cord to rope, and he still had what he had purchased on his first meeting with her. Duct tape! He'd used the last of it and forgotten to get any more. He could stop at the DIY shop on the way to collect Samantha. Was there anything else? The anticipation of the meeting clouded his mind, preventing clear planning. Stanley knife, cable ties . . . he thought. Cable ties! He would need his side-cutting pliers to cut them. In the end he simply put his toolbox into the van.

Samantha called him before he could contact her. She sounded depressed. 'Well, Amanda's gone. It was awful in Reading. I had to come home.'

Harold felt better because she had called to share her bad feelings about the empty nest. 'Hold the fort. The cavalry is on the way. I'll be there in twenty minutes. Come with me to your old house and we'll collect the last bits.'

He hung up before Samantha could refuse. At the flat he found her still dressed (he presumed) as she had been for the drive to Reading. Not dressy, but with a skirt and blouse rather than jeans, and shoes with kitten heels. It was an outfit for a mother saying farewell to her daughter, rather than for an attractive woman to greet her lover. She was indeed depressed, and Harold guessed that tears were not far from the surface. It was hardly the time to whisk her off to the country for sex and bondage in a van. He was glad he had been discreet with the duvet and pillows and the rest of his stuff.

He kissed her lightly on the cheek and stepped back to look at her. 'You're beautiful,' he told her, and was rewarded with a faint smile, though she shook her head in denial of the compliment. 'You are, you know. I've been trying to remember just what you looked like, and all I could think was, what a beautiful woman.'

The smile returned, a bit stronger. 'Keep telling me that and I'll begin to believe you.'

Harold embraced her, smelling the fragrance of her perfume and the scent of healthy woman. He bent close to her ear and began to sing 'Pretty Woman'.

'You'd never make it as a singer,' Samantha said, but her smile was stronger. 'I'm so glad you came. Come in.'

She stood aside and Harold went into the front room. There were curtains at the windows now, and the furniture had been arranged to suit her tastes rather than his idea of them. The mounds of things had mostly disappeared. Only a few boxes remained to be unpacked. She and Amanda had been working hard. 'I don't recognise the place,' he said in wonder. That brought another smile to Samantha's face. It reached to her eyes as well.

'We have been busy,' she admitted with a touch of pride. Then she remembered that it was not 'we' any longer. Tears threatened again.

Harold closed the door and took her into his arms. He pulled her head down onto his shoulder and held her while silent sobs shook her. He had never felt this loss as children grew up, left home, made their own lives. But he saw that it could be intense. He held Samantha while the tears of loss and separation flowed, doing his best to be a rock amid the tumbling sea of her emotions. She clung to him. Not the time, he decided, for a bit of the other. Maybe later, his darker side added hopefully. Console the grieving woman in the best way. Harold was not proud of himself just then.

Eventually she raised a tear-stained face to look at him. Harold looked steadily into her eyes.

'I must look frightful.' He shook his head while holding her glance. He bent to kiss her lips and drew back before his darker side asserted itself. 'You were beautiful when I first saw you and you still are. I know this sounds glib now, but Amanda won't stay away forever. She loves you; she'll come back as often as she can.'

Samantha looked startled. 'How do you know how she feels? You hardly know her!' She looked as if she were about to accuse him of . . . what?

'She does, you know'. Harold thought he could at least that aspect of Amanda's conversation without revealing the rest of what she had said. 'When we were packing up at your old place we spoke a few times. She said you deserved whatever happiness you got, and she hoped you got a great deal of it.' He didn't say that Amanda seemed to have appointed him as the bringer of joy to her mother, nor her opinion that he would be good for Samantha. 'She told me to look after you.' That was as far as he could go.

Samantha looked quickly at him. 'You must have impressed her. She doesn't impress easily. I know.' Then she smiled lopsidedly. 'It sounds as if Amanda was handing me over to you before going away.'

'I can think of worse fates,' Harold told her with a smile of his own. 'But if I'm going to be any use to you, I should take you out and feed you and tell you bad jokes and try to make you laugh.'

'I'm not fit to be seen in public.'

'Well, go make whatever repairs you think necessary before we go. I'll wait.' Harold sat down on Samantha's sofa, feeling the strangeness. His sofa had been across the room. The TV set was more visible from the new location. There was less light from the window to block out the picture. The flowers and plants were entirely new, different touches that he would never have thought of. Samantha was making herself at home in his place. That felt good to Harold.

She came back with her short hair brushed and shining with coppery highlights in the light from the window. She wore a dress. Her stockings or tights – Harold couldn't tell which – were darker, with a coppery sheen that matched her hair. The shoes had higher heels. A transformation in his honour? At any rate the tears seemed past. This Samantha looked more the mature woman and less the vulnerable mother of a few minutes ago.

'You *are* good for me,' Samantha said. 'I feel better than I have since I left Amanda in Reading.'

'I'm glad. And you're beautiful.' Samantha's smile was his reward.

'Where are we going?' She sounded like a girl on her first date.

'Burger King, I suppose,' Harold said.

Samantha burst out laughing. The sound of her merriment was an even greater reward than her smile. 'Should I put on my diamonds, then? I don't want to feel under-dressed.'

'They used to say,' Harold told her, ' "be a hero to your kids – take them to McDonalds." So for grown-ups it has to be Burger King. Their hamburgers are much better than those from the Golden Arch restaurant. I eat there all the time. I can't wait to show you off to my friends behind the counter.'

He drove them to the fast food restaurant.

'You really meant it,' Samantha said in surprise.

'Well, we can go just about anywhere you'd like. How about McDonalds?'

Samantha laughed again. 'No, let's eat like grown-ups.

Inside, Harold nodded to one or two of the customers. Two of the counter staff he knew by name. No

76

hard, Samantha thought, since their names were on badges pinned to their uniforms, but they seemed to be genuine acquaintances. They greeted Harold by name, and looked at Samantha more closely than she liked.

'See, I told you they'd like you,' Harold told her as they took their order to a side table. 'You've passed the Burger King test.'

Samantha smiled again. 'I'm glad.' And, suddenly, she was. It began as a feeling of being able to breathe again, and went on to become a new sense of being an independent woman who could attract and interest a younger man like Harold.

Harold too saw the change. He reached across to take her hand and give it a squeeze. She returned the grasp, and they ate one-handed like love-struck teenagers.

As they left, Samantha said, 'I'd never have believed fast food could be so therapeutic. Too bad it's so fast.'

'Feeling better, then?'

'Definitely. It could have something to do with the company, too.'

Harold leaned close and kissed her cheek. 'In full view of the counter staff, too,' he said. 'They'll all want to know about you now.'

'I'm to be the talk of the Burger King chain, then?'

'Well, maybe not the whole chain. They probably won't know who you are in Newark – New Jersey, that is, not the one up the road.'

They passed the drive to Samantha's old house in companionable conversation. There they loaded the last of her belongings into the van.

'The new owners move in in two days' time. They're coming from Manchester,' Samantha said, as they stood gazing out at the back garden. Beyond the privet hedge there was farmland, looking green and lush now as the fields waited for the harvest.

'That's corn, isn't it?' Harold asked. 'I'm a townie, hopeless at matters rural.'

'It is,' Samantha agreed. 'Over there is sugar beet.'

Suddenly she turned away from the window and went up the stairs. Harold followed, curious to see the house again before leaving. Samantha toured the upper floor, looking into each of the bedrooms and toilets and closets.

'Just making sure I've left nothing,' she said with an edge to her voice.

Saying goodbye, Harold reckoned, and not enjoying the process. He had felt something like this on moving house for the first time after the divorce.

Samantha turned to him, her back to the window and her face in shadow, so that her expression was unreadable. 'This is . . . was Amanda's room.' Her control broke again.

Harold held her once again as she cried for the ending of her former life. The empty nest reaction must be a strong one, he thought – with a certain detachment and relief. Glad I'm not facing that. From his detached position he was still able to feel Samantha's distress. Her distress, not the cause of it, distressed him. She shook with sobs as he held her tightly to him.

Eventually the tears passed. Samantha raised her head and caught his glance. The back garden was growing shadows as the sun set. Against the failing light he saw the diamond points on her eyelashes and the wet streaks down her face. But she faced him steadily.

This time it was Samantha who held his gaze. 'I've never thanked you for helping . . . for being there through all this.' She raised her face and kissed him on the mouth. Her lips opened and suddenly she was holding onto him and kissing him with her whole body.

They clung to one another as evening fell over the garden and the future approached.

Finally Samantha broke free to continue the goodbye tour of the house: dining room, front and back sitting rooms, cloakroom, the closet under the stairs. The last stop was the kitchen. With the cabinets and sink and appliances still in place it was the most normal-looking room in the house. Samantha stood with her back to the sink and let her eye travel the familiar room. She had a faraway look in her eyes, as if she were remembering the countless breakfasts and teas with Amanda. It went on for a long time. Finally she shook herself and reached for Harold's hand. She led him from her house, from her old life, toward the next chapter in the story. Samantha locked the front door and, as a final token of goodbye to the house and the past, she pushed the key through the letterbox.

'Let's go,' she said.

They went, not to the hamburger bar, but to a quiet pub for their evening meal. The bar was not crowded. They had several drinks. Samantha, predictably, had a vodka and Coke. Harold, equally as predictable, drank lager. Life seemed to be getting back to normal. The food was good but unpretentious – roast beef, baked potatoes, salad and two veg. They left as the bar began to fill up.

'My place or yours?' Samantha asked him as they reached the car. 'Yours,' she decided abruptly. 'I've never really seen where you live. It's time I did.'

Harold shrugged and headed towards his own house, thinking that he really should have put things away when he had the chance. Now it seemed to him that he had been postponing decisions about his own future. So long as he continued to live out of boxes and cartons, he did not have to decide about settling. He had been camping out in his house rather than living in it.

As they entered Samantha noted the clutter. Harold was glad that he had at least made the attempt to keep the kitchen clean. The sink was not overflowing with dirty dishes and the counters were clear. The coffee maker and the coffee were in their places.

'I'm glad to see you're not living in typical bachelor squalor,' Samantha commented as she filled the kettle. They sat on the sofa to drink their coffee, the TV turned on low to the evening news. Samantha relaxed, and, seeing that, so did Harold.

'Why are you being so nice to me?' she asked abruptly.

'Because I want to be. I like you a lot. And,' with a grin, 'because you're perverted.'

Samantha smiled at his use of her word. 'You've never run into anyone with my particular kink?'

'I wasn't talking about your preference for being tied up, though I like that too. And, to answer your question, no, you are the first. What I meant was your whole approach to sex. Your enjoyment of it. Your headlong style. No woman has ever got so quickly from hello to fuck me. And I've never enjoyed sex so much before.'

'So I'm just a sex toy?' Samantha's question had an edge to it.

'Not just, as you should know. But since you brought it up, what's so bad about enjoying sex? A lot of people don't, from what I've seen. You do. I do. I enjoy it with you. Can you think of a better way to get to know someone? We all have to start somewhere.'

'So the best way to a woman's heart is through her pussy?' Samantha sounded easier now.

'Sometimes,' Harold replied. 'But I see nothing wrong in that. Does having sex worry you?'

'No.' This time Samantha was smiling. 'I just wanted to see if you would start to talk of love and commitment and higher longings. I detest that kind of cant. Let it come later if it comes at all. Enjoy what you have first. But tell me again that I'm beautiful.'

'You are.'

Samantha smoothed her skirt over her thighs. 'Look,' she commanded. Beneath the taut material the outline of her suspenders was revealed. 'I wore these for you. Would you like to look?'

'In a minute,' Harold said, glad that the difficult moment had passed. 'First, come nearer. Sit beside me and kiss me.'

Samantha slid across and nestled against him. Harold put his arm around her shoulders and hugged her to him. They sat for long moments enjoying the nearness.

'See? No groping hands.'

'What are you waiting for?' Samantha asked.

'I just wanted you to see that I don't have to make a grab for your tits in the first five minutes.'

'Well, the five minutes are up,' Samantha said, grinning.

'So they are.'

Harold stood and lifted Samantha to her feet. Then he undressed her. She raised her arms as he slid her dress off over her head. He released her full breasts from her bra and let it fall to the floor. Carefully he slid her pants down to her ankles and she stepped out of them. Wearing only her stockings and suspenders, she posed for him.

'Glorious,' he said, looking at her nakedness. 'Thank you.'

She caught his mood. Stepping forward, she undressed him. There was a moment of difficulty as she manoeuvred his pants over his erect cock, and then he stood naked before her. Samantha too looked him over, then knelt to kiss the head of his cock.

'Glorious,' she whispered in turn.

Harold raised her and led her toward the bedroom. 'Get on top of me,' Samantha told him as she climbed into bed, 'and fuck me stupid.'

He did. Harold found it necessary to stop her mouth with his own when she cried out in release. The silky material of her stockings created a delightful friction against his legs as he rose and fell above her. She matched his ardour with her own, and they clung to one another as the waves of pleasure swept over them both.

Later, lying entwined, Harold raised his head to kiss her lips. Taking her naked body in his arms, he held her until they both fell asleep.

Samantha woke him in the morning with a kiss, and they made love again as the light grew in the room. Afterwards, Harold told her that she had taken the virginity of his house.

'Really? You've never had a woman here?'

He shook his head.

'Then I am honoured,' she told him.

They rose, naked, and ate a breakfast of boiled eggs, toast and tea. The early morning sunlight slanted through the kitchen window and tipped Samantha's breasts with gold. He stood before her and kissed her crinkly nipples while Samantha stroked the back of his head and his neck, holding him against her. They cleared up together, touching and kissing as they bumped into each other at the sink.

Then Samantha asked him to tie her up. He was expecting that, but he had to get into his trousers and go to the van for the cord. When he returned, Samantha was coming from the bathroom, her hair brushed. She still wore the stockings and suspenders.

'I'll have a lie-in,' she told him as he was tying her hands behind her back.

Harold knew now what Samantha liked, and he tied her as he had on their first meeting: wrists and elbows, ankles, knees and thighs. Struck by inspiration, he tied her thumbs together.

Samantha approved. 'I'll never get loose now.'

When he had gagged and blindfolded her Harold stood for long moments regarding the bound woman lying in his bed. Then he hogtied her and pulled the covers over her helpless body. The autumn mornings were getting chilly. Samantha moved slightly as she settled down. He kissed her taped eyes, and her mouth over the gag. Then he left her to her fantasies.

Harold tried to put her out of his mind as he began tidying up the place. Samantha had looked askance at the bachelor-clutter, and so he set about clearing it up. He worked happily, anticipating her surprise when she saw what he had done while she was *hors de combat*. Of course, he couldn't quite forget about her. Who could?

Harold looked in from time to time to check Samantha was all right. Each time he entered as silently as he could, in case she was sleeping – or doing something else. Once he found her doing something else with a great deal of energy, and he stopped to watch in fascination. He doubted that Samantha would mind very much, but even if she did not like to be seen indulging her fantasies, he could not tear himself away. She was pulling and jerking at the rope, and making muffled but unmistakable sounds through her gag. It was the noises she made that told Harold when she came. She did so quite often, heaving and jerking against the cords and moaning deep down in her throat when her orgasms swept through her.

Harold wondered where she got the stamina. She seemed inexhaustible, but of course she was not. After what seemed like a very long time Samantha grew quiet. Her tense body relaxed, and she appeared to sleep. Harold could not tell from that distance, and he did not want to disturb whatever fantasies she might be having about being abandoned in a deserted house. That seemed to be one of her strongest fantasies, and when he closed the door quietly Harold began to think of places that would fit the scenario she had described.

He was trying to think of a place to take her in the van, and he was ransacking his memory of the surrounding countryside for a deserted house (or a barn) where he could leave her while she lived out her abduction fantasies. It occurred to Harold again that Samantha was getting a lot more out of this than he was – if one went by orgasms alone. But he had to admit that he took much satisfaction in knowing that he had a naked woman in his keeping – one who could not free herself unless he untied her. And, of course, there were the fucks when he finally did let her go.

It was not such a bad bargain after all, he concluded, though it was not one he would have accepted with any of his former lovers. Something in him had changed without his knowing it. At some point in the past few days he had ceased to care just about fucking a woman and had begun to think of sex in terms of what he had to offer her in the way of pleasure. He had met Samantha at just the right time. She had crystallised these feelings by making him tie her up and leave her to work out her sexual release. He might have come to that position on his own, but it would have probably have taken longer.

By late afternoon the house looked tidier. Samantha had been tied up for nearly six hours, alone except for his quiet visits. He began to feel the urge for her company, for proximity, even if she only lay next to him bound and gagged. He was beginning to take a certain proprietary satisfaction in her – which he put off for another half-hour. When he entered the room Samantha lay on the floor beside the bed, tangled in the duvet. Somehow she had managed to move close enough to the side of the bed and, Harold guessed, had overbalanced and fallen, unable to stop herself. He could see her hands and arms, held tightly behind her back by the cords. The duvet was twisted round her legs, but had slipped down far enough to reveal her thighs and the tops of her stockings.

The overall effect was erotic, he thought: bound woman struggling to free herself falls to the floor and is revealed in her helpless nakedness. She twisted slightly, moaning. He saw her breast, the nipple erect. Sanity returned in the next moment. He crossed the room hurriedly to check that she was uninjured. Samantha was breathing normally. She moaned softly but did not seem to be in any pain. From the smell of sex Harold knew that she had worked herself up to her usual multiple orgasms.

Samantha, he guessed, would prefer to remain bound as she was and to pursue her fantasy, but he had to assure himself that she was all right.

He peeled off the tape over her mouth and pulled her pants out. Samantha worked her jaws to relieve the cramp left by having them held open for so many hours.

Harold asked anxiously if she were all right. Samantha nodded, working her tongue around inside her mouth to moisten it so she could talk. 'Toilet,' she croaked. 'In a hurry, please.' This came out accompanied by a faint smile.

Hurriedly he removed the hogtie and picked her up in his arms to carry her through to the bathroom. There the problem of untying her legs arose. 'Do I have time to get you loose?'

'I don't think so,' she replied with another faint smile. 'We've left it too long. Better lay me in the bathtub and let nature take its course.'

He hesitated. Then he felt Samantha clench her legs even more tightly and knew that she was going to piss herself in a moment. He knelt awkwardly with her body in his arms. Somehow he got her balanced sitting on the side of the bathtub while keeping her from falling in. That way lay broken bones – or worse. The care and feeding of helpless women was not an easy task. Harold lifted her legs over the edge and allowed her to slide down until her bottom touched the tub's bottom. He held her in a sitting position, leaning against the near side of the tub, with both arms around her upper body.

'Ahhh,' Samantha sighed as she relaxed. A golden stream ran from between her bound legs, making its way to the drain. Even with her legs tied together so tightly Samantha managed to piss the insides of her thighs. When the cascade ended, her stockings were soaked, dark with her urine.

'God, that felt good,' she said. 'Get me a glass of water if you don't mind.'

Harold filled a tooth-mug at the hand basin and held it while Samantha drank.

When the glass was empty she was able to speak more plainly. 'Don't give me too much, or I'll have to go again.' There was a laugh somewhere in the remark.

'I'll have to untie you now,' Harold told her.

'I know,' Samantha sighed. 'It's a pity, but there it is.'

'Will you be all right while I get the knife to cut you loose?'

'Yes, I can manage, but I'd feel better if you kissed me first – if only to show me that I'm not such a pain.'

Harold kissed her. Samantha kissed him back, ardently. There was a danger that things would go on from there. Samantha moaned as the kiss drew out and showed no sign of wanting it to end.

Harold at last drew back. He balanced Samantha in the sitting position and went to the kitchen for something to cut the cords that held her. She sighed again as they fell away. Harold removed the tape from her eyes and helped her to stand up. Samantha's legs weren't cooperating, and he asked her if there was any problem.

'I'm just stiff from being tied up for so long. It will pass. No need to worry.'

86

Harold allowed that she knew more than he did about her recovery time. He stopped worrying about injury and began to worry about his erection. Samantha naked in his bathtub save for her stained stockings was a powerful aphrodisiac.

She noticed. 'You still want me after all this? I must look a mess.'

'Yes, I do,' he croaked.

'Then you shall have me. Get undressed while I rinse myself.'

Samantha turned on the shower taps and adjusted the water temperature while Harold shed his clothes. She turned around under the stream, keeping only her hair dry. She turned off the water and stepped dripping out of the tub and lay down on her back on the carpet in the bathroom. 'Get on top of me,' Samantha told him.

When he did she guided him into her and lifted her legs. The wet nylon made a slithery sound as she crossed her ankles behind his back and pulled him against her body.

Harold sank gratefully into her and lay gazing down into her eyes for a moment.

Samantha smiled at him and lifted her hips, beginning the steady in-and-out rhythm that could lead to only one conclusion. When her climax was near, she told him, 'Kiss me. Cover my mouth. I'm ... I'm going to scream.'

So he did, and she did, and they both did. And when it was over she held him atop her with her arms around his shoulders.

'Mmmmm,' Samantha said contentedly.

'Another lost virginity,' Harold said.

'Do you mean that you don't fuck regularly in the bathroom?' Samantha smiled ironically.

'No, you're another first. This is getting to be a habit.'

'Then I'm honoured again, I think.'

Samantha uncrossed her ankles and allowed her legs to lie along the floor. Harold stroked them, liking the feel of the wet nylon against her warm flesh. Then he made as if to rise. 'I don't want to squash you,' he told her.

'No. Stay there,' Samantha commanded.

And so they lay on the bathroom floor as the shadows lengthened in the room. . This time it was Harold whose head lay on Samantha's shoulder. He occasionally lifted it to kiss her eyes and nose and throat, or to nibble at her earlobe. This last caused Samantha to giggle.

'It tickles,' she said.

At length she raised her legs and once more crossed her ankles behind his back. She tightened them, pulling him against her. At the same time she rolled her hips on the floor, causing his cock to nudge into her. Then she began a slow series of internal clenchings and relaxations, making him fully erect. As she felt him hardening inside her, Samantha changed from rolling to thrusting. Harold picked up her rhythm, and they made slow love on the tiled floor once more. This time, he didn't need to stop her screams with kisses, but he kissed her nonetheless. There seemed no urgency this time. Samantha moaned softly as she came, and when he joined her at the last, she used her legs to hold him firmly inside, against her, as he spent himself. Outside, Sunday evening came, but it brought none of the usual post-weekend *triste* Harold remembered from a few months ago.

4

Safe as Houses

October came, and the Hunter's Moon. Harold and
Samantha saw one another nearly every weekend.
Occasionally they met for lunch or drinks during the
week. Samantha continued to rely on Harold to satisfy
her 'perversion'. Harold came to rely on Samantha for
the passion and the tenderness that had been missing
from his life. He thought he might be falling in love. She
called it falling into lust – which, thankfully, she said,
showed no sign of lessening. Samantha refused to act
like the conventional woman, angling for the safety of
marriage. As she put it, she didn't want to give up
passion for security. She felt most secure, she averred,
when tied up. No other form of security appealed to her.
Harold thought that she simply liked to live dangerously
(if that were a simple desire). As time went on, he began
to enjoy the danger too. He was always careful not to
leave Samantha in circumstances where she could be
injured, while she pushed gently at his self-imposed
limits from time to time.

'Experiments,' she called her ideas. Harold became
her experimenter. The proposed bondage-in-a-van
weekend never happened. Neither of them had any idea
where to stage it, though both continued to look for
likely spots. The main trouble was that a parked van

invited exploration, if not outright theft, which neither of them wanted. The plan became an unattainable goal, even as it spurred them to strive for it.

Samantha revived the idea of being left tied and gagged in a barn. 'Just drag me up to the loft, tie me up and throw me into the straw,' as she put it. Autumn in England was not a good time to be left naked and bound in an unheated barn, straw or not, as he put it. But she clung to her fantasy even as the days grew colder and shorter.

Eventually Harold found an old barn (with straw in the loft). He took Samantha to see it on a cold but sunny October Sunday. The countryside seemed deserted for miles around. Samantha was excited by the prospect of being left there. The isolation appealed to her; no one would know she was there, she insisted. Harold agreed with the last, but pointed out that the wind was both strong and cold.

Samantha accused him of being afraid. Not so, he said. Just careful. Inevitably, though, he acceded to her wishes, partly because her idea – her fantasy – had begun to arouse his interest as well. Her suggestion for a *denouement* was also interesting. When he came back for her he was to act as if he had come upon a bound and naked (and attractive) woman by accident, and to let nature (in the form of an erect cock) take its course. Play-acting had never appealed so strongly to him as it did then. To Samantha play-acting formed a good part of her fantasy life.

No one's around, she argued. The cords are in the car. Samantha had got him to leave a quantity of the thin cord she preferred to be bound with in the car, along with the duct tape. Ear plugs had joined the collection, and a leather welder's hood which he sometimes put over her head back to front. When it was tied around her neck, she was effectively blind. It was not as hard on her eyelids as the duct tape he often used. Samantha preferred the tape. 'More authentic,' she described it. 'Spur-of-the-moment stuff.' In the end he agreed to try it. The plan was to leave Samantha there until around three in the afternoon, when he would return and 'stumble' upon her.

In the shortening days there would not be much daylight left if he did not return by three or three-thirty. 'I could do all night,' Samantha told Harold with evident excitement. He thought that was too much. It would be really cold then. 'You won't be able to move around to keep warm,' he pointed out. Samantha accused him of being a kill-joy.

The barn was in an open space that must once been a farmyard, though it was overgrown now. He left the car near a footpath and they walked across the intervening space. Even if they could have driven up to the barn, the car standing outside would give the game away. Samantha was clearly excited as they approached the building.

The doors were partly open, the hinges rusted from years of neglect. They forced them open and stepped inside. Concrete covered the ground floor, not an inviting place to be left helpless. The loft looked more promising. It had a wooden floor. Harold saw that there was straw and hay there, and Samantha said that it would do. The windows were covered with dust and cobwebs, as was most of the interior. Not much of the weak daylight filtered in. Samantha went up the ladder eagerly. Harold admired the play of her leg muscles under the sheer nylon of her stockings as she climbed up ahead of him. The loft was thick with straw from broken bales. It looked as if no one had been there for quite some time. From this, Samantha immediately concluded that no one else would come and find her. Harold had gone along with her plan without considering that danger. Deserted barns (in fantasies at least) stayed deserted. Now he weighed the possibility of someone else coming upon Samantha while she was helpless. Samantha did not seem concerned by the possibility. Maybe, Harold guessed, it didn't matter much to her who found her. That was part of the fantasy. However, her fantasy did not seem to include the possibility that her finder might be considerably less considerate of her than Harold was.

Samantha began to undress. The plan was to leave her naked save for her stockings and suspenders (which had become a kind of uniform for their sex-and-bondage sessions because Harold liked that touch.) She had not even finished undressing when she began to shiver. Goose flesh broke out all over her body, but she appeared ready to carry on, a measure of her excitement and her pride. Her nipples stood out hard and tight in the cold air. Harold was about to protest that it was too cold when the matter was resolved for them. The distant baying of hounds broke in upon the silence of their rural retreat. They came closer. The discordant, tuneless notes of the huntsman's horn were heard. Through a crack in the side of the barn Harold saw a large group of horsemen and women in red and dark green field jackets following a large pack of hounds, who in turn were in hot pursuit of a frightened fox. And the fox was making straight for the barn.

'It's the local fox hunt,' he told her, 'they're coming this way.'

Samantha looked alarmed, as well she might.

The fox came into the barn at a dead run, paused, and looked about for a safe haven. There were none. After wasting a few moments in his search, he began casting about for an escape route that did not lead into the jaws of the pack.

'How beastly!' Samantha was instinctively on the fox's side. 'We've got to save him.'

'Well,' Harold suggested, 'you could wait for the huntsmen to come into the barn, and remonstrate with them. I'm sure they would at least pause to listen to a naked woman telling them that they should cease and desist. That might give the fox time to make a run for it. Of course, you'd have to get the dogs to listen as well. They will get to him before the hunt crowd do.'

Samantha began to see the difficulties in coming to the fox's aid. She ceased bristling and continued shivering, wrapping her arms around her breasts and hugging herself. 'Well, they shouldn't set dogs onto helpless animals.'

Harold imagined that if the dogs got a whiff of Samantha in heat they might be distracted from their bloody pursuit. The image of Samantha knee-deep in interested fox hounds, tails a-wag, nearly caused him to burst into laughter. Fortunately he contained it, for the huntsmen would certainly have heard, and, hearing, investigated. But Samantha had noticed.

'What's so funny?' she asked in a furious whisper. She was not amused when he told her.

The pack followed their quarry into the barn. The huntsmen did the same, the followers remaining outside. Harold prodded Samantha. 'Aren't you going to tell them to stop?'

She shot him a furious look but kept quiet.

Fortunately for the fox, there was a hole in the rear of the barn and he slipped through. Fortunately for them, the pack noticed the fox making his escape. They set off in pursuit, followed by a chorus of tally-ho!s and a bloodthirsty group of hunt enthusiasts. The noise quickly receded as the hunt turned away and followed the pack.

Samantha was shaken, both by the hunt and by the narrowness of their escape. The cold was getting to her as well. Perhaps she was beginning to think that this was

93

not such a good idea after all. What finally caused her to abandon the scheme was something much more prosaic than being discovered by the hunters or put off by the cold. She moved to the wall of the barn to peer through a crack at the departing hunt. There was a rustle and a series of squeaks, and mice fled in every direction from her feet. One of them ran between them, paused, then continued its flight. 'Eeeekkkk!' Samantha screamed, oblivious to the possibility of being overheard by the retreating hunt. She stood rooted to the spot, eyes wide in horror and legs clamped firmly together. She had assumed the classic Venus de Milo pose instinctively, and (unlike Venus, who already had a pedestal) was looking for something high to stand on.

There were only a few bales of hay among the straw. She clambered up onto one of them without moving her arms from their protective positions (a feat that impressed Harold considerably). Atop the bale she resumed her legs-together stance while looking anxiously for more threatening mice.

She did not have to look very far. A grey furry head poked up from the bale beside her foot. She probably would not have noticed, for the terrified rodent was as quiet as ... well, a mouse. Its relatives were not so circumspect. There was a renewed chorus of squeaks and a second horde of mice fled in all directions. Samantha looked down and saw the mouse beside her foot. She launched herself into the air, perhaps expecting Harold to catch her and hold her safely above the tide of rodents she had loosed. It was not a good plan.

Harold was doubled over with laughter. Samantha's hurtling body caught him completely unawares. The impact knocked him to the floor. Samantha landed atop him.

Harold raised his head and regarded the naked woman lying across his chest – and broke into renewed gales of laughter. Samantha looked furiously at him, and then fearfully around for more mice. There were none. She looked very carefully, while Harold's laughter subsided to chuckles.

'How could you ... !' she began, and then was overtaken by a fit of the giggles. Perhaps she laughed in relief. Perhaps she really saw the funny side now that the panic was over. Her laughter was infectious. It set Harold off again. They rolled together, laughing and hugging one another. He seized Samantha's head between his hands, holding her still while he covered her laughing mouth with his own. Still Samantha laughed, into him, gasping and snorting. Harold too laughed.

When finally they stopped, Samantha had given up the idea of being left bound and gagged in the hay-loft.

'Why?' Harold asked. 'I would have tied your legs tightly together. No mouse on earth would have stood a chance of entering your mouse-hole.'

Samantha gathered up her scattered clothing and got dressed. So ended their rural expedition. They descended the ladder and returned to the car. They would have stopped at the first pub down the road, except that the car park had been turned temporarily into a horse-and pony-park: the local hunt celebrating the bloody end of yet another fox, as Samantha put it in renewed fury.

The next pub was hunt-free, and there they had lunch and some calming drinks. Several of the customers, as well as the landlord, looked at them curiously; probably, they thought, because they were not local. Samantha only discovered the source of the merriment when she went to the ladies' room. There she discovered strands of hay and straw caught in her hair and clothing. She blushed hotly, and then became furious with Harold again. He could have told her, and saved her from making a fool of herself. She stormed out intending to collect him and vent her anger on him in the relative privacy of the car.

Harold too had hay and straw in his hair and on his clothing. He was oblivious to it. Luckily for him, Samantha saw the funny side of it all. Luckily for her, she was able to contain her laughter until they were once more on the road.

'Oh my dear,' she said, simultaneously hugging him and plucking straws from his hair while laughing uncontrollably. When she sat back in her seat, she turned to him and explained the latest cause for merriment. Harold saw the funny side at once. He smiled at her. She smiled back.

'I'm sorry you didn't get to leave me there. It might have been fun,' she said.

'I'm sure the mice would have enjoyed it,' Harold retorted with a chuckle.

'Never mind, we'll make it up at home,' Samantha said. 'In the meantime, you can stare at my legs.' She pulled her skirt up to her waist and settled in her seat, leaving her long shapely nylon-sheathed legs on display.

Many long-distance lorry drivers had their Sunday afternoon gladdened by the sight of Samantha's legs as they overtook the car. And several of them honked their air-horns and waved in approval. Samantha grew accustomed to the salutations. She made no effort to cover herself up. Harold was pleased by her healthy attitude and by the display – which was, as she said, for his benefit. His cock grew erect several times on the drive. Whenever Samantha noticed she smiled at him. Finally she reached over and unzipped his trousers. She plunged her hand inside and emerged holding his cock, in contravention of the Road Traffic Act. Without covering herself she leaned across and down to take him into her mouth. What she did then certainly contravened the Road Traffic Act. Harold was less displeased, though there were several times when he had to bring his attention forcibly back to the road. One of the lorry drivers, overtaking, saw what was happening inside the car that was moving so erratically. He honked his horn and gave them the victory sign as he passed. Samantha returned the salutation before returning to the business in hand. In both hands. Harold tried to drive straight.

She made him come despite himself. And she swallowed his semen again. When she sat up there was a shiny trail at one side of her mouth. Samantha licked it away.

Amazing, Harold thought. What an amazing woman. In the past, when something like this had happened, his partner had been spitting and gagging for an hour afterward.

Samantha did not zip him up again. Like her legs, his cock was on display to whoever could see. It felt strange at first, but gradually Harold felt himself begin to enjoy the experience.

Back at her flat Samantha pulled her skirt down and helped Harold zip up before they got out of the car. They ate ham sandwiches and drank coffee and laughed anew at the misadventure of the barn. And later Samantha kept her promise to 'make it up.' Naked once more save for stockings and suspenders, she lay on her bed while Harold tied her wrists and ankles to the four bed posts. 'Boring but effective,' Samantha pronounced as she tugged at the cords that held her.

'Would you like a mouse to liven things up?'

Samantha shook her head, giggling.

Harold taped her eyes and gagged her with her pants and more duct tape. She sighed in pleasure when he was done. He left her then, knowing that she wanted to be allowed time to fantasise and to test her bonds. This was the hardest part for Harold – finding ways to fill the time while his mistress was enjoying her fantasy life and trying to make herself come. He doubted that she would be able to manage that, tied as she was, but her fantasies would at least offer some compensation.

The time dragged. When they were at his place he could at least pretend to tidy up or perform some domestic chores. At Samantha's, where everything was tidy all of the time and where he did not feel free to pry, there was nothing to do but watch television. Television at the best of times was no match for having Samantha. Sunday afternoon television was not the best.

When he went to Samantha, therefore, he brought with him a good deal of pent-up sexual desire. He knew he was being rougher than usual with her as a consequence, but Samantha seemed not to mind. If her own responses were any indication, she liked his abruptness and energy. Samantha was not one to enjoy the same lovemaking time after time. Her fantasy of being 'found' and then fucked in a deserted barn suggested that she was playing out some kind of rape fantasy. This was another version of the same fantasy. Warmer, safer, but the same idea. She came several times before he did, thanks to the blow job in the car and to her own postponed release. She bucked and heaved as he plunged in and out, moaning whenever she reached a peak. Samantha was not a passive fuck.

Nor did she seem to be 'passionate for a purpose,' as the writer John Fowles once expressed it. She enjoyed passion for its own sake. Most of the other women he had known had been passionate in the initial stages, and then, as security of tenure set in, had become less so. He had begun to expect this process, much as he disliked it. With Samantha the passion did not lessen as they became regular lovers. She asked not for security but for novelty (within certain limits), and gave in return her wholehearted cooperation in making sex a satisfying adventure for them both. Harold was forced by her example to look for new ways to please her, and so was kept from becoming stale himself.

When she felt him tense up just prior to coming Samantha reared up, tugging against her bonds until the bed creaked as she came along with him. When he had spent himself she remained tense, her internal muscles clenched around his cock until she had finished coming. Only then did she lie back on the bed and relax her taut muscles. She was covered with a sheen of perspiration and there were deep red marks on her wrists where the cords had dug into them. But she made no protest save when Harold began to remove her gag. Samantha shook her head, indicating that she would like to remain as she was.

Harold left her again. This time, however, with nothing to do for another indefinite time, he did snoop. Samantha had never forbidden him to look around her house. He reminded himself of that as he guiltily began to pry into her private life. He was looking for nothing in particular, and for anything that would tell him more about this woman with whom his life was being woven tighter each day. It occurred to him that she was binding him even as she was bound. He could not simply walk away from her. Not today, when she was helpless, nor any other day, when he hoped she would call and ask him to come tie her up and make passionate love to her.

So he searched for clues to her private life. Curiosity: pure, simple, indefensible. But not fatal, as it was to the proverbial cat. He knew that he could not be interrupted.

First the desk. A collection of the usual bills told him only that Samantha paid by direct debit, mainly, and owed no substantial sums. There were some old snapshots of a younger Samantha. When he studied then, comparing them to the Samantha he knew, there was no great physical difference. In the older photos she was somewhat thinner. Perhaps too thin, by his standards of beauty. He preferred her as she was now. Amanda appeared, a young girl indistinguishable from a young boy of the same age save by dress. Amanda growing up,

Samantha not always in shot now. Several shots of Amanda at the Pony-Club stage, wearing jodhpurs and a determined look, riding crop in hand. No pictures of the husband, though there were many empty spaces in the albums that might once have contained his likeness. They only served to emphasise his abscence now. Harold was oddly gladdened – relieved – by that.

An old diary of Amanda's. Girl-thoughts, saved out of sentimentality rather than for any profound insights. Samantha apparently kept no diary. He turned to her computer. No diary there either, though a calendar contained several references to meetings they had had. Nearly always Samantha had recorded her pleasure at his calling, or after a meeting. It was flattering to his ego to know that she was glad of his presence and, presumably, of their mutual pleasure (carnal and otherwise) in one another's company. There were no longings for a more permanent arrangement, nor any evidence of a desire to terminate the one they presently had. That was OK with him. Harold was not yet ready for a more official arrangement either.

Samantha had not protected her computer with a password, but she had been forced to do so for her Internet connection. In her calendar she had recorded it: Amanda. Easy to remember. He wondered if Amanda had made the discovery yet. Probably she had. Harold signed on to her Internet service provider and had a look at her favourites menu – a good sign of where the user's interests lay. There he found that Samantha had taken his advice and investigated various sales outlets for bondage equipment. Whether she had bought anything he couldn't say, but she had looked at several handcuff and leg-iron sites. One of them advertised medical restraints and equipment.

She had looked at bondage wear, as well as several more conventional clothing sites – fashion shopping, no doubt. Harold wished she had not investigated the handcuff sites. He had determined to buy her the leg-irons she had not had the nerve to buy for herself, as a birthday present. He couldn't ask her without giving the game – and his snooping – away. But he could snoop further around the flat to see if she had taken delivery of anything lately. He closed down the computer and set off to investigate the hiding places in the flat. He knew these as well as she did.

His search revealed nothing that jingled or clinked other than the handcuffs he already knew about. In the cupboard under the stairs he came across an umbrella stand that held, among the umbrellas, a riding crop. It was probably Amanda's, but he remembered Samantha saying that she already had a whip of her own. Was Samantha into being whipped? The next discovery suggested she did. She had purchased a short-handled whip, light in construction, with a dozen short knotted leather thongs. The box in which it had come contained an illustration of its use – on a bound woman who was apparently screaming in pain. The literature described it as a 'pussy whip,' and the woman was being struck in the designated area. In a nod toward women's liberation, the makers added that it worked just as well on penises. Had she bought it for herself, or for him?

The idea of being whipped on his penis caused mixed feelings in Harold. He didn't want to analyse them just then. He replaced the whip where he had found it and went to check on Samantha.

She was still securely bound and gagged, showing signs of recent exertion. The red marks at her wrists and ankles looked deeper. Her body was covered in a thin sheen of perspiration, and he thought he could detect the odour of arousal. He imagined her struggling to free herself, and her feelings when she could not. Unbidden, there came an image of her body covered in red welts of

101

the kind the pussy whip might make. They covered her breasts and stomach and belly and trailed off between her legs . . . Harold shook himself mentally.

'Samantha,' he called softly, 'are you awake?'

'Ummmnng!' she said through the gag.

'I'll take that as a yes,' he said lightly, kneeling beside the bed and planting a kiss on her mouth, feeling again her lips working beneath the tape as she did her best to return it. He stroked her hair, pushing a few damp strands back off her forehead. With his free hand he stroked her left leg from bound ankle to sheer stocking-top. Samantha made approving noises.

'Toilet?' Harold asked next.

Samantha shook her head.

'Hungry?'

'Oo.'

'Thirsty?'

A shake of the head.

'Want to get loose?'

Another shake. Samantha raised her head and looked (if one could use that word of a woman whose eyes were taped shut) in the direction of her widespread thighs. Samantha emphasised her demand by raising her hips as far as she could in her position.

That meaning at least was clear, and Harold wondered anew at her stamina and appetite while at the same time feeling the first stirrings of his own desire. He guessed that Samantha had not been able to bring herself off while tied in this position. He climbed onto the bed and knelt between her legs. He used his lips and teeth on her labia, and his tongue on her clitoris.

Samantha sighed with pleasure, and her breathing became shallow and rapid as he aroused her. She tried to spread her legs even further, without much success. Harold thought of untying her ankles, but she probably would not want that. He sat back on his heels and

102

inserted a finger into her cunt, teasing and rubbing her clitoris. He slid another finger into her anal passage. That was harder, but when she was doubly penetrated Samantha moaned loudly – the first sign of an orgasm. Harold continued to arouse her. Samantha obligingly became more excited. Inevitably she came, jerking and struggling against the ropes, her hips thrusting against the invading fingers, moaning deeply through the gag.

When she lay back Harold continued to touch her. Samantha would have none of it. She raised her head and shook it vigorously. 'Ooooo!' she said, pointing with her chin vaguely in his direction.

Flattered (and erect), Harold lay down on top of her and guided his cock into her cunt. Samantha sighed deeply as he slid into her.

Harold supported himself on his elbows. His fingers were just able to reach her engorged nipples. She approved of that too, raising her hips and then lowering them again quickly so that she made him slide in and then partially out. Harold took this as a sign that she wanted to be (as she had frequently put it) 'fucked stupid.' He did his best, holding himself back through several of her orgasms. Samantha, restrained as she was, was much less restrained in her response. Her body heaved and bucked as she came. The gag muffled her vocal responses, but they were still loud. She was having a good time.

Harold, observing what he could of her movements, and feeling the internal ones, was also having a good time. Part of it was due to Samantha's obvious pleasure. As he rose and fell he remembered Amanda's injunction to give her 'as much pleasure as possible.' He concentrated on that. So when he came himself it was the cause of much mutual pleasure – if Samantha's movements and incoherent noises were any indication.

Harold lay atop her as lightly as he could while heartbeats slowed, breathing became less frantic and bodies cooled. This, too, was one of the many delights of fucking Samantha. She did not expect him to climb off instantly, untie her and let her retreat to the bathroom for repairs to her dignity. Samantha in rut was Samantha satisfied. Samantha tied to the bed was more so.

They spent the rest of the evening quietly. Samantha, still naked save for her stockings and suspenders, made an omelette for them. Harold did not get dressed either. After they had eaten he sat on the sofa and she came to lay her head in his lap. He found a curious satisfaction in the aftermath of sex. He stroked her hair and face and neck and ears (despite her giggles) and she occasionally stroked his cock, or kissed it lightly. It was a quiet end to a busy day.

5

Birthday Gifts

After that weekend, barns seemed less likely venues for their sex games, though Samantha continued to dream of fulfilling her fantasy. When she called him one Thursday about the plan for the weekend, she wondered again if they might find a suitable barn, *sans* mice and *sans* hunters. Harold said probably not. At best they might escape the hunt. Mice were common to all barns. He asked her why the idea of mice disturbed her, as it seemed to disturb most women. Samantha said something vague about not liking their tiny claws on her, and finally admitted that she was terrified that a mouse might run up her leg and enter her.

To no avail, Harold pointed out that any mouse would run a mile before getting that close to a human. He told her that he would find suitable plugs for her 'mouse holes' if she still wanted to try it. Samantha asked him what he meant.

Dildoes, he replied succinctly. She might like that.

Yes, she might, Samantha admitted with a touch of excitement.

We'll see, he told her, mentally adding a pair of dildoes to his shopping list. Samantha's birthday was not that far away. He wondered what she would get for him when January came.

In the meantime they continued to pleasure one another with variations: his house, her flat; thin cord or thicker linen line; handcuffs, gags and blindfolds. She moaned and cried out, he felt more fulfilled after having her than he had ever felt before. The affair became a relationship. They became an item, albeit unacknowledged.

Amanda came home for a weekend. She did not bring her boyfriend, if indeed she had one. She didn't say, and neither Samantha nor Harold asked. Her arrival moved the love affair from hers to his, a fact that Amanda did not fail to notice.

'Don't mind me,' she told Harold.

'Has your mother spoken to you about us?' he asked in reply.

When Amanda said she hadn't, he told her that then they would have to mind her still. 'Even if she tells you about us, we still wouldn't want to do what we do before a witness. Would you like to have it off with your boyfriend while we watched and commented?'

'I hadn't thought of it that way,' she said. 'You're right. He's too shy.'

Despite the partial hiatus in the affair, Harold was glad to have Amanda home. Samantha felt better. Her fears of losing her daughter forever were allayed. Amanda enlivened their evenings together with stories of her time at uni, Samantha by turns worried about what her daughter was doing and proud of her for doing it – or most of it. Amanda made no comment about the relationship between Harold and her mother. Samantha was relieved and even more pleased with her daughter. Pepperoni pizza and hamburgers at Burger King (the grown-up place to eat, Samantha informed her daughter) were interspersed with more conventional meals and a visit to the local safari park, where Amanda gleefully pointed out the zebra's 'wang.' Samantha was suitably horrified – and enthralled.

'I wonder what the lady zebras think of all that tackle,' Amanda remarked. Samantha blushed and tried to shush her. Amanda retorted that there was no one to overhear them. 'Don't be so square mum,' she advised.

One evening toward the end of her holiday Harold went to see Samantha, but found only Amanda at home.

'Mum will be late. She phoned to say she'd bring pizza, so you needn't do the domesticated-male act today. Anyway, I'm glad you came. I want to talk to you without mum around.'

Harold glanced at her warily.

'Stop looking so worried. I'm not going to seduce you,' Amanda remarked with typical brashness.

'You make bulls in china shops seem subtle by comparison,' Harold said, though he felt relieved – and just the least bit disappointed. Whoever became Amanda's lover would have a handful, he thought.

'It's about mum,' she continued. When he remained silent, Amanda grinned . 'And, no, I don't intend to give you a ticking off for fucking her. She's looking happier than I've seen her in a long time. So keep on doing whatever you're doing for her. If you hear faint cheers from time to time, it'll be me applauding from Reading. What I want to know is, what are your long-term plans – yours and hers?'

'We don't have any,' he replied. 'We just go on from day to day.'

Amanda looked amazed. 'I thought all grown-ups thought of was marriage and family life and bills and things. You mean you two don't?'

'No. It's as much your mother's idea as mine. We enjoy what we have every day. Isn't that what you do?'

'I suppose I do, but that's because I still think I'm going to live forever. But you're right. I'm prouder than ever of mum. And you too. I'm glad for you both. It's

107

such a relief to know she's happy.' Amanda managed to sound as if she had been trying to arrange her mother's life for ages.

'Tell her what you've just told me,' Harold suggested. 'She'd be glad to know you feel that way.'

'I couldn't say that!' Amanda seemed taken aback at the idea of expressing approval to her mother. Daughters just didn't do such things.

Harold shrugged. 'Whatever you say. But I think she'd be happy to know.'

Amanda changed the subject abruptly. 'I suppose she's still getting you to tie her up?'

'Don't pry, Amanda. If you want to know what she likes, ask her. I'm still keeping your secret, so let ours alone.'

Amanda grinned. 'All right. But I'll just go on thinking the worst anyway,' she said.

Samantha came home and broke up the tête-à-tête, to Harold's relief. She asked what they had been talking about.

'Uni,' Samantha replied at once. 'Harold said he's sorry he never had the chance to go himself. He told me he once wanted to be a writer.'

'That's more than he ever told me,' Samantha said. She sounded alarmed at the exchange of confidences, though false, between her lover and her daughter.

'Well, I do like the Victorian poets,' he said lamely.

Amanda helped her mother set the table and they sat down to eat in companionable fashion. Harold went home later, leaving mother and daughter to exchange whatever confidences they might wish to share. Amanda gave him a brief goodbye peck on the cheek as he was leaving, and winked broadly at him, knowing her mother couldn't see her face. She was going back to Reading the next day.

When Samantha returned there were fewer tears than at the first parting. Either she accepted that Amanda

108

had to do this, or she had begun to take more comfort in her ongoing relationship with Harold. Or both. He was relieved.

As Samantha's birthday approached Harold began to think about a suitable gift. She probably already suspected about the leg-irons, so that would not be much of a surprise. He surfed some the Internet sex-and-bondage sites for inspiration, and at last settled on something he thought she would like. Samantha had responded with curiosity to the mention of a dildo, and so he chose for her a leather panty with both anal and vaginal dildoes (usable together or separately, whichever turns her on, said the advert). It was available in removable or non-removable (lockable) styles. He chose the lockable, as much for himself as for Samantha. He thought she would enjoy wearing something under her clothes that both stimulated her and reminded her that she was locked up.

For his part, he knew that the idea stimulated him. This bondage stuff is catching, he told himself wryly. He bought the leg-irons as well, knowing that she would like them. His purchases came in the first week in November, and he planned to invite Samantha out for dinner after giving her the present. In the meantime he hid them away.

On Samantha's birthday he showed up at her flat an hour before their table was booked at the restaurant. Harold planned to let Samantha choose whether to wear the leather pants or not. He hoped that she would wear them, and that she would invite him to help her get into them before they went out. The leg-irons they could use afterward. Samantha let him in, still half-dressed. She wore her bra and slip and, he hoped, stockings and suspenders, rather than tights.

'You have a one-track mind,' she told him when he asked which it was. She admitted to stockings and

109

suspenders. 'But why? Wouldn't tights do as well when you know that I'm going to go to bed with you anyway?'

'Are you?' Harold asked in mock surprise. 'I've been trying to get into your pants ever since we met. What made you change your mind tonight? Anyway, happy birthday.' He handed her the wrapped presents.

'I wonder what this could be,' Samantha said as she felt the weight of the gift-wrapped leg-irons. She was as mystified by the second present as she was knowing about the first. She kissed him lingeringly. 'Thank you so much.' She unwrapped the lighter of the two gifts first.

The leather pants shone dull black amidst the tissue paper. The dildoes were wrapped separately in the box, as yet unseen. Samantha held the pants up and saw what they were made of. 'I think you might have some trouble getting into these pants,' she said. 'I thought you liked the silky kind.'

'Maybe you won't want me to get into your pants when you see what goes with them. You might not want to take your pants off at all.'

Samantha looked even more mystified. 'Not want to take my pants off? Why ever not?'

'Allow me to demonstrate, madam.' Harold showed Samantha how the pants went on, and how they could be locked in place.

She looked even more mystified. 'Locked? Why?'

'The better to hold these inside you, my dear,' he said as he showed her the two rubber dildoes that came with the pants. 'Your very own chastity belt, and I have the key.'

Samantha was taken aback by the sight. She caught her breath on a gasp. 'So big! I'll never get them inside me.'

'Would you like to try?' he asked.

110

'Oh, yes!' Samantha said, recovering her voice.

That was one of the many things that Harold liked about his older mistress. She was willing to try almost anything. Her surprise and delight – and her eagerness to try out the dildoes – pleased him.

Samantha took off her underwear there in the entrance hall and took the leather pants as Harold held them for her. She discovered with delight the two internal connections designed to hold the dildoes in place and to prevent them from slipping too far inside her. 'How clever,' she said weakly, her fingers trembling as she held up her slip for him to put the pants on her.

Harold made her wait while he went to the bathroom. He returned with a jar of petroleum jelly.

Samantha's eyes widened in comprehension. 'For my . . . back passage?' she asked in a shaky voice.

Harold nodded, pleased with her quick comprehension. 'I don't suppose you'll need much lubrication for the other one.'

'Oh, my, no,' Samantha said softly.

Harold could smell her pussy as he inserted the dildoes into the pants. He greased the anal dildo and held the pants for Samantha to step into.

She held onto his shoulder as she lifted first one leg and then the other into the leg openings. She was shaking with excitement. When the shaft penetrated her cunt, Samantha leaned heavily on Harold, moaning with the sensation. She moaned even more loudly as he applied some petroleum jelly to her anus and slid the second dildo into her back passage. He thought her knees would buckle with the exquisite pleasure of being penetrated back and front. 'Harold, I'm going to come,' she moaned.

'All right.'

And she did, trembling as he slid the dildoes home and closed the zipper at the back of the pants. The pants fit Samantha like a second skin, with just the right amount of give in the leather to allow movement. She moaned again, signalling another orgasm as he locked the zipper behind her back. She let her slip drop from trembling fingers and held onto Harold as she came. He held her in his arms as she shuddered and moaned.

'I take it the gift is a success,' he said as Samantha held onto him.

'Ohhhhh, yesss!' she sighed. She looked up at him. 'I don't think I can go out in these. I won't be able to . . . control myself.'

'But wouldn't it be fun to try?'

Samantha strove for control, and after a moment she looked up with an impish if still shaky grin. 'Yes, it would,' she agreed. 'And if I fail, I'll have to conceal the signs.' She straightened up and let go of him. At once her eyes darkened as the dildoes stabbed her again. She looked doubtfully at him as she stumbled toward the bedroom to finish dressing.

Harold allowed Samantha to take her time, and when she emerged she looked stunning in a green silk dress and matching high-heeled shoes. Her glossy off-white stockings showed off her legs beautifully. Her control looked wobbly, but she seemed ready to try going out in public with her twin penetrations.

'You'll take me home if I lose control?' She sought reassurance from him.

'Of course not, you silly woman. I'll simply abandon you to your orgasm in the street. You can find your own way home.'

Samantha smiled at the joke. 'All right, let's test my control.'

They walked slowly to Samantha's car, Samantha wincing slightly at each step. Sitting in the seat brought on another orgasm as the anal dildo stabbed into her. 'Oh, god, Harold, I can't stop!'

'Do you really want to?'

Samantha looked doubtful, but only about the wisdom of going out wearing what she later wryly called her get-stuffed pants. She fastened the seat belt and tried to compose herself for the journey.

Getting into the driver's seat, Harold remarked that he was going to take the bumpiest route to the restaurant. Samantha looked swiftly at him, alarm showing in her face and in the tension of her body. She was holding herself as still as possible. She relaxed slightly as Harold grinned. 'You wouldn't really do that, would you?' she asked. When he did not reply, she sighed fondly, 'Beast.' The sigh changed abruptly into a cry of alarm. Samantha gripped his arm. It was not necessary to tell him that she was going to come again. She grasped his free hand convulsively and moaned loudly as the orgasm shook her body.

Harold moved their intertwined hands until they were resting over the vaginal dildo. He pushed gently, feeling the tight leather pants beneath Samantha's dress give slightly under the pressure. Samantha felt the pressure on her clitoris as the dildo moved under his hand. With a wail of despair and release she came again, bucking in the seat and breathing in shallow gasps. Samantha was oblivious of the other motorists who might have seen her. Harold had some trouble with his driving.

When the storm subsided, Samantha said, 'I don't think I can face an evening at a restaurant. I wouldn't be able to keep quiet, and I must look a wreck already just from the ride.'

Harold assured her that she looked just fine, but agreed about the inappropriateness of the restaurant. 'Maybe we should take the grown-up's option,' he suggested. 'We can eat in the car park at Burger King.'

Samantha agreed that this was the best idea, and they headed for the fast-food outlet. Harold went in to get

113

the food, and Samantha saw him talking and laughing with one of the counter staff. She remembered that he was a regular here, and she wondered if she were the subject of the conversation she could see but not hear. She blushed as she imagined what they were saying. When Harold returned bearing hamburgers and fries, she hissed at him, 'I know you were talking about me in there!'

Harold was surprised at her fierceness. He denied the charge, but Samantha took some convincing. She warned him (needlessly, from his point of view) never to mention what they did to anyone else. Harold thought of having kept their secret so close that even Amanda could not get it out of him. He was on the verge of telling Samantha so, but at the last moment he remembered that a secret had to remain unknown – if it was to remain a secret. He did not want to sow discord between mother and daughter, nor do anything to jeopardise the relation with the mother – Samantha, sitting beside him now, looking beautiful and desirable as ever even as she strove to control an incipient orgasm.

'I have an idea,' Harold said, changing the subject, he hoped, to one that would make Samantha less suspicious and angry. 'Let's find a local lovers' lane, where we can neck and you can get warm and excited, and we won't be able to do anything about it – just like we used to do when we were kids in love with no place to take our lovers.'

Samantha liked the idea, but asked why they wouldn't be able to fuck.

'I left the keys at your place,' Harold confessed. I don't suppose you would want to ruin those pants by having me cut them off you.'

Without waiting for a reply he started the engine and drove toward the outskirts of town. Lovers' lanes were few in number, and his memory was rusty from disuse. Eventually they found a place to park and eat their impromptu meal. When they were finished, Harold suggested that they get into the back seat of the car. They slid the bucket seats as far forward as they could go and climbed onto the wider seat behind.

'Now, do you remember how we go about this?' he asked Samantha. He took her face between his hands and kissed her lips. He felt them open beneath his, and her breath caught on a gasp. Definitely better than his first girlfriend. Martha had never learned to kiss as well as Samantha did.

When the kiss ended, Samantha was breathing heavily and squirming on the seat. 'Oh god, Harold, it's going to happen again!'

'Good.' He slid his hand up her leg, liking as always the feel of the sheer nylon stockings. When he reached her crotch, Harold pushed gently against the leather pants. Samantha gasped and shuddered as the dildo was pushed further inside her. She squirmed on the seat, driving the anal dildo in as well. No, Martha had never become this excited. Thank heaven for older women.

Samantha held him tightly against her as she came, moaning, her mouth once more seeking his. She came as they kissed, shuddering with the pleasure of her release. Samantha didn't stop for a long time, and when she did, she was sweaty and exhausted. She lay against him, small tremors shaking her body.

Despite her multiple orgasms, Samantha's body still felt tense as he held her. No doubt she was as conscious as ever of the internal arrangements, and was trying to calm herself down instead of surrendering once again to the dildoes' effect.

'Darling,' she said finally, 'I can't go on any more. I came so often I feel worn out. And,' she continued contritely, 'you haven't even come once.' She reached for the zipper of his trousers. 'Let me ... Oh! Oh god, it's happening again. What can I do?'

'Relax and enjoy it, my love. That's why I gave you the present.'

'But what about you? I feel so self . . . Oh! Ohhhhh!'

Once again he held her tightly as she came. This was a smaller one. Samantha must have been tired. The windows were frosted over. They were alone in their private steel cocoon. Gently Harold extricated himself from Samantha and got out of the car. The interior light went on as he opened the door, revealing her *dishabille* and her exhaustion. He switched the light off and brought out the cord she insisted he keep in the car. Getting back in with Samantha, he told her what he wanted to do, though his intentions must have been obvious. Samantha turned her back to him and brought her hands behind her. Harold tied her wrists tightly and she sighed with pleasure as the thin cord bit into her flesh.

'We'll just make this a quick one – until I get you home,' he whispered to Samantha. He crossed her ankles and tied them together. He did this deliberately, knowing that Samantha would not be able to stand with her ankles crossed. She appreciated his effort. Her smile was a quick flash of teeth in the darkness as he tied the last knot.

'Will you gag me? Please?' Samantha asked softly.

Harold taped her mouth with the duct tape, and used more to tape her eyes closed. He arranged Samantha on the back seat so that she was propped into the corner with her bound wrists in the space behind her and her bound ankles out of sight on the floor of the car. She turned her face away from the window so that no one would notice the gag and blindfold.

Harold got into the driving seat and started the engine. As he did, Samantha whimpered softly. She must be fantasising like mad about abduction and rape, he thought as he drove away from the secluded spot. In the rear view mirror he could see that her body shook with occasional tremors. Her progress toward what sexual release she could still attain in her exhausted state was marked by her sighs and moans and the shifting of her body on the seat as the dildoes did their work.

Harold was painfully erect as he considered his lover's state. At the same time he surprised himself again at the satisfaction he had taken in giving her such a good time. Three cheers for forbearance and artificial sex aids. He did not add, though Samantha might have, for tolerance and sensitivity and . . . lust.

He took the long way to her flat to allow Samantha to fantasise for as long as possible. He kept carefully within the speed limits and obeyed all the laws he could think of. It would not do to be stopped by a zealous and inquisitive bobby tonight.

At the flat he looked carefully around before opening the door and untying Samantha's ankles. Once more he caressed her legs. Samantha made a sleepy noise of comfort. The car was parked in shadow by her back door. No faces showed in the nearby windows. Harold opened the door to the flat and helped her inside. He waited by the door for a sign that they had been seen. When there was none, he helped Samantha to her bed. There he re-tied her ankles and left her sleeping. He felt that he had done a good evening's work as he settled down on the couch to sleep.

So, apparently, did Samantha when she awoke and made summoning noises through her gag. The morning outside was sunny as Harold went to her. Despite the tape over her eyes and mouth, he could see that she was smiling. She stretched like a cat, and Harold paused to admire the sight of a beautiful woman bound and gagged in bed. Then he removed the tape from her eyes and mouth, and untied her. He unlocked the leather pants and helped her get un-stuffed. Samantha rested

117

her arms on his shoulders as he knelt between her legs to remove the tight pants. When they lay on the floor, she bent down to kiss the top of his head with a sigh. Harold looked up, and she kissed him on the lips. That threatened to turn into something more serious, but Samantha broke it off and said, 'Toilet!' urgently.

Harold released her hastily and helped her into the bathroom.

'How would you like your eggs?' he asked as she peed noisily.

'Hold on,' she said, looking up at him with a smile. 'Thank you for a wonderful birthday present. For a wonderful birthday,' she added.

'If you enjoyed this one, just wait until the next one.' He had no idea what he would get for her next November, but was confident that something would occur to him in the interim.

Samantha undressed down to her stockings and suspenders – her indoor uniform when he was there. She hung up her dress while Harold took off his clothes. Samantha looked at her birthday present lying on the floor with a concerned expression. 'Last night was wonderful for me, but what about you? It was terribly one-sided.'

'Breakfast first,' Harold said. 'Let's find something to eat.'

After Amanda's visit and Samantha's birthday, the affair changed subtly. The chief difference in their relationship was that they took to spending more time at one another's houses. What had been weekends together often stretched to three or four days. In practice their different residences became just different places for them to meet, live, make love.

Amanda took to calling Harold's place when she got no answer at her mother's flat. She became accustomed to having either of them answer no matter where she called. 'So you two are still together,' she remarked each time she called. Not that she called every week. She was busy becoming her own young woman. Samantha no longer felt devastated when her daughter did not call. Harold came to know Amanda better through her calls, for if her mother was not wherever she telephoned, she spoke to him. They learned that she now had a live-in lover, and that so far things were OK. Amanda seemed to base her own relationship on what she knew of Harold's and her mother's. Samantha took the advent of the lover with admirable self-possession. She kept her misgivings from Amanda. Only Harold knew of them. Amanda told him that she was pleased at her mum's reaction. 'I expected tears and sermons,' she said.

After that momentous birthday Samantha took to testing herself, asking Harold to take her out while she wore the pants and dildoes under her clothing. She seemed to accept the challenge posed by her leather pants in place of her fantasy about being left in a deserted barn. Fortunately for them both, Samantha did not lose her sensitivity to sexual stimulation by dildo – or by any other means. They continued to enjoy the illicit nature of that and all the other aspects of their relationship.

She learned how to lock the zipper behind her back, keeping the open padlock and leaving the keys with him. Samantha was enthralled by the idea of having to go to him to be released.

A fortnight after her birthday she showed up unannounced and in a state at Harold's house on a Saturday afternoon. He could see that she was aroused – highly aroused, sweating and shaking and breathing like a locomotive.

'Oh god!' She breathed a shuddering breath as he opened the door. She was holding onto his handrail –

and her control – with white-knuckle intensity. Samantha staggered inside, signalling him wildly to close the door. He guessed the cause at once. Samantha held onto him, her knees threatening to buckle as he led her to the sofa. He admired her fortitude in coming out like that. Driving while in the throes of orgasm was not easy – as he remembered from the time she had given him a blow job while they were driving home from the abortive deserted-barn scenario. And he had only come once. For all she knew, he might not have been at home. He wondered if she would have found the keys on her own.

She sat down, but jerked erect as the anal dildo stabbed her. 'Oh!' she gasped. But she did not ask him for release. When Samantha asked him instead to tie and gag her, Harold guessed that she had deliberately set about getting herself into this state. She may have miscalculated the difficulty in getting herself from her flat to his house, but now that she was here, Samantha wanted to get into even more of a state.

While Harold went to fetch the cords and the duct tape, Samantha undressed down to her indoor 'uniform,' this time with the addition of the all-important leather pants and their interior accoutrements. She opened her handbag and with shaking hands took out the pussy whip. Harold recognised it at once when he returned, but said nothing. Officially he knew nothing of its existence. The fact that Samantha now revealed it to him suggested that their relationship was about to take another unexpected turn.

In a voice shaking with excitement Samantha asked him to lash her thoroughly – 'all over,' was how she expressed it – with the short whip, once she was tied and gagged. 'There might be . . . screams,' she explained.

A masterly understatement, he thought.

'But ignore the noises. I want to try this.' She seemed determined. 'You decide when to begin and when to stop,' she directed him. It seemed important that she should not have control over this part of the act.

Harold had originally intended to tie Samantha and leave her lying on the floor to work out her own release. It was one of her favourite positions, the one they used most often in fact. The addition of the whip, and her request to use it, caused him to revise his plan. He led Samantha upstairs and into the rear bedroom. There he made her stand beside the bed while he tied her hands behind her back. She did so, her knees threatening to give way as she shuddered with rising excitement. He tied her elbows as well, pulling them close together behind her. As an afterthought he tied Samantha's thumbs. She gasped as she felt the cords tighten around them.

Outside the window, the sun shone onto the back garden and, across it, on the windows of the other houses. The ordinariness of the scene, the tidy gardens and sheds and garages, the houses with their curtained windows, the clothes drying on the lines, contrasted sharply with what he and Samantha were doing. As he finished tying her thumbs together, he wondered what was going on in those other rooms, behind the walls of the other houses in his neighbourhood. Probably nothing as bizarre as this. Was Samantha thinking the same thing as the cords tightened?

Harold could see that her control was slipping as he tied her up. He hurried, for her sake as much as his. The gag (a pair of her pants, kept for the purpose, held in with duct tape, as she preferred) and a blindfold increased her agitation. Harold had a sudden inspiration. He turned Samantha with her back to the bed, a half step away from the side. Then he pushed her, roughly, so that she staggered and fell back across it. Samantha squealed in surprise as she fell with her bound wrists and arms under her body. Harold had

121

never before offered her any violence, but this time he was thinking of the whip she had brought. Samantha was apparently ready and willing to move on to more trying fantasies.

He knelt to tie her ankles, jerking the cords tight. He tied her legs above and below the knees, the cords biting deeply into her legs. Samantha moaned with excitement as he did so, her breath coming rapidly and her bare breasts rising and falling with her arousal. As a final touch Harold wound more cord around her breasts, pulling the loops tight and causing them to stand out tight and shiny from base to erect nipples.

When he leaned over to take one of those engorged nipples between his teeth, Samantha exploded into a shattering orgasm. He struggled to hold her down as she writhed and jerked. The moans that escaped from her gag left no doubt that she was pleased with her treatment – so far. The whip might prove too much, but there was only one way to find out about that. When she subsided, Harold lifted Samantha's bound legs and arranged her on her side in the bed. From there, he knew from experience, she could work herself up to as many orgasms as she liked. He left her alone to do so, going down to the front room to examine the whip more closely before he had to use it.

The pussy whip, as its makers called it, was about eighteen inches long. It consisted of a braided handle with a loop for the user's wrist to go through. The remainder, about twelve inches in length, consisted of leather thongs that would strike the usee. The whole affair was lightly made, designed to sting rather than to inflict damage, though the makers suggested coyly that the whip could be made 'more effective' by tying one or more knots in the thongs.

Faintly from upstairs came the sounds of Samantha working out her destiny in the bed: faint creakings; the occasional thump; muffled (though fervent) moans of pleasure. Harold had left the door ajar so that he could keep track of her progress without having to disturb the self-imposed isolation that was an important part of her fantasy. Since deserted barns seemed to be off the menu, they had to make do with what was available. To heighten the illusion of abandonment and isolation, Harold often went out for a greater or lesser interval, leaving Samantha bound and gagged to fantasise about deserted barns, houses, parked vans and strange men who might stumble upon her therein. He sometimes wondered if she was disappointed when the finder always turned out to be him, and the deserted spot turned out to be the old familiar residence. Still, it was the best that they could do.

Now he climbed the stairs, the noises from the bedroom becoming louder. At the door he paused, postponing for a moment the pleasure he always took at the sight of his lover bound and gagged, struggling in their disordered bed, as Samantha luridly described it. The bed *was* disordered, and Samantha was struggling lustily against the cords that held her captive, and enjoying the experience thoroughly. This was the first time she had been left alone with the dildo-pants to spur her on.

Samantha was on the point of rolling from one side to the other when Harold walked in. She was on her back, her back arched and her breasts pointing to the ceiling as she struggled to reach the balance point that would let her fall onto her left side. And she was obviously having another orgasm. Her hips thrust up and down as she worked the dildoes inside her. Loud incoherent sounds, gasps and grunts, leaked past the gag to accompany her release. Harold stood watching in fascination as she bucked and jerked on the bed.

Then the spell broke. He went to the bed to help Samantha roll over. He realised suddenly that he had the pussy whip in his hand. Somehow the loop was around his wrist. It was as if it had followed him upstairs on its own. And there was Samantha, straining and jerking against her bonds and having an orgasm. He raised the whip and struck her across her upthrust breasts, drawn like lightning to the highest point, as he described it later to her.

The sudden unexpected blow to her tits seemed to galvanise Samantha. Her body grew taut and she let out an explosive 'Nnnnnnggggg!' Harold did not know whether it was a cry of pain or of ecstasy. Certainly it did nothing to interrupt Samantha's release. He struck her repeatedly, the lashes sounding softly against the background of her cries. Samantha went wild, jerking against the cords and moaning loudly as the blows landed on her stomach and thighs, on her breasts and her engorged nipples.

Once he had started, he found it impossible to stop. Samantha rolled wildly so that the backs of her legs were exposed. Thin red lines appeared on her thighs beneath the sheer nylon stockings. He struck her on her bottom, but the tight leather pants merely absorbed the lashes. Wearing the pants, and with her legs tied together, he could not reach her pussy, but the whip nevertheless drove her to orgasm, her screams muffled only by her gag.

He stopped when his arm grew tired. Samantha lay still on the bed, drenched in sweat. The exposed parts of her body were covered in thin red stripes. She dragged in great gulps of air and moaned softly. Her legs twitched and her bound hands twisted behind her back.

Harold was appalled at what he had done. Hurriedly he stripped the tape from Samantha's mouth and eyes. He rolled her over and lay beside her, holding her tightly while she slowly grew quiet.

'I'm sorry, love,' he said softly. 'I don't know what came over me. Once I got started I just couldn't stop. Are you all right?'

Samantha murmured, 'I'm so glad you didn't. That was magic. I think I'd have killed you if you had stopped.'

Harold was astounded. 'You mean you *liked* that?'

'Ummmm,' she murmured. 'It was wonderful! I wish I'd thought of it sooner – had the courage to do it, I mean. I've had that whip for ages but couldn't bring myself to tell you about it.'

Relief swept over him. This was not the time to tell her that he had found it earlier, and wondered about using it.

More urgently, worried by his silence, she asked him if he now thought her a real pervert – beyond the pale, she meant.

'Yes, you are a pervert,' he said, 'But you're *my* pervert.'

'Oh!' she gulped. Tears trickled from the corners of her eyes and down her cheeks. 'Oh, I'm so relieved. Hold me! Tight!'

Samantha slept in his arms, and he dozed with her. When she awoke she insisted that he untie her and get the pants off her. In stockings and suspenders Samantha lay on her back in the bed and asked Harold to 'fuck her stupid.'

And he did, several times during the course of that night. In the morning he asked her if she felt stupid.

'Yes,' Samantha said at once. 'Thank you!'

'That proves I'm good for something, at least,' he grunted.

Samantha got up and made for the toilet. When she returned it was his turn. When he returned, Samantha was waiting for him, still wearing her stockings and suspenders. She had brought her handcuffs and the leg-irons he had given her from downstairs. 'Put them on me,' she asked him. 'Please.'

Harold began to cuff her hands behind her back, but Samantha demurred – for the first time. 'In front, please. Otherwise I won't be able to make breakfast.'

He complied.

'Now the leg-irons, please,' she said.

Harold locked them around her ankles and looked up to see her smiling at him.

'That's wonderful. I feel like a proper kept woman now.' Samantha clinked to the door and beckoned him to follow. 'Omelettes or fried eggs?' she asked over her shoulder as she descended the stairs in her shackles.

Breakfast was a slow affair, Samantha hampered by the handcuffs in preparation and eating, but she insisted on wearing them throughout. 'Good practice,' she remarked enigmatically. She did not say exactly what she was practising for.

While she did the washing up, Harold watched her slow progress with abiding pleasure. Done, Samantha asked him to cuff her hands behind her back. 'We have all day to play games now,' she said.

Harold left her in the house while he went to the newsagent's for the Sunday paper. When he returned, Samantha insisted that he take his clothes off – 'so we'll be even,' she said. They spent a companionable couple of hours reading the papers, Harold sitting on the sofa and Samantha lying with her head in his lap. Occasionally she took his cock into her mouth and licked or sucked it.

That led by a natural process to an erection, and that led to Harold taking Samantha atop him and guiding the erection into her cunt. That led in turn to Samantha making more disgraceful noises. The paper lay neglected beside the sofa.

6

Christmas

The onset of Christmas was heralded by Amanda's phone call to announce that she would be home for a week just before the holidays. She had planned to spend the holidays with them all along, she said, but now she was coming a week earlier. After the holidays she would go back for some partying with her new friends before the next term began. Samantha was surprised by the earlier visit, and as close to being angry with her daughter as Harold had ever seen her. The revised visiting date would put their own plans on hold. She could not tell her daughter not to come home – nor why. Harold learned of the impending visit and Samantha's displeasure on Thursday evening. It was good to learn that Samantha valued their time together so much.

'Why not tell her you'll be away for a few days but that she is welcome to the flat? She might like the chance to be on her own.'

Samantha could not get it out of her head that she should be around when Amanda came home, even if it ruined their plans. Harold did not mind waiting, but she evidently did. She directed some of her resentment at him. Sooner or later, he knew, she would see that the postponement was just that, and would go back to her

127

usual self. In the meantime he planned to make himself scarce and give mother and daughter a chance to spend time together without an outsider around. He told Samantha that he would work that weekend. She objected.

'Amanda said she was looking forward to seeing you,' she said. It came out almost as an accusation.

Harold was not sure whether she blamed him for Amanda's visit, or whether she was accusing him of working his way into her daughter's good books. Perhaps both, he decided. Women were strange creatures. Reluctantly he agreed to come around on Saturday evening to see the returning prodigal. He would call first, he said. Perhaps they could all go to dinner. Being out in public might discourage further recriminations, if Samantha still harboured any.

On Saturday he called and got Amanda. 'Mum's gone to the butcher's for a Sunday joint. Did I ruin your plans for a dirty weekend?'

'What makes you think that?'

'Mum seems put out. She tries to hide it, but I know her too well.'

'Well, we did have plans, but they can wait. It's not the end of the world.'

'Shall I tell mum you said that – or is she giving you enough trouble without that information?' Amanda did not sound penitent.

Harold determined not to sound put out. 'She's your mother. You can tell her whatever you like.'

'Oh, don't worry. I won't make any trouble for you. I still think you're good for her. Is she getting enough of the old in-out to keep her happy?'

'You'll have to ask her about that,' he said, smiling despite himself at her direct approach to her mother's sex life. 'How are things between you and your boyfriend?' A counter-attack might work.

'We're not seeing one another any more, before you ask again. For the record, I am desolate. Deserted.'

'Oh.' He could add nothing more. She did not sound desolate, but that may have been her defence mechanism.

'Anyway, when are you coming over, and where are you taking us?'

'Around seven, seven-thirty. We can decide where to go when I get there.'

'All right. See you then.' Amanda hung up brusquely as always.

When he arrived Amanda opened the door.

'Mum's putting on her war-paint,' she announced. 'I can't decide if she's doing it for me or for you. She's been taking more trouble with herself since you've been around. And she still looks happy. Whatever you are up to, it suits her.' Amanda did not look heartbroken. She gave him a brief peck on the lips.

Harold was both surprised and pleased. Except for verbal *badinage*, it was the first intimate contact between them. It seemed that he had at least Amanda's approval.

She wore a dress and heels. Despite himself Harold noticed that she had nice legs and a stunning figure – most of which she got from Samantha. What was the matter with her partner, he wondered. Was he blind? Amanda gave a twirl, revealing more of her legs. She wore tights, he guessed, unlike her mother. He applauded. She smiled.

'Something to drink?' she asked. 'We have beer or whisky, as you probably know. Which do you want?'

Harold chose beer. Amanda did likewise. They sat at the kitchen table to drink while Samantha finished dressing.

'Mum won't say anything about where I can get a pair of handcuffs,' Amanda began without preamble. 'Do you know where to go?'

'Why do you want handcuffs?' he asked, naturally enough.

'We're having a fancy dress party next week at uni. A group of us are dressing up to go see *The Rocky Horror Show*. I plan to go as a tart who likes a bit of rough. Mum was horrified when I brought it up. She clammed up at once. Honestly, you'd think she would approve – daughter following in her mother's footsteps and all that.' Amanda smiled ironically. 'Anyway, she won't say anything. She just gets red in the face and warns me about the danger of going out looking for trouble. I don't know where to turn. I can't ask to borrow hers, since she doesn't have any, officially. So, where do I go?'

'Try the Internet,' Harold suggested. 'You can buy nearly anything there if you look.' It was the same advice he had given Samantha. 'Are you going to follow in your mother's footsteps?'

'Aha, so you admit you've been using her handcuffs!'

'Well, you've known about that ever since we met.'

'Tell me what she does,' Amanda demanded.

Harold replied, 'I have to invoke the Official Secrets Act. You'll need to ask your mother.'

Amanda sighed. 'You're both so square. I despair of you.'

Samantha entered. Amanda looked at her and said, 'Wow!' Harold turned to look as well. 'I agree,' he said.

Samantha smiled at them both. She wore a pencil skirt, sheer blouse and high heels. She seemed to have got over her disappointment. Harold was relieved.

They decided on a Thai restaurant in the town centre. Several of the other diners paused to look at the two women as they entered. It was not lost on Amanda. 'They all want to take you home and ravish you,' she told her mother. Samantha blushed and scolded her. 'Well, the men do, at any rate.' Amanda insisted. 'Their wives seem less enthusiastic.'

Samantha made a hopeless gesture: what can I do with her? Harold smiled and replied, 'She's right. I'm jealous.' Amanda beamed at them both. Samantha seemed proud of her daughter despite her brashness, and the evening went smoothly after that. Back at the flat Harold prepared to say goodnight to them both, but Amanda would have none of it.

'Surely you're not going home because of me. Stay the night. Don't mind me. I won't embarrass you. I'll wear ear plugs.'

In the face of Amanda's knowledge it seemed silly to pretend any further. They went inside and sat in the front room to watch the late news. Amanda made coffee for them, and regaled them with tales of university life, some of which made her mother look askance at her daughter's growing independence. At about eleven o'clock Amanda ostentatiously stuck her fingers in her ears and went to her bedroom. Shortly after that Harold and Samantha went to bed, Harold watching admiringly as she undressed. He was pleased when Samantha left her stockings and suspenders on.

'Thanks for a lovely evening.' She got into bed and embraced him.

Harold drew back. Amanda saying she would hear nothing was one thing, but reality was something else. Samantha pulled him closer. 'Fuck me stupid,' she told him. 'Amanda knows you do anyway.' She climbed on top of him and guided his cock into her, clamping down as he slid in. They made love as if there were no one else in the next bedroom. In the hour before dawn Samantha woke him and they fucked again. Her only concession to Amanda's presence was that Samantha did her best not to cry aloud when she came.

Harold was first up in the morning. As he made coffee Amanda joined him, in nightgown and tousled hair. 'Had a good night?' he asked her.

131

'Not as good as yours. The bed squeaks.'

'Most of them do,' he replied. 'I hope we didn't keep you awake.'

'I tossed all night with frustrated desire while you two enjoyed one another. Surely you didn't think I could sleep knowing what was going on next door? It sounded as if she enjoyed it.'

'She' chose that moment to come into the kitchen. Samantha's face glowed with the aftermath of the night, but reddened instantly when she heard Amanda's remark. She would have made her escape, but her daughter heard the sound of her slippers and turned to face her mother. She smiled, and Samantha eventually returned it. Amanda jumped up. 'You two sit down. I'll make breakfast – that'll show you I've learned something at uni. And you're allowed to look yearningly into one another's eyes while my back is turned.' In the face of Amanda's acceptance of the status quo, Samantha gradually relaxed.

Amanda scrambled eggs, fried bacon, made toast and tea. She seemed proud of her cooking. Samantha and Harold both complimented her. 'Student food,' she said deprecatingly, but nonetheless looked pleased by their approval. 'I can actually do spaghetti Bolognaise and chili con carne too. Practically an entire single person's repertoire.'

'What, no beans on toast? You used to love that.'

'I'm at uni now, Mum. I'm supposed to learn new things. But I've got the number of the local Pizza Hut in case of an emergency.'

'Oh, good,' Samantha said. 'I was beginning to worry that you'd starve in your flat.'

'Do you mind if I ask a few mates around this afternoon?' Amanda asked them both. 'Only, I haven't seen them since I went to Reading. We used to stay at each other's houses all the time when we were all at school.' This last was directed at Harold.

132

'Of course not, dear,' Samantha replied. 'I had intended to have a Sunday roast for the three of us, but I don't think they'd want that. Is there anything special I should make for you and your friends?'

'Just make yourselves scarce,' Amanda said with her usual tact. 'Go out, have fun. Or stay in and do the same if you'd prefer. We'll play loud music and pretend we can't hear the cries of passion.'

Samantha reddened again. Amanda looked impatient.

'Grow up,' she said. 'If it really bothers you, go to Harold's place. Stay overnight. We won't wreck the joint, and I promise not to tell my friends where you are, or who you're with.'

'It seems we're being thrown out,' Samantha said with a wry smile.

'No, just invited to be elsewhere temporarily. Why not take the food with you and have your Sunday dinner in your spare time – if you have any? You can come back on Monday or Tuesday if you want to.'

'That's a relief. Being homeless is not much fun.'

Harold was likewise relieved. Amanda had certainly learned something at Reading. Samantha, out of habit, cleared up, remarking that there were still some gaps in her daughter's education. Amanda went to her bedroom to dress. Shortly afterwards she emerged and began to call her friends.

'I think that's our cue to leave,' Harold said.

Samantha waved goodbye as they left. 'Let's take a drive in the country,' she suggested to Harold.

Amanda, on the doorstep, looked exasperated. 'It's December. It's cold and rainy. Go to Harold's and curl up together.'

Samantha shrugged helplessly as they left. Once they were in her car, Samantha immediately asked Harold what to do about Amanda. 'She's asking about getting a pair of handcuffs for some student outing. I can't let her do anything foolish.'

'Like her mother, you mean? Take her advice – grow up. She's already doing that. Let her make her own decisions. You never came to any harm.'

'Not yet,' she replied with a rueful smile. 'But I'm still hoping.'

'Lend her yours,' Harold suggested. 'Keep it in the family. At least you can save her from falling into the hands of some unscrupulous handcuff dealer. There are a lot of them about, you know.'

Samantha smiled, but insisted that lending hers to Amanda was not on. 'She'll know what we're doing.'

Harold suggested that that might not be such a bad thing, but Samantha was adamant. Once again he was tempted to tell Samantha that the cat was already out of the bag, but did not. Telling the truth needlessly was not always a good idea. 'Do you want to drive out into the country? That way you can convince yourself that you're being virtuous.'

'And get more excited the longer you make me wait.' Samantha thought for a moment. 'Amanda knows,' she said finally. 'And I'm already excited. Let's skip the cold and damp and go straight to your house. We won't answer the phone in case Amanda calls to check up,' she added with a grin.

'We could unplug it,' Harold suggested.

'She'd know why at once,' Samantha demurred.

Harold shook his head. If Samantha wanted to keep up the pretence he would play along, but he saw no need. Then again, Amanda was not his daughter. At his house they both undressed at once, Samantha as usual leaving her stockings and suspenders on. She wore no pants. 'No more pants from now on,' she declared. 'An early Christmas present for you.'

Harold kissed her by way of thanks.

134

Samantha said, 'Tie me up really tight and we'll lie on the sofa and watch Sunday television. Something else will no doubt occur to you if that's too dull.'

Harold used the thin cord Samantha preferred. As he tied her wrists behind her back, he remembered too late that they had left her dildo-pants at her flat. Nothing to be done about that now. Besides, Samantha could work herself into a state without them, as she had proven repeatedly.

'Tighter,' Samantha commanded. 'Make it really tight.'

Harold cinched the cord between her wrists, making the skin stand out around the binding. 'Much better,' Samantha sighed. He tied her arms above the elbows, making those cords tight as well. He noticed that her elbows came very close to touching now – the result of practice, he guessed. Her thumbs and breasts received the same treatment. Samantha pronounced herself satisfied. Her breasts were jutting out, the nipples taut and erect, tightly confined by the cord tied around them. She sat on the sofa and watched as Harold tied her at the ankles and above and below the knees. Samantha nodded in satisfaction as he cinched these cords tightly between her legs. 'You'd make some slave-type a good master,' she complimented him when the job was done. 'And now, since I am completely at your mercy . . .?'

'Yes, that thought had occurred to me as well,' he replied, 'but I have to get a few things for later.' He left Samantha sitting on the sofa, trying to get comfortable in her bonds. In the bedroom he took the duvet from the bed, along with the pillows.

'Are we having bedroom-thoughts?' Samantha inquired brightly when she saw what he was doing.

'You have a one-track mind sometimes,' he said with a grin. 'But as it's on the same track as mine, I don't object.' Harold laid the bedding on one end of the sofa and set the remote control for the TV on the floor nearby. He sat beside Samantha and pulled her tightly to him, savouring her helplessness and her obvious eagerness as much as she did. They kissed, open mouth meeting open mouth. Harold was excited by his power over Samantha. He could arouse her, whip her, do anything to her – and she could not stop him. That's power, he thought. His cock hardened at the thought.

Samantha began to breathe rapidly. She moaned when Harold used one hand to cup her bound breast and tease the swollen nipple. It began as another of the usual bondage sessions so familiar to them both, until Samantha changed the scenario abruptly: 'Hurt me,' she begged Harold, a trifle breathlessly. She flushed as she made the suggestion.

Taken aback, Harold asked, 'What? How? Do you want me to whip you?'

'If you want to,' Samantha said unsteadily, 'but you could also put clothes pegs on my nipples, or shove something big up my arse. You could sodomise me.'

Harold stood abruptly, inflamed at the idea. He had put his finger up her anus several times, but this was something different. He went to the bathroom, returning with a jar of petroleum jelly. Then he arranged Samantha on her knees with her breasts on the sofa cushions and her bottom sticking up in the air. He knelt astraddle her bound legs and spread the jelly in and around her arsehole. Without further ado he guided his cock into her from behind. Samantha resisted instinctively, clamping her anal sphincter shut against the self-suggested invasion. Harold continued to push. The jelly made things easier for both of them, but it was clear that the invasion was causing her some discomfort, at least.

Samantha struggled, her bound wrists jerking against the cords and her body taut with excited anticipation

When he finally got past the sphincter, Samantha moaned loudly. It did not sound like a moan of pain. Now fully aroused, Harold pushed harder. Samantha struggled as his cock slid into her anus until he was fully inside her. She bucked and shuddered, the muscles of her anal passage gripping his cock convulsively. He could not tell if she was trying to expel him or let him all the way in. Harold reached around with his hand and forced it between Samantha's bound thighs. When he touched her clitoris she screamed and quivered.

'Fuck me, oh god, fuck me!'

He did, plunging in and out rapidly while Samantha grew steadily more excited. Then she came in great shuddering spasms. Her mixed cries of pain and release formed a background to their excited coupling. Harold lost track of time as he fucked her. When he came, Samantha screamed again. Gradually her moans subsided and she lay still, her body shaken by diminishing shudders.

Harold withdrew from her arsehole, not without difficulty. He was shaken by the intensity of his response to her plea. She had asked for pain, and he had supplied it without pausing to consider whether he should. The intensity of his own orgasm, the response to Samantha's pleas for more pain, showed him something new about himself. He had enjoyed inflicting this pain on her. It did not matter that she had asked for it and enjoyed it. His enjoyment was the issue. Anxiously he looked at his lover, this older woman who seemed to have worlds more experience than he in the nuances of sexual arousal. She seemed unchanged from the woman he had bedded the night before, and countless times before that. But he had changed. The change was unsettling.

Harold lifted Samantha to the sofa and lay beside her, drawing the duvet over them both and holding her body against his own. Samantha settled down against him with a sigh and drifted off to sleep. While she slept he examined the new Harold. He was forced to acknowledge that he had a strong streak of sadism in him. The question was, what would he do the next time Samantha demanded to be hurt? He had no doubt that she would. And as he considered the matter, he acknowledged that he would do as she asked, and enjoy it again. The trick, he guessed, was knowing where to draw the line – in effect, when to say no to her and to himself, in order to avoid serious harm. How to satisfy his own enjoyment of power over her. And he had no answer. His own sleep was slow in coming, and it was not untroubled.

He awoke when Samantha stirred against him. Anxiously he scrutinised her face for signs of revulsion, disgust, fear, rejection.

'Mmmmm' she said softly, 'that was wonderful.'

She was not angry. She was not going to leave him. But this, or something like it, was going to happen again.

'Toilet, please,' Samantha said. Harold took refuge from his troubled thoughts in action; extricating himself from her, he untied her legs and steered her toward the bathroom. He waited anxiously while she peed. He wiped her dry, noticing the thin streak of semen that trailed from her anus. Samantha said nothing when he cleaned that too.

'Feed me,' she commanded next, again submerging his thought in action. While he fed her, Harold searched again for bad signs. There were none. Samantha, fed, leaned forward and kissed Harold as intensely as she could, lacking the use of her hands. He embraced her, closing his arms around her and holding her breasts against his chest. Samantha sighed in contentment.

'Let's go back to the sofa,' she commanded when their passionate kiss ended, 'and tie my legs again.'

Restrained once more to her own satisfaction, Samantha asked to be gagged and blindfolded too. Harold

138

recognised the signs. Responding to her mood, he added ear-plugs to his lover's bondage. Once more he laid her on the sofa and lay down beside her. Samantha slept softly beside him, occasionally pulling against the cords that bound her, but mainly just tired, well fed and well fucked.

The ringing of the telephone awakened Harold. Samantha appeared not to have heard it. Gently, not wanting to wake her, he got up to answer it. It was dark outside.

'Harold?' A woman's voice, sounding tentative and unsure.

'Yes.' A sigh of relief came down the wire.

'I'm so glad it's you who answered. Mum would have had a fit.'

Recognition came. Amanda. But this Amanda sounded less brashly self-confident than the one who had told them to leave and to curl up together at his house. She sounded almost tentative, a little breathless; at a loss for words.

'Are you at a breaking-off point with mum?' Without waiting for an answer, she continued, 'Only, I've got myself into a bit of trouble and need your help. Can you come over without her knowing about it?'

Harold wondered what help he could give that Samantha could not.

Amanda told him. He hung up thoughtfully and went back to check on Samantha. She still slept, secure in her bonds. Harold drew the duvet over her and took his clothes into the bathroom to dress without waking her. Amanda had specifically asked him to keep this a secret. Harold looked once more at Samantha before going out and locking the door behind him. He consoled himself with the thought that this was what Samantha liked so much, being left helpless in some place where no one could find her except by accident. He started her car and drove through the late-evening streets of Weybridge. The rain had slackened but not stopped. The lights gleamed in the puddles. Tyres swished on the damp roadway.

The flat was in darkness as he parked the car. 'Draw the curtains before you put on any lights,' Amanda had warned him. Harold let himself in. From the darkness Amanda called, 'Harold?' She sounded frightened.

'What would you do if I were someone else?' he replied.

'Swoon with desire,' she responded, recovering something of her usual manner. 'Come in and close the door,' she commanded.

He locked the front door and drew the curtains in the front room. Harold turned on the standard lamp and turned to Amanda. She was seated on the sofa, naked save for her mother's handcuffs and dildo pants. From her state it was clear that she had experienced the same sort of pleasure her mother got from the pants, but now she was wary and tired and on the defensive. It was also clear why she had called for help, but she explained anyway. 'I dropped the damned key behind the cushions and I can't get it out,' she said, relief and frustration and embarrassment blended in her manner. 'Get me loose,' she commanded, 'don't just stand there staring.'

Harold smiled. Amanda looked furious and nervous at the same time. 'You'll have to stand up,' he told her.

'Why? So you can stare at me?' she snapped.

'Nice as that might be, there is actually another reason.' Harold was doing his best not to let his own arousal show, for Samantha's daughter nearly naked and helpless had a strong effect on Samantha's lover. 'I have to take up the cushions to find the key,' he explained. 'Can you stand up alone?'

Amanda struggled to her feet, looking so much like a younger version of her mother in the same situation.

140

Samantha must have looked like this at twenty. He wished he had known her then. Amanda moved nervously away from the sofa while Harold removed the cushions one at a time. Naturally, the key was behind the last one, deep in the angle between seat and back.

'You'd never have found it,' he told Amanda consolingly. 'Turn around so I can unlock you.'

Instead of doing what he asked, Amanda turned toward him and drew back her shoulders. Her firm breasts, so like Samantha's, excited Harold as Samantha's always did. He strove to hide his arousal.

'You want me, don't you?' Amanda asked challengingly. 'You're all hard and red in the face. Take these pants off me and have me. I can't stop you.' She sounded like Samantha too.

'Yes, of course I do,' he began, 'but you can't always have what you want, as the song says.'

'You just have to want what you get,' she finished the quotation for him, looking relieved and piqued at the same time. She turned away and presented her manacled hands to him.

Harold unlocked her and Amanda fled to the bedroom. He turned to leave so that Amanda could recover her poise in privacy. Things might be difficult between them for the foreseeable future, he thought. As he was going toward the door Amanda's voice called him back.

'Don't go, please. I want to talk to you.'

Amanda in polite mode was a rare change. He sat down on the sofa where she had waited for him to free her and wondered what she had been doing and feeling while the dildoes and handcuffs did their work on her. Evidently she had felt as her mother did in the same situation. Heredity played strange tricks.

Amanda returned wearing a dressing gown and looking a bit more at ease. She sat in the armchair across from him and crossed her legs. 'Sorry,' she said, an apology which seemed to take in everything: the trouble, the embarrassment, the bravado of her offer of herself. 'Now I know you really like mum. I don't think anyone else would have passed up an opportunity like you did.' Amanda spoke without false modesty, but she looked at the floor as she spoke.

Then she looked up at him with a flash of the old Amanda. 'You may regret it. I hope you do, anyway. You passed the temptation test with flying colours, even though I didn't intend to ask until the last minute. It was a spur of the moment thing – the damsel in distress offering the ultimate payment to her rescuer. But I meant it. You could have had me.'

'I'm flattered, but you must know why I said no. It wasn't easy,' Harold said, feeling embarrassed in his turn.

'Mum's a lucky woman,' Amanda told him. 'And I know a bit of what she must feel when you leave her tied up wearing those pants. Is she tied up now, at your place, waiting for you to come back and fuck her stupid?'

'Official secret, Amanda. We agreed on that. But why don't you ask her? It might take a bit of getting used to for her, your knowing about her preferences, but she could tell the story from the inside. At best I'm only observing her reactions.'

'And having your own, no doubt,' Amanda said with a smile.

'How did you manage to use the phone with your hands out of action?'

'Teeth and nose,' she replied, adding, 'It was awkward.'

He nodded understandingly. There was another awkward silence. Harold tried again. 'So what happened with the boyfriend?

'I asked him to tie me up before sex,' Amanda said in

142

her direct way. 'I wanted to see what it felt like for mum,' she added.

'And did he?'

'He asked me if I was some sort of pervert. We argued. He left. I felt relieved. Life with someone as square as him would have been hell. He was Italian, dark and handsome and Catholic. It felt like love, but I suspect that it was just fascination. I suppose I wanted to see if I could seduce him – despite his early toilet training. Anyway, he would probably have expected me to stay at home, keep house and raise the kids while he had his career and his life. And probably a bit on the side.'

While he thought that Amanda was probably overdoing the sour grapes bit, she was probably right. He had certainly never expected a woman as undomesticated as Samantha to enter his life, but he was glad that she had. 'Yes,' he said, 'I can see that it might have been dreary. You sound like your mother.'

'I'll take that as a compliment,' Amanda said dryly. 'If you won't tell me about mum, then I'll tell you what it felt like to me. You can make your own mental comparisons.'

Harold guessed that Amanda needed to explain why she had tried her own experiment. The talking cure, the shrinks called it. He didn't know that he could offer any absolution, should she be seeking any. Probably she just needed to talk. He thought of Samantha, bound and gagged and waiting for him to return, if she even knew of his departure. He guessed that she did. She would be all right, he decided. She was a veteran. Harold settled back on the sofa, an invitation to her to say what was on her mind.

'It was fantastic,' Amanda began. 'I knew it was going to be different with two things inside me. I just never realised how different, even though every woman

143

knows about dildoes. Since they belong to mum, I'm guessing that she likes it too.' Amanda paused.

Harold did not rise to the bait.

She resumed. 'I suppose the initial shock of having something up there,' Amanda indicated her back passage with a gesture, 'was what did it. I've had dozens of things up the other place.'

Harold hoped that was an exaggeration, but he let it pass. Amanda had a strong need to sound experienced, if not actually blasé.

'It was amazing. Fireworks and fun fairs, and all on my own. With the handcuffs it was even better. I understand why mum likes it so much. Perversions needn't be awful, even if one chooses to keep them secret.'

It sounded like a pronouncement. Harold greeted it with a respectful silence.

'Damn it, say something!' she demanded. 'And wipe that knowing smile off your face!'

'I wasn't smiling,' Harold said with a smile. 'Or at any rate not at you. Go on.'

'If mum were here, she'd be having fits. Why aren't you scolding me?'

'Because you're your own person. You have to find out what you want to do and then do it. Do you remember the first day we met, when you were moving from the old house? You told me that you had to be tolerant, with a pervert for a mother. That sounded very grown-up. I have taken your advice. So should you. Do what you like as often as you can, and if someone else objects, try not to notice them. As for me, well, pots and kettles should cooperate, not argue about relative blackness.'

'I wish I were as lucky as mum,' Amanda told him.

'Keep looking. I didn't have any luck until your mother bought this flat.' A thought occurred to him. 'What happened to your mates?'

144

'Oh, they'll be here tomorrow. I just wanted to have some time on my own to try out the handcuffs. The pants were an unexpected bonus. Where did you get them?'

'The Internet,' he replied. 'If you use your mother's computer, just go surfing. You can find almost anything you want there.'

'Does mum ever wear the pants under her clothes when you go out? Oh, I know you don't want to talk about her, but I guess she does. I know I would. In fact, I will. Tomorrow. The mates can wait until later. I can't wait to find out what it feels like to be secretly stuffed in public.'

'I'd better go now,' Harold said. 'Good luck with the boyfriend – and the pants.'

'What will you say to mum when she asks where you've been?' Amanda sounded worried once again. 'Better take something back – hamburgers or a pizza. Say you were hungry. The returning hunter bringing back sustenance for his mate. That sort of thing.'

'Good idea. I won't say anything about tonight if you won't.'

Amanda walked him to the door. There she planted a more substantial kiss on his lips. Harold was tempted to try his luck, but went instead to the Burger King and bought some grown-up food to take back to his older lover.

When he got back, Samantha was awake and struggling against her bonds. She sounded as if she was on the verge of an orgasm as he silently opened the front door. In the flickering light from the television screen he saw that she had rolled over onto her stomach and was driving her hips against the cushions. Her moans of pleasure were loud despite the tight gag. She thrashed on the sofa, nearly falling to the floor as she came. Harold watched her, not wanting to interrupt such a satisfying performance. When Samantha eventually subsided, he rolled her over onto her back and kissed her over the strips of tape that gagged her. Samantha returned the kiss as best she could. It was good to be back on familiar ground, Harold thought.

He removed Samantha's gag and offered her a hamburger and soft drink. The people at Burger King, he thought, would never guess the use to which their fast food was being put. He left her lying on the sofa while he cleared up the paper cartons and cups. When he returned, he undressed, sat down and held her head in his lap. Samantha snuggled against him with a sigh of contentment.

'Where were you? '

'I had the midnight munchies. You know how sex always makes me hungry. You too, apparently' Harold was thankful that he had followed Amanda's advice to stop for some food. 'Did you enjoy yourself in my absence?' he asked in his turn.

Samantha nodded. 'Can't you smell me?'

'Well, yes, but I thought it indelicate to bring it up. But now that you have, I'll admit that the smell of sex is one of my favourite odours. Next to hamburger, that is.'

They slept that night on the sofa, Samantha still bound hand and foot. Harold dreamed of Samantha writhing and screaming as he lashed her, and woke several times in a nervous sweat. Each time he was reassured by her weight and solidity as she slept. Samantha sighed when he bent to kiss her hair but didn't wake up, unaware of his dreams. In the daylight his dark dreams retreated and Harold said nothing to her about them as he untied her and they both got ready to begin another week.

Samantha decided to stay at Harold's place for a few days, until Amanda was ready to allow her to return home. Harold told her he liked the idea of her waiting for him – 'just like the little women of the Victorian era.'

Samantha retorted that the 'little women' probably did not dream of doing what they were doing. 'But, tonight we'll have the roast,' Samantha promised. 'I'll be a dull little woman for a bit.'

'Think of next weekend. We're not exactly reduced to screwing in the back of your car in a country lane, exciting as that might be. Or does the fear of being caught turn you on?'

'A little,' Samantha admitted, 'but the things you do to me turn me on more. Were you thinking of finding a secluded spot for a bit of rural seduction? I wouldn't mind it if you tied me up and had your way with me in some suitable place.' Samantha looked interested in the idea. She had insisted on leaving some of her favourite cord in her car as well as in his van. 'Just in case,' she had explained, putting a coil in the boot.

'There aren't many places that secluded,' Harold told her. 'And it's winter.'

'I know,' she sighed.

147

7

Deserted House

In the week leading up to Christmas, Harold had a bit of luck in his work. He was asked to do some extensive renovations to a family house at Flexford, out in the country. The owners explained, when he met them, that they were taking an extended holiday just after Christmas, in order to escape the full horrors of the English winter. They would fly off to sunnier climes, leaving the repairs to Harold, with whom they would correspond or telephone to get progress reports. As he had done some work for the same owners at their previous house, they were inclined to trust him with this larger project. He was asked to keep in touch in case there were any problems.

It was a large, rambling house, with a complex roof that covered many wings, and out-of-the-way rooms which had no doubt been the abode of servants – before servants became extinct with the advent of death duties and other confiscatory tax schemes. There was also a cellar to be cleaned up and converted into dry storage space. The work was to begin after the New Year.

The owners took him on a tour of the premises, discussing what they wanted done. As the renovations were all internal, he could work in the warm and dry. There was an extensive list, ranging from the bathrooms to the attic bedrooms. It would keep him busy until spring, he realised. As he walked through the many rooms, he thought that this would be almost as good a place to leave Samantha as the barn she desired. He wondered what the owners would think of the idea. Probably not very much, he guessed. And what would Samantha think of it? Would the house be an acceptable substitute for the barn? It would at least be warm, dry and mouse-free. She would probably like the warren of rooms and halls and stairs; it was a good place to be left in.

Harold decided to say nothing to Samantha about the project until after the coast was clear. If he told her now, he reasoned, she would be in a fever at least to see the place, if not to put it to the planned use. Amanda was going to be with them until after the holidays anyway, and the owners of the house would not be leaving until the same time.

Christmas came and went, the usual three wet Sundays in a row. Amanda announced her intent to visit her grandparents for the New Year. She would return to Weybridge and spend the last few of the holidays at home before going back to Reading. Samantha drove her to catch the train and returned feeling both relieved, and saddened by her relief. Harold told her about the deserted house idea to cheer her up. They could try it out after Amanda had gone back to university. What did she think?

'What about doing the deserted house plan this Saturday and Sunday? Amanda will be going back to Reading on Saturday.'

'I'd rather a barn,' Samantha said, but she looked eager. She asked Harold to describe the house to her. 'Yes, let's do it! Take me there right after we drive Amanda back to Reading,' she said. He had not known that he was going with them.

'Amanda asked if you'd like to come along,' Samantha told him.

Harold thought that that could prove awkward after his recent encounter with Amanda, but there was no way to back out gracefully. Samantha meanwhile was making plans of her own.

'As soon as we drop Amanda off, we can go directly to the house. I can hardly wait! And you can tie me up for the drive there.'

Samantha's inventiveness continually surprised him. Her imagination worked much better than his own.

Amanda duly returned to Weybridge on the Friday after New Year. They started early on Saturday morning to drive to Reading. The plan was to arrive in Reading before lunch. Amanda wanted them both to see her rooms at the university. They would all have lunch and then they would start back homewards.

The first sight of her daughter's lodgings dismayed Samantha. She immediately set to tidying things up. Amanda asked her to stop, but her mother insisted.

'You and Harold go and get some food in for the week,' she commanded, handing Amanda some money. 'I'll be done when you get back. There's nothing in the fridge, and the place looks as if a troop of monkeys had been living in it.'

They went, Amanda in her turn shrugging hopelessly.

'Let her be your mother again for a bit. She's missed you around the place ever since you left.'

Amanda looked pleased, but covered it at once by asking, 'What about you? Did you miss me too?'

'I hardly knew you when you left. I'll make up for it by missing you this time, all right?'

That seemed to satisfy Amanda. They drove to the supermarket and stocked up on student food, Harold making no attempt to guide her selection. Amanda knew her own tastes well enough. As they filled the cart,

150

Amanda found time to ask Harold what they were going to do when they got back home. 'Are you going to take Mum back to yours, or will you conduct your revels at her place?'

He did not reply, and Amanda finally gave up.

Samantha had finished when they returned. Amanda guided them to a good restaurant near the university, where they ate an unpretentious dinner of roast beef and three veg.

Mother and daughter both looked tearful as they parted. Samantha was quiet as they drove out of the city and started back home. It was nearly an hour before she roused herself and reminded Harold of their plans. It was nearly as long again before they found a place deserted enough to accomplish the first stage. Samantha had wanted to be bound and gagged and locked into the boot of the car. Harold thought she would be too cold and uncomfortable there. 'Besides, I want to look at you.' Samantha smiled at the compliment and they agreed that she would ride up front with him.

They stopped in an empty lay-by screened from the road by trees. Samantha took the cords from the glove box, handing them to him wordlessly.

He bound her wrists together in front of her, palm to palm, making the bindings as tight as she liked them. He tied her thumbs as well. Then he made her sit in the seat while he raised her skirt to her waist. He took a moment to admire Samantha's legs and her shiny grey stockings, bending to plant a quick kiss on her pubic mound, feeling the familiar ripple of excitement. Samantha spread her thighs invitingly, and the kiss moved to her labia. Harold licked her cunt lips and his tongue slid inside her. Samantha sighed with pleasure.

Pleasurable as all this was, the lay-by was much too public to go any further. He crossed Samantha's ankles and bound them tightly. Then he bound her back against the seat with several turns of cord under her breasts and around her waist, trapping her arms against the front of her body. Harold hoped that this would not be visible to overtaking lorry drivers, while at the same time letting Samantha knew that she could not escape. He draped her scarf so that it covered her bound wrists.

Samantha wriggled like a puppy as he finished tying her up. Harold again knelt beside the open door and planted another kiss on her exposed cunt. With her ankles crossed Samantha's thighs were spread invitingly. It was too good an opportunity to miss. She sighed in excited anticipation. Then, his captive secured to his (and her) satisfaction, Harold got into the driving seat and resumed the journey. He glanced appreciatively at Samantha's exposed legs and cunt from time to time. Not all the overtaking lorry drivers noticed her condition, but those who did occasionally honked their horns in salute. 'You've got them all so horny they're honking. Me too,' Harold remarked to his mistress. Samantha smiled.

It was a longish drive from Reading to Flexford. The fine afternoon turned into a clear evening. The first stars were appearing in the sky as they drew up in front of the house. It was going to be a frosty night. 'Aren't you glad you won't be freezing in some awful barn tonight?'

'I suppose so,' Samantha retorted, 'but that doesn't let you off your promise to look for a suitably deserted barn or stable before spring.'

Harold switched off the lights and the engine. In the light of the half moon the house looked dark, but not forbidding. 'Damn,' he said, 'where are those bats? I had arranged for them to be flitting around the eaves as we drove up.'

'Perhaps Count Dracula needed them elsewhere. But not to worry. It looks spooky enough in the dark.'

Harold untied Samantha's ankles and removed the ropes that held her to the seat. To her surprise, he also untied her wrists. The reason became clear when he ordered her to strip. The drive in front of the house was a cleared space of about one hundred feet across, surrounded by gradually thickening woodland. Samantha was a bit apprehensive, this being her first experience of outdoor nudity. She hesitated.

'Do it!' Harold commanded. With a quick glance at the surrounding darkness, Samantha did so. She let her clothing fall to the ground: skirt, blouse, and bra. The moonlight on her naked body made shadows in the hollows he knew so well. As usual, she left her stockings and suspenders on. At Harold's suggestion, she also kept her high-heeled shoes on; the ground was too rough and cold for unshod feet. He gathered her discarded clothing from the ground and put it into her car.

Samantha shivered as he turned back to look appreciatively at her. The shiver was not entirely due to the cold night air. Not only would she be left helpless here; she now knew that she would have no clothes even if she somehow managed to get loose. Harold broke the tableau by motioning for her to turn around. Samantha brought her arms behind her back without having to be told. She shuddered with excitement as he bound her hands behind her, palm to palm as she had shown him on their first encounter. As she had explained then, it provided for better circulation when she was going to be tied up for a long time. It also facilitated the tying of her thumbs whenever the notion struck – as it did again. Samantha's elbows nearly touched when her bound her upper arms together. In another few months, Harold reflected as he finished the last knots, they will touch.

With her arms bound behind her, Samantha's shoulders were pulled severely back. Her naked breasts stood out prominently, the nipples and areolae dark in the silvery light. Her pubic hair made another inviting well of shadow.

Without hurrying, Harold gagged her, stuffing the pants she kept in the car into her mouth. She had kept to her resolve not to wear pants. It was a delicious secret they both enjoyed. Samantha grimaced at the stale smell of them – not so much in distaste as for effect. She wanted Harold to know that she appreciated his efforts. The tape was next, covering her mouth from nose to chin. Harold wound it twice completely around her head, making it impossible for her to loosen it. More tape covered her eyes. 'Mmmm,' Samantha sighed, lost in her helpless nakedness.

Harold bent to kiss her erect nipples, and Samantha sighed once again. She stood still awaiting whatever he wanted to do to her, and seemingly loving every minute of it. Taking her by the elbow, Harold steered her toward the dark house. Unlocking the door, he led his bound mistress across the dark entrance hall. There was enough light from the moon to make interior lighting unnecessary, and for Samantha it would have made no difference anyway. Harold closed and locked the door behind them, and then turned his blindfolded captive several times round, effectively disorientating her. She could have no idea which way she was facing. Samantha swayed slightly and then steadied herself. Harold took her into his arms, his hands holding her bound hands behind her, and he kissed her long and deeply over the tape gag. Samantha as usual did her best to return the kiss, her lips working against his through the tape. They both found this handless and helpless kissing exciting. Harold felt his cock grow stiff. So did Samantha, pressing herself against it and exacerbating his erection.

Harold knelt before Samantha and ran his hands over her naked body, caressing her bottom and her hips. He moved on, down her nylon-sheathed thighs to her knees, over the swell of her calves and to her trim ankles. And then back up again. Samantha shivered at the touch, and Harold knew that it was going to be very hard to leave her tied up alone while he went home. A part of him knew that the excitement came from thinking of Samantha waiting helplessly for him to return to her, but another part of him was reacting strongly to the woman who stood before him here and now. He hoped that it would be at least as hard for her as she lay bound and gagged through the night.

But a promise was a promise. He stood and led Samantha to the stairs. Up they went, past the main bedrooms, to the room that he had chosen for her. There was nothing in the room but a bed. The moonlight fell on the floor, lucent silver, and the shadows were deep in the corners. Though Harold had left the central heating on to allow Samantha to lie naked through the long night, the room was distinctly chilly.

Samantha's breathing was ragged by the time they reached the room, not entirely from climbing the long flights of stairs. Harold thought he could smell her arousal. A quick check with his hand found Samantha wet and parted. She moaned as he touched her. He changed the plan abruptly. He seated her on the side of the bed and knelt between her thighs, his hands on the smooth nylon of her stockings. He bent and kissed her cunt, sliding his tongue inside to tease her swollen clitoris. Samantha moaned again. She lowered her head until her chin rested on his, a sign of her acquiescence and eagerness. Harold licked and kissed her cunt, biting her labia and breathing in the scent of her arousal. He felt his cock stiffen painfully in his trousers. His clothes felt like a suit of armour, restricting his movements.

Hurriedly he stood and undressed, then lay on the bed and pulled Samantha atop him. When he guided himself into her, she shuddered. She was wet and hot around his cock, and he thought she came almost as soon as he entered her. He held still as Samantha shuddered again. Her parted legs lay on either side of his own, her stockings smooth against his flesh. The feel of them excited him immensely. Harold turned her head to face him and planted a long kiss over her gag. He felt Samantha tighten around him and he couldn't hold back any longer. He shook as he spurted inside her, Samantha moaning and squeezing his cock as she climaxed at the same time. He had always been able to make their coupling last much longer. Now he had allowed himself to be caught up in Samantha's fantasy, and this was the result. He felt more drained than he could ever recall after such a short fuck. Shaken.

Samantha was breathing rapidly. She was still excited. She clenched herself around his cock and thrust with her hips. She came once more, and continued moving until she felt him growing hard again. This time it went on for much longer. Samantha seemed to be having climaxes one after the other. Harold was able to hold back this time, the earlier climax delaying him. Samantha bucked and jerked. Harold, holding her with both arms, could feel her fighting against the cords that bound her hands and arms behind her back. She moaned continuously, and no doubt would have been screaming but for the gag. Her impending abandonment seemed to be working on her as it had on Harold.

They lay joined for a long time after he came. Harold was reluctant to get up and leave Samantha alone. And it was nice to lie in bed with her. For a moment he wished he could stay the night, but he knew that Samantha did not want that. They had, after all, gone to some trouble to get her here. She would not want to waste it all.

After a while, Harold got up and got dressed. He helped Samantha sit on the side of the bed so that he could tie her legs as she liked: ankles, knees and thighs, the cords pulled tight and cinched between her legs. Samantha moaned contentedly as he finished tying her up. Harold arranged his helpless mistress on her side in the bed before hurriedly leaving. He knew that he would not be able to go if he spent too much time looking at Samantha lying bound and gagged in the moonlight.

He left the house, locking the door as he went. He started the engine and drove away, knowing that Samantha would be able to hear the receding sounds of her car as he drove away into the night. She would be certain that she was alone and helpless in a strange house. No one knew where she was. No one would come to her rescue. It was as close as she could come to realising her fantasy. From Harold's point of view, he knew that she was as safe as the circumstances allowed. And as accessible.

The drive home was pleasant. The night was clear and fine. The heater kept the interior of the car warm and comfortable. Samantha would not be quite so cosy. Harold hoped, as he had jokingly remarked, that her fantasy would keep her warm. He went to Samantha's flat rather than to his house. There he slept fitfully, waking often to see if it was time to retrieve her. His dreams, when he slept, were filled with lurid images of her struggling to free herself, and making herself come as she tried. He had seen her do it on many occasions, so it was not hard to visualise her struggles and climaxes in dreams. The night seemed to last forever. It probably seemed longer to Samantha.

When Harold got up and made coffee, he seemed to settle down. The worst part of the adventure was past. There was suddenly no hurry to drive back to check on Samantha. She had got through the night, and now he found himself inventing reasons to leave her a bit longer. Harold had begun to share her fantasy. So he prolonged it, looking at her computer to see what she had been doing. He found a diary this time. It began soon after her birthday. He read it, feeling slightly guilty but unable to stop himself. Amanda's remarks were confirmed – Samantha admitted that she loved him. Being loved made him feel oddly pleased. It was not a word men used easily, but Samantha had no such reservations. Harold also found the record of her fantasies. The deserted barn scenario was at the top of the list of things to do. He was glad he had been able to manage that for her.

'I hope he stays,' Samantha had written at one point. She went on to talk about the age difference. She seemed quite concerned about it. Harold was tempted to type, 'It doesn't matter!' but did not. Better, he thought, to let Samantha believe her secrets and her worries were unknown. And better if he showed her that the difference did not matter – showed her by staying and by making her as happy as he knew how to do.

Switching off the computer, Harold had a look through Samantha's clothing and lingerie. Might as well violate all secrets, or none at all. In her absence the sight of Samantha's clothes made him feel closer to her. Most of her underwear he had seen at one time or another, but he found this secret viewing arousing. He found a black corset and a dark-blue basque among her things. Samantha had never worn either of them when she was with him. She did not need the corset, for her body was firm and slim. Nevertheless he imagined her wearing it with a pair of black shiny tights, and grew excited at the image. He toyed with the idea of taking it with him when he returned for her, but in the end he put it away again. Some other time, he promised himself.

Harold selected a clean pair of stockings and a suspender belt from the collection before leaving. He guessed that Samantha might need these items after her long night in bondage.

When morning came, Harold tried to drive slowly back to the house, but arrived too quickly. In the low sun of morning it looked undisturbed. No signs of a break-in. He slammed the car door, wanting Samantha to know that someone – though not necessarily him – had come for her. That was an essential part of the fantasy. She would be waiting uncertainly now to see who was here. For the same reason he made as much noise as possible opening the front door. Up the stairs, down the hall, into the attic room, making no attempt at stealth.

Samantha lay on the bed as he had left her, bound and gagged, blindfolded, helpless. She was smelling of something a bit less pleasant than sex. There were dark stains on the mattress, and on her stockings. She had pissed herself at some time in her struggles. Harold had no idea how long she had lain in her own urine, but he guessed that she had managed to enjoy that humiliating experience, too. Helpless captive, unable to get free, forced to wet the bed and herself, and then lie in it until someone came to set her free – it was all part of her fantasy. Harold studied the scene before him, enjoying what he saw and reluctant to end the experience. Samantha's scenario called for ravishment by her discoverer. He looked forward to that, but still delayed breaking the tableau.

Samantha was facing the door, her head raised as if she wanted to see who had come for her. The blindfold, Harold imagined, hid the anxiety in her eyes. And the anxiety would be real enough: there was no guarantee that it would be Harold who had arrived. As she had said, that was an important aspect of her fantasy. So for that reason too he delayed going to his captive – and found himself enjoying being the cause of her anxiety. He gazed at her for a few more minutes in silence, then strode across to the bed and knelt beside it.

Harold took her face between his hands and kissed her gagged mouth. He felt Samantha relax as she recognised him. She did her best to return the kiss.

'Mmmmm,' she said as he drew back. When he cupped her breasts and squeezed the nipples she was more demonstrative, emitting a long sigh of pleasure.

Harold felt himself growing erect as he caressed her. His ex-wife had never been able to arouse him so strongly; partly, he suspected, because she had never been this aroused. Unlike her, Samantha never held back. When she was pleased, she showed it. As she did now.

Harold shifted his attention from Samantha's breasts to her legs. He untied the cords quickly and helped her to stand. As usual, her legs were shaky after being tied for so long. He had to steady her to keep her on her feet. Harold wanted her there and then, but he knew that she would like a shower first. He led her into the bathroom down the hall. That was the trouble with servants' quarters: no ensuite facilities. He left Samantha standing in the middle of the floor while he undressed. She heard the sound of the water as Harold adjusted the temperature of the shower and nodded appreciatively. He led her into the shower, undressed and got in with her, the warm water cascading over them both.

Samantha rotated under the jet, soaking herself from her hair to her toes, her stockings going darker as they absorbed the water, gleaming dully. Samantha turned to face him and he began to soap her body, her naked flesh slippery and wet. She liked that. Harold soaped her legs and stockings, washing away the urine. He paid special attention to her cunt. She liked that too. So did he. Samantha was becoming aroused as he touched her. The sight of her, her body all slippery and her arms bound behind her back, aroused him. She rubbed herself against him, arousing him even further. There was only one way this could end.

Harold turned her away from him and applied soap around her anus. Samantha stiffened as she realised what he intended to do, but seemed eager for him to sodomise her again. 'Ummm,' she said softly as she felt his cock nudging against her arsehole. This time there was less difficulty as he slid slowly into her. As before, Harold reached around to tease her clitoris once the penetration was complete. And, as before, Samantha moaned with pleasure at the dual stimulation. She relished the novelty, the slightly illicit pleasure, of being penetrated there, as much as he enjoyed being there.

Harold could feel her internal muscles clenched around him. They clenched and relaxed, clenched and relaxed as her arousal grew. Samantha's moans were almost continuous, reduced in volume by the gag, but an unmistakable sign of her pleasure. Her clitoris swelled and grew hard as he teased it between thumb and forefinger. He caressed her breasts in turn with his other hand until the nipples were likewise swollen and erect.

Samantha's first climax jolted them both. She stiffened at the onset, and then began to thrust with her hips, causing him to slide in and out of her as she came. She went into her second climax almost without pause. He saw Samantha fighting against the cords, her fingers clenching and the muscles in her arms standing out as she came. Harold had to hold back hard in order not to come himself. He wanted this to go on for as long as possible – for both their sakes. Samantha moaned through the gag as she bucked and shuddered. Finally he could not wait any longer. The hot spurt when he came made them both groan as Samantha joined him.

Harold dried Samantha and stripped off her wet stockings and suspender belt, He sat her on the toilet while he dried himself. Presently there was the sound of a woman pissing. Reward enough for his efforts. He wiped her clean and kissed her over the gag. Samantha reciprocated enthusiastically. He found a toweling bath robe to drape around her to keep her warm, intending to keep her bound and gagged for a while longer because he enjoyed looking at her and because he knew that she simply liked being tied up. He knew that sooner or later he would have to untie her; in the meantime, she made a beautiful animal.

He told her so, and she smiled behind her gag and blindfold. The adventure looked like being a success.

8

Country Life

Samantha took to the deserted house idea as if born to it. She also took to arriving unannounced, with predictable results. She was always dressed provocatively, and she enjoyed being left tied up in various rooms. While Harold worked, Samantha worked herself up to climax as she had so often done when left alone. When he came for her, she could look forward to Harold doing more of the same before untying her. He could look forward to furious sex with his mistress at the end of the day.

One day she showed up wearing a long coat with knee-high laced leather boots with high heels. She looked fetching indeed. He came down to meet her. She kissed him in the front drive, then stepped back and unbuttoned her coat. She wore nothing under it except the by now inevitable stockings and suspenders. Samantha dropped the coat to the ground and embraced Harold in full view of whoever might be lucky enough to be in the vicinity. He was surprised, as well as pleased and excited, which was doubtless her intent.

'You have a decision to make,' she told Harold. 'You have to decide whether to stop work and have me now, or to have me later if you can't square it with your conscience to break off yet. Or you could have me both now and later, if you have a really well-trained conscience.'

He led Samantha indoors and they went straight up to the bedroom in the attic space. Harold had developed an erection almost from the time she had dropped her coat. By the time he had followed her up the stairs, admiring the rear view of a nude woman ascending a staircase, it had grown. He nearly threw her onto the bed. Samantha, laughing at his eagerness, was also excited by it. She lay back on the bed, spreading her legs and reaching up with her arms. Harold lay down beside her and they embraced, kissing and nuzzling one another for a long time. Samantha's nipples were hard and tight against him as he held her. His erection poked her belly insistently. She guided him into her and crossed her ankles behind his back, pulling him fully inside.

Samantha smiled up at him as he began to thrust in and out. 'Kiss me while you're fucking me,' she commanded.

He did, keeping his mouth pressed down on hers as she groaned and squealed in release. His mouth made an effective gag, a much more enjoyable one than the tape they usually used to stop her mouth. Samantha's perfume was in his nostrils, along with the odour of her arousal. The aroma of healthy, willing woman drove him on. Samantha matched his ardour, thrashing beneath him as she came and moaning against his mouth.

When Harold came she clamped down on his cock and rode him to the end. Afterward they lay together recovering.

'Now, wasn't that more fun than hanging doors?' she asked him teasingly.

'Hanging doors isn't everything,' he replied, 'but I'll have to get back to it for a while.'

Samantha nodded. 'Tie me to the bed and get on with it,' she told him.

Harold used a ball of twine from his tool kit to tie Samantha's wrists and ankles to the bed posts. Samantha lay spread out on her back, the cords biting into her wrists and ankles just as she liked them.

'I'll wait here, then, shall I?' she asked with a grin. 'Don't be too long.'

He was not very long.

Winter passed, and still the work on the house continued. One bright March day, Samantha arrived, unannounced as usual. The blue sky invited outdoor sports.

'Nearly spring,' she said as she took off her clothes in the back garden. Harold took off his clothes and picked up Samantha's coat. He led her to a patch of lawn, excited at the prospect of yet another different experience. Samantha continued to amaze and challenge him even now. He spread her coat on the ground and they lay on it. It was a lumpy bed, but that did not matter. Samantha lay on her back and reached eagerly up to pull him down to her. This was their first outdoor fuck. She spread her legs and they made love under the open sky. Samantha's excitement was contagious.

Afterward, when they had recovered their breath, Samantha asked Harold to leave her tied to a tree while he got on with his work. 'I imagine you'll think of something pleasant to do to me when you return,' she said, 'and I will commune with nature while you're away.'

He led her to a birch tree at the edge of the wood. There he tied her hands together behind her back and around the trunk of the tree. 'Wouldn't it be nice if all trees came with a beautiful woman tied to them?' he told her as he tied her ankles and knees as well. He left her

165

there and went back to work in the house. He found himself looking often at her through the windows, both to ensure that no one wandered by and found her (though Samantha probably would not have minded that), and to enjoy the sight of his lover tied up helplessly waiting for him to return. That afternoon he had an almost continuous erection. Quitting time seemed a long time away as he forced himself to work as nearly normally as possible. Samantha seemed to be enjoying her exposure to nature – and to whoever else might be in the area.

When he finished for the day his cock led him to Samantha. Without speaking, Harold removed his belt and whipped her naked body with it, being careful not to strike at full strength as he had recently taken to doing with the lighter pussy whip. Samantha urged him to hit her harder, and seemed to be enjoying the beating. Her nipples were erect, even after he had struck them several times, and she moaned with pleasure. She screamed when he struck her on her lower belly, tugging at the cords, and then asked him to untie her legs so that he could lash her cunt. He wondered if even her protests would stop him. She screamed again when he did as she asked, but those screams quickly changed to moans of pleasure. Harold grew more excited as he beat her, and he found it difficult not to lash her as hard as he could. Her excitement drove them both on. Finally he dropped the belt and his trousers and nailed Samantha to the tree trunk. She jerked and shuddered, and moaned with pleasure.

'Ahhhhh!' she screamed as she felt him tense up and spurt inside her. She came again as he did.

Samantha was reluctant to be untied, but it was getting dark and the warmth of the day was nearly gone. They got dressed and drove their vehicles to a nearby pub for an early dinner. The rope marks on her wrists and ankles were red. Harold hoped that no one would notice. Samantha seemed oblivious to them. 'That was marvellous,' she told him. 'Can we do it again soon?'

Harold agreed with her assessment. 'Bring the pussy whip tomorrow,' he told her.

Barely a week had passed before Samantha was back at the site, this time, she said rather tentatively, with a surprise for Harold.

'Not another one!' he said with mock-exasperation, Wondering why she seemed so diffident. She insisted on undressing indoors. It was a cloudy day, but dry. He thought she would have preferred outdoor sex, to which she had taken enthusiastically. Well, he admitted, so had he, and he had been rather looking forward to another al fresco fuck.

Wordlessly, she turned her back to him and stripped down to the stockings and suspenders. She wore high-heeled shoes that showed off her long, full legs to advantage. He admired the view from the rear. Samantha's bottom, outlined by the suspender straps, looked very attractive; he considered kissing it, but just then Samantha turned toward him and he saw her 'surprise'. A thin plastic tube hung down between her thighs, its origin somewhere under her pubic hair. Harold stared uncomprehendingly at it for a moment. Then he saw that the tube was held shut by a plastic clamp, and he recognised the device as a surgical catheter. She looked uncertainly at him, wondering what he thought. But Harold did not know what to think. It was bizarre, despite the fact that their whole relationship leaned rather heavily in that direction.

'I'm beginning to enjoy humiliation,' Samantha explained enigmatically. When he remained silent, she went on, hesitantly, as if unsure herself, or of what she meant, 'I like it when you do things to me that would be embarrassing if others knew about them. You know: leaving me tied up, and whipping me . . . this house . . . what we do here and at home.'

Harold nodded. It would be embarrassing if others knew about what they did together; even more embarrassing than a revelation of ordinary sex between two people. But he could not imagine giving it up.

'I thought that this,' she said, indicating the catheter, 'would be another way of giving you control over me. I mean . . . even more control than when I'm merely tied up.'

Harold thought that 'merely' was not quite the right word.

'With this, you can control when I pee as well. When you tie my hands I won't be able to wee unless you release the clamp for me. It will be your decision, not mine. So you have even more control. I rather like that idea. Do you?'

His reply seemed important to Samantha. Harold recalled the sense of power he had felt while whipping her, or knowing that she was lying helpless waiting for him to come to her. This was yet more power over the body of the woman he had grown to . . . love. There, the word was out, even if only silently. He felt relieved at the final admission. Slowly, he nodded, and opened his arms. Samantha closed the distance between them and they embraced long and silently. Holding her body to his, Harold thought of his former wife. They had never reached any such understanding of one another. Perhaps there was a greater wisdom in older women. Samantha held him tightly, her head against his shoulder. Finally she looked up, and they kissed lingeringly. Harold put his hands on either side of her face and held her head still while the kiss drew out. Samantha sighed with contentment and relief. He understood her so well, she thought gratefully.

'Can you tie me up now?' she asked when the kiss ended. Her voice trembled with an unusual, shy eagerness as she looked into his eyes.

'Is the Pope a Catholic?' he retorted.

They went upstairs hand in hand, leaving her clothing strewn about the sitting room, Samantha clutching her handbag as they went. In the bedroom Harold got the cords from the cupboard where he had taken to leaving them. Samantha produced another length of tubing from her handbag, and a joining piece. She fitted the two tubes together, so that the catheter now reached the floor. Indeed, she had to be careful to avoid stepping on it. Harold imagined that such an abrupt pull would be painful.

'How did you get it in?'

'I asked a friend who's a nurse to show me,' Samantha replied. 'She thought it was a bit odd, but I told her that I had to look after my mother who was becoming incontinent. If I knew how to insert it myself, I said, I could do if for her. She showed me how to remove it too.' Samantha flushed as she spoke of the experience, and Harold guessed that she had enjoyed the humiliation of these intimate attentions from her friend. He tied her hands together behind her back, pulling the cords tightly around her wrists.

Samantha sighed in relief and satisfaction. 'When you've tied me, I want you to examine my cunt. See where the catheter goes in, and how. So you can do me the next time.' She paused. 'You will do me, won't you?' she asked with an edge of anxiety. 'I mean, it won't put you off, will it?'

This too seemed important to her. 'Of course not, silly. It would take a lot to put me off you. You should know that by now. Anyway, who else would put up with a pervert like you?'

'Another pervert?' Samantha suggested, relief and happiness evident in her face and voice.

169

Harold felt a certain tension leave her body. He kissed the top of her head, inhaling the clean fragrance of her hair. Yes, he thought, it would take a lot to put him off Samantha. And he would enjoy performing this further, intimate service for her. He told her so. 'I like the idea of controlling you that closely,' he said. Samantha wriggled like a puppy.

Harold sat her on the edge of the bed and she spread her legs. He knelt between her nylon-sheathed thighs, pausing only to stroke the smooth stockings and to kiss the insides of her thighs above them. Then he traced the plastic tube to where it ended inside her. Looking closely, he saw that it entered a small hole he had never before looked at, within her vagina, tucked up in the folds of her upper labia. He examined a woman's urethra closely for the first time. Then he kissed her there, where the tube disappeared up inside her. Samantha moaned softly.

'You have to push a bit to get it past the muscle,' she told him, her voice shaky. 'But then it stays in place. I could show you – only my hands are tied,' Samantha said archly.

'Show me next time,' Harold replied. 'But doesn't it hurt?' He tried to imagine a similar tube being fed into his urethra.

'A little, but you can apply some lubricant to the catheter. I may wince a bit, but just keep on feeding it into me. It goes in about two inches before the sphincter will hold it. There's a little ridge in the tube you have to push past the sphincter. Once it's in I won't be able to remove it, and you'll have to decide how long it stays and when I can wee. The clamp is closed now. If you open it, there will be a small flood. You see, I clamped it before I set out, and I drove the whole way here like that.' Samantha indicated the plastic clamp by nodding her head toward her crotch. 'If you leave the clamp open, then whatever's in there will run out. I won't be able to do anything about that, either.' Samantha sounded as if the idea excited her.

Definitely a pervert, Harold thought with wry amusement. 'Okay,' he said. 'It sounds like fun. Do you want to wee now?'

'That's up to you,' Samantha replied. 'You have control. It doesn't matter if my legs are tied together. I can still wee. I tried before I came here,' she added.

A very thorough pervert, Harold thought. And an unabashed one, thank heaven. He moved back from her inviting cunt and tied Samantha's ankles with more of the cord. He stuffed a pair of her pants into her mouth. Using duct tape, he taped her mouth shut and left her sitting on the bed while he went back to work in the kitchen. His erection accompanied him, reminding him at every moment of Samantha bound and gagged just a short distance away. He recalled their first encounter at the flat. It must have taken a great deal of courage for Samantha to begin a relationship such as this with a complete stranger. And a great need too. How had she known that he would respond? That, he supposed, was like asking what made any two people respond to one another, and there was no answer to that.

The time passed swiftly for Harold. He was busy, and thoughts of his lover waiting for him upstairs made a pleasant background to his work. At the end of the day he went to her. Even before he got to the door, he heard Samantha working herself to orgasm as she usually did whenever he left her bound and gagged. Apparently the presence of the catheter did not interfere with that aspect of her sexuality. He wondered if anything would. He wondered if it would interfere with more normal sexual activity, smiling a little at the word 'normal'.

Samantha lay on her stomach, working her cunt against the mattress as she drove herself to orgasm. Her

171

hips bucked madly, and she emitted a maddened humming sound through her gag. Harold wondered how much the new feature had contributed to her arousal. She had seemed quite excited earlier by the catheter. The tube hung over the side of the bed and down to the floor. Struck by an idea, Harold went along to the bathroom to collect a plastic bucket. He set it beside the bed and placed the end of the catheter in it. Then he took off his clothes. He placed the palm of his hand in the small of Samantha's back and pushed her down against the mattress, grinding her cunt into it. She opened her eyes and looked wildly at him, aware that she was no longer alone. 'Ummmnnng!' she said. He did not know if this meant 'go on', or 'get inside me'. He chose the former, helping Samantha to come. Which she did in a series of spasms that shook her body. When they died away, he untied her ankles and lay down beside her.

Carefully he pulled her atop him and helped her to straddle his hips – standard procedure for fucking when her hands were tied behind her back. Samantha cooperated with enthusiasm. He guided his cock into her, conscious of the catheter as he slid past the point of entry. Once he was fully inside her, he did not notice its presence – except as a contribution to his own arousal. He wriggled until Samantha sat comfortably atop him, impaled on his erect cock, and apparently content to remain there. Harold quickly checked that the end of the catheter was still in the bucket, and that it ran clear of their joined bodies. Then he began to fuck his lover, seeing the echoes of her pleasure in her facial expressions.

When he could not hold off any longer, Harold relaxed and let himself come. As he did so, he felt and saw Samantha beginning another orgasm. He found the clamp and opened it. Samantha opened her eyes in surprise and delight as she came and peed simultaneously. 'Ahhhhhh!' she said. Her orgasm went on long after he had finished, helped seemingly by the simultaneous release of sexual tension and the pent-up flood from her bladder. The catheter was most definitely one of her better ideas. He liked the sense of power as he released the clamp and let her pee as she came.

Samantha made a supreme effort to hold herself upright as the flood and the orgasm ended, but Harold could see that she was nearly exhausted. Evidently she had been very busy indeed before he came to her. He helped her to slide off him and to lie on the bed. Harold tied her ankles, knees and thighs together and clamped her catheter before joining her on the bed. Samantha sighed happily as she snuggled against his body. He embraced her and they drifted off to sleep.

It was dark when he awoke. Samantha lay beside him, awake already. She made inarticulate noises through the gag. Harold sat up and rolled Samantha to face him. Carefully he peeled off the tape and removed the pants from her mouth. Then he went down the dark, unfamiliar hallway to the bathroom for a glass of water. He bumped into an uncharted obstruction on his way back to the bedroom, nearly dropping the full glass. Samantha drank greedily while he held the glass with one hand and massaged his toe with the other.

When she finished drinking, Samantha spoke. 'That was wild!' she exclaimed.

'You liked it, then?' he asked, already knowing the answer.

'Mmmm, yes. Definitely. Whatever gave you the idea to unclamp me just at the moment of truth?'

'I don't know. It just seemed like a good idea at the time.'

'It was one of your better ones,' she assured him.

The countryside was dark and silent outside the window. It seemed late. Harold was conscious of the open door downstairs, and of Samantha's clothing lying all over the sitting room floor. If anyone visited the house, there were ample signs of a naked female on the premises. He understood something of Samantha's fascination with being found by a stranger. Glancing at the end of the catheter, Harold noticed that it had fallen out of the bucket. He guessed that Samantha would want to piss again by now, but was unable to do so. He wondered again at her appetite for what she had called 'humiliation.' Being unable to control one's bodily functions must be humiliating, even though the inability was largely self-inflicted. Harold toyed with the   idea of letting her wet herself again by unclamping the catheter and spraying her with her own urine, but instead he merely held the end in the bucket and opened the clamp.

Samantha sighed as her bladder emptied. When she was empty, and the bucket rather full, she moaned softly with pleasure. Harold wondered if she had come. Silently he untied her hands and feet. Samantha stretched to relieve her cramped muscles. She said nothing about removing the catheter, and Harold felt a shiver of excitement as he contemplated her driving home with the thing in place. He reached down to close the clamp. Samantha acknowledged his control with a small shiver of her own. He removed the extension and she put it into her handbag. They went downstairs in the dark, and dressed in the sitting room. Dressed, Samantha's new accoutrement was invisible, but they both knew it was there. They went to their vehicles and Harold followed her back to her flat.

Inside, he asked her whether the catheter bothered her. Samantha shook her head. He decided to leave it in place. 'Don't take it out,' he ordered her. She nodded. 'Let's eat,' she said, leading the way into the kitchen. Samantha made an omelette with bacon, eggs and toast. Harold undressed as she did so. Noticing, Samantha paused to do the same. Wearing nothing but her heels, stockings and suspenders and an apron to prevent burns from the cooking, she seemed the more bizarre in the domestic surroundings with the catheter sprouting from her crotch and dangling between her legs. Samantha appeared not to notice its presence, but he knew she must be acutely aware of it. He certainly was. It stirred him again. When she served the food, Samantha stood close to him. He grasped her appendage and tugged gently, feeling the resistance of her sphincter. Samantha grimaced slightly but did not object.

Afterward they watched television, and Samantha submitted quietly to having her wrists and ankles tied before going to bed. She slept easily. Harold was again troubled by dreams of inflicting various tortures on his lover.

In the morning Samantha showed him how to remove the tube. There was a surprising amount of resistance as she sat on the bed with her legs spread while Harold pulled the catheter out of her. She shuddered as it came free but appeared to be in no pain – unless she was concealing it from him. 'I'll show you how to put it in this evening,' she promised. Harold dressed for work. He kissed her goodbye and drove out to the country house. His thoughts were filled with inserting the catheter again that evening.

Not long afterwards, Samantha asked him about leading the end of the catheter to her mouth while she was bound and gagged. It would be the ultimate humiliation, she said, having to drink one's own piss. Harold vetoed the idea on health grounds. Nevertheless he

175

found it exciting. He vaguely knew about urophilia and coprophilia, but shied away from the idea. Samantha, clearly, did not.

9

New Job

Toward the end of March, Samantha announced that she was bored. 'Not with you – or with what we're doing,' she told Harold hastily. Amanda, she said by way of explanation, was safely at university, making something (though exactly what was not certain) of herself. 'You have your work; it's different every day. I go to the same place every day. I only really get out when we do things together.'

'Do you think that wanting to be tied up all the time might have something to do with the lack of mobility you complain of?' Harold asked with an ironic smile.

'It might,' she agreed ruefully, 'but you know what I mean. I need something new to occupy my mind.'

'As opposed to your sweaty body?' Harold asked her with a grin. This kind of talk made him uneasy. One never knew where it might lead.

Samantha refused to be deflected. 'I've applied for another job,' she told him. Naturally he asked her what sort of job. 'Book editor,' she answered, somewhat defensively. Hurriedly she added, 'If I get it, I can work from home a fair bit, set my own hours – within reason. There could even be some travel involved – book shows and such. I've got a good education, and it's mainly going to waste.'

'You mean screwing your brains out is beginning to pall?' Harold said, half seriously. He was worried a new job might take Samantha away from him. Jobs had a way of growing on one, changing one's outlook and driving people apart. That prospect worried him more than he wanted to admit, either to Samantha or himself. But he would not stop her. He had seen her grow accustomed to having Amanda living away, seen, in short, her boredom, without being able to suggest a remedy. Reluctantly he conceded that she had a point. 'But will you really be able to work from home?'

'I'd have to go in from time to time, and maybe attend the odd conference or book fair in another city.'

'So in theory,' he said, seizing on the working-from-home aspect, 'you could spend the entire day wearing nothing but your stockings and suspenders, chained to your computer, and still earn the odd crust?'

'In theory, yes,' she replied, glad to see that he chose to joke about the job prospect. Adopting the same tone, she continued, 'It would have to be a rather long chain, of course. Long enough to permit trips to the bathroom and kitchen.'

'Suppose you wore just your leg-irons? That – and being naked – should be enough to keep you from straying too far.'

'It would be a bit chilly.' she replied. An early spring had given way to April showers, and the days could still be breezy and cold.

'I suppose we could allow you central heating on the worst days,' he said with mock seriousness.

'So you approve?' Samantha asked.

'In general. Let's see how it works out. See if you're happy with the work,' he said. If she began working from home, there would be more time for them to pursue their bizarre sex games. Look on the bright side, he admonished himself.

She hugged him tightly. 'It will be OK. You'll see.' Then, 'You don't think I want to change our sex life, do you?'

'Do you?'

'I don't,' she said firmly.

'That's my sweaty little pervert,' Harold said with a smile.

Samantha seemed happier than she had in weeks. Harold concluded that he would just have to adjust to the new job, if and when she got it. As it happened, she didn't, but within a fortnight she had applied for another and been hired. She was ecstatic. Harold welcomed her with an elaborate meal: prawn cocktails, tossed salad, lemon sole. There were candles on the table in the early evening dusk, a bottle of champagne cooling in a bucket.

'How did you know I'd get it?'

'I had faith in you,' he replied.

'You're good to me,' Samantha said as she kissed him.

As they ate Harold looked at Samantha in the candlelight across the table. The flames made shifting shadows on her face. She was beautiful, he decided for the hundredth time. She smiled when he said so. The age difference did not show. Why did she even worry about it?

Thus Samantha began to spend much of her time in stockings and suspenders and leg-irons. On the colder days she sometimes put on a dressing gown, but always tried to anticipate Harold's arrival so she could look her most provocative when he came in.

Their sex life was changed by the altered routines, but showed no sign of tapering off – or of becoming less bizarre. Samantha spent more time at home than she had before, but made up for it on the occasions when she had to go to the office. Occasionally she varied the routine by travel. There were overnight stays in places like Inverness and Bristol. Often she passed through Reading. Amanda was well, she reported with relief after one such visit.

One Friday Harold drove his van to Samantha's flat after work. He let himself in with the spare key. Samantha would not open the door when she was in her working clothes. True, she could always put on more clothes when Harold was not there, but there was no way to conceal the leg-irons. That would have raised the eyebrows of any caller. But she tried to keep to her word, though he never asked her about it. It was something they did for one another, without coercion.

Samantha was waiting for Harold to collect her. She had been waiting for nearly two hours, unable to do any more work, anticipating his arrival and the things they would do. The week's progress paled before that, though she was pleased with what she had accomplished.

She rose to meet him as he came in, turning up her face to be kissed, for all the world like any suburban housewife welcoming her husband back from a hard day at work. When the kiss ended, Harold produced the key to her leg-irons from his pocket.

'Freedom at last!' Samantha exclaimed as he knelt and unlocked her. He grinned and planted a kiss on her pubic mound. She thrust her hips forward, pressing herself to his mouth. The kiss threatened to grow into something more serious. Harold broke it off and stood to hold Samantha in his arms. That was nearly as satisfactory as kissing her cunt. He held her for a long while before breaking off to allow her to gather her things for the weekend. Samantha checked the pussy whip was among them. She had been thinking about another lashing for several days, she said. The dildo pants and locks were also among their paraphernalia. They took her car, leaving Harold's Transit van in her drive. It was more convenient that way, because his tools occupied most of the space in the van.

At his house Samantha prepared spaghetti Bolognaise, which Amanda had scornfully called student food – as though she herself were into *cordon bleu* cuisine. Amanda had phoned her during the day to check on the new job, she reported, and had pronounced herself satisfied that her mother was keeping busy. She had sent her regards to Harold, Samantha said.

They took the student food into the front room to eat on the low table in front of the sofa. 'Like students,' Harold observed.

'Amanda asked about handcuffs again,' Samantha said, not hearing his remark. 'What do you suppose she wants them for?'

'Something like what you use them for?' Harold suggested.

Samantha was scandalised – and worried. 'You didn't tell her anything about us, did you?'

Harold said no, of course not. Once again he did not add that Amanda already knew about her mother's sexual preferences. He wondered if Amanda was working around to telling her mother what she knew. He hoped not. The results of that revelation might put Samantha off for some time – though he doubted that she could permanently give up her perversion. 'Lend her yours,' he suggested again. Samantha still knew nothing of Amanda's earlier adventure with the handcuffs. Her response made him glad he had kept silent.

'Oh no! What would she think of me if she knew?' But Samantha continued to worry. 'Why handcuffs?' she asked.

'Like mother, like daughter?' Harold suggested.

She looked horrified. 'Do you think she's turning into a pervert . . . I mean, into . . .?' she trailed off.

'Someone like you?' Harold asked with a smile. 'I can think of worse things for a daughter to do. Besides, didn't someone once say that imitation is the sincerest form of flattery?'

'But suppose she takes up with someone . . .'

'Someone like me? Someone unsuitable?'

'Someone dangerous, I meant, of course. There aren't many men like you.'

'Thanks for the compliment, if that's what it was. But she's growing up. She is nearly independent. She'll have to make a great many decisions without consulting you.' Almost as soon as he said it he regretted the words. Samantha did not need to be reminded of the emptiness of her nest.

Fortunately, that implication was lost on her. She was more worried about what Amanda might be doing – and with whom.

To distract her, Harold asked her where she had got her preferences from.

Samantha did not answer at once. She appeared to be thinking back to her childhood – that proverbial source of all hang-ups. 'I don't know,' she said finally.

'Well,' Harold changed the question, 'when did you first get yourself tied up? Why?'

'It was playing games with my brothers, of course but I still don't know why it affected me so strongly. I suppose I was thirteen or fourteen. One day my brother Richard tied me up and left me in their den. And I came while trying to get loose. It was my first orgasm. At the time I was frightened out of my wits, not knowing what those strange feelings were. I didn't connect it at once with being tied up. Only when it happened again did suspect that the two were connected. The second time it was a very nice feeling indeed. Not scary. After that the two were inextricably connected, and they got more inextricable the more often we did it.'

182

'At first I thought that everyone – all girls, anyway – had the same reaction, but something kept me from asking my friends about it. Just as well I didn't, as I soon found out that not everyone was as interested in rope games as I was. That was just for perverts – like me.' Samantha smiled wryly at the word, as she nearly always did.

'I went on enjoying the games until my brothers grew out of them. I never did. But I didn't have the nerve to ask anyone else to help me until my husband did it – and we both know how that ended. I tried other things, like tying my feet and legs, but I couldn't do anything with my hands. It's the old problem of trying to pull yourself up by your own bootstraps. I finally got the handcuffs, but I didn't like having the keys accessible. I didn't feel as helpless as I might if someone else were to tie me up. And then you came along. We were alone, and I had seen the ball of twine you had in your toolbox. So I took the chance, and here we are!'

Harold noticed that her explanation did not explain her 'perversion,' nor why she had suddenly pitched upon him to become her accomplice. But he was glad that she had. He said so.

Samantha smiled and hugged him. 'So am I.'

She continued, 'All this talk about my perversion has made me horny. Can you tie me up?' She produced the whip from her bag and laid it on the coffee table. She would not meet Harold's eyes.

'You have a one-track mind,' Harold said with a smile. He was glad to be back on familiar ground. 'I suppose you'd better get undressed,' he suggested. 'It seems a waste to get dressed up only to take it all off again. Maybe next time you could just put on a long coat for the trip over here.'

'Sounds like a good idea, but that will be just the time we have an accident – and I won't be wearing any pants.'

'You didn't let that stop you from driving out into the country wearing nothing under your coat.'

Samantha put down her plate and took off everything except the stockings and suspenders she had been wearing all day at her flat. She posed for Harold. 'See anything you like?'

They went into the bedroom. Harold took the whip along, Samantha noticed. Her breasts heaved excitedly and her breathing became shallow and rapid. Harold, walking behind her, admired the way the light played on her sheer stockings, and on the thrust of her shapely legs and hips.

Immediately, Harold ran into a practical problem. Samantha obviously expected to be tied up. If he were going to use the whip on the place for which it had been designed, he would not be able to tie her legs together. He considered stringing Samantha up to something so that he could strike her all over. A hook in the ceiling would be ideal, he thought, only there was none. Too late now. He would have to do something later.

For now, the simplest way would be to tie her to the bedposts. That would leave her crotch exposed, as well as her stomach, belly and breasts. And the fronts of her legs. So he did, Samantha tugging at the ropes to ensure that she could not escape before submitting herself to pleasure. He gagged her without being asked, knowing that she would scream when he lashed her. Samantha's eyes were dark and expectant over the tape, with just the right hint of trepidation.

He decided to blindfold her. Originally, Harold had intended to leave Samantha to commune for a while with whatever spirits she invoked when she was enjoying her fantasies. But, as usual, the sight of her was too much for his intentions. He sat beside her on the bed and stroked her breasts. 'Ummm?' Samantha said. She too had expected him to leave her tied up before he

184

administered the beating she so craved. Nevertheless, her nipples soon grew erect. He pinched one of them and bent to kiss the other.

'Ummmmmm,' Samantha said.

Thus encouraged, he extended his range to stroke the taut muscles of her stomach. She liked that, too, squirming and twisting on the bed. Harold kissed her lips beneath the tape gag, while Samantha did her best to return the kiss and encourage him further. He kissed her taped eyes, her cheek bones, her throat and breasts. He kissed her stomach and belly, and then got onto the bed and crouched between Samantha's legs. She moaned loudly when he kissed her labia and probed her cunt with his tongue and a forefinger. He used his free hand to caress and tease her breasts and nipples. It was not easy to be doing three things at once, but Samantha obviously appreciated his efforts.

She twisted again on the bed, tugging against the ropes that held her spread open for him. Harold was reluctant to stop, but he had to break off to get undressed. When he was naked, he was as excited as she was. He found himself shaking as he guided his cock into her. Samantha groaned as she lifted her hips to receive him. She was wet and parted and she began at once to thrust up and down. They matched rhythms and Samantha fought the ropes as she came for the first time. As usual, the restraints had the usual effect of making her more excited. Harold rode the storm of her release. Samantha moaned loudly as she came. With only the briefest interval she began another series of orgasms. Her excitement drove him over the brink with her. Samantha bucked and shuddered as they came together. Samantha shook for a long time afterwards as he lay atop her. Finally she seemed to doze.

Harold could not. Thoughts of lashing Samantha kept him wide awake. Eventually they drove him to get up and fetch the whip. It felt heavy in his hand as he came back to the bed. Samantha still dozed, unaware of what was coming. Harold gazed at her, growing more excited as he anticipated her reaction. When he could hold back no longer, he raised the light whip.

The first blow, across her nipples, woke her with startling suddenness.

'Nnnnggggg!' she said. She jerked against the ropes, straining to pull free. Or was she just proving to herself that she was helpless? It was no matter. The sight of her futile thrashing excited Harold even more. He struck her again, this time across the stomach. This produced another grunt from Samantha, but seemed not nearly as effective as the first blow. Harold struck her again across the breasts. Samantha reacted more energetically. Thereafter he alternated between her erogenous breasts and the relatively neutral territory of her stomach. He settled into a rhythm. Samantha seemed to like it, becoming steadily more excited as the lashing went on. She jerked and thrashed and moaned as he lashed her. When he paused, Samantha twisted on the bed, as if begging him to continue.

Harold changed his aim, striking low across her belly, perilously close to her cunt. That was the ultimate target, but he intended to save it for the climax. Samantha reacted explosively, raising her hips as if offering her crotch to the whip. However, he continued lashing her belly and the tops of her thighs, thin red stripes appearing on her stomach and belly and legs as the beating went on.

Suddenly he struck Samantha sharply across her exposed nipples, and she moaned loudly. He struck her again, and he guessed that she was going to come soon. The whip roved over her body from breasts to thighs, but always avoiding the real target. Harold enjoyed withholding that pleasure from her as much as he enjoyed lashing her and seeing her struggle. Then he gave her two quick slashing blows between her parted thighs, the whip striking her exposed labia.

Samantha reared and bucked, moaning and fighting the ropes but obviously enjoying what he was doing to her. She was making the sounds she always made when she came. Her excitement was infectious. Harold struck harder, moving over her body, finally returning to her crotch. When she came, Samantha's body went rigid, her muscles standing out in relief as she fought the ropes. She would have screamed aloud but for the gag. Samantha gasped for breath, and her breasts were heaving as she struggled. Harold paused to watch the results. Samantha appeared to experience a long series of orgasms. She heaved and bucked and moaned as he watched.

Finally the storm died away. Samantha's taut muscles slowly relaxed, and she lay in a sweaty heap on the bed. Harold let the whip trail over her from breasts to knees. Samantha jerked to attention as he teased her. She moaned and shook her head, seemingly begging for a respite. In the past, Harold would have allowed her to rest, but he was still excited. The sense of power as he lashed his helpless lover had grown too great to resist.

He knelt astride her, and with his hands and mouth he aroused Samantha once more. Her muffled cries of protest gradually became moans of pleasure. She came alive under his hands, her muscles becoming taut as she strained toward him. The mingled aromas of her sweat and her rut aroused him as he moved over her helpless body. Harold could no more have stopped himself than Samantha could escape from her bonds. Briefly he considered removing the gag so that Samantha could take his cock into her mouth and give him some of the pleasure she had received, but instead he stood and again took up the whip. The urge to lash her won out.

187

This time he concentrated on her breasts and crotch, alternating between light strokes and punishing lashes as Samantha rose toward orgasm. Which she did steadily, to the accompaniment of moans and the sharp crack of leather meeting flesh. When he judged that she was on the crest of yet another orgasm, he struck her between her straining thighs, squarely on her cunt. Now that he had found the target, he lashed it steadily. Samantha lost what little control she had left, moaning loudly and thrashing wildly as she fought the ropes in her ecstasy. Her hips rose and fell and her pinioned body twisted as far as the ropes allowed. That was not much, but it was clear to Harold that she was enjoying the experience. He went on for a long time, enjoying the sense of power this gave him. He was in control of her body, of her pleasure. No one else. She could do nothing to influence him. Her surrender of all control, and his assumption of it, was heady stuff.

What stopped him at last was weariness. Samantha was still twisting and moaning when he let his arm fall to his side. She went on for a long time. Once more he was struck by her ability to do without him. Tie her up, whip her, and she had wild orgasms while he watched. But he knew they had both derived pleasure from his efforts with the rope and whip. The excitement he had felt as he drove Samantha to orgasm was startling. He suspected that it would not diminish.

He took his erection and his new-found knowledge downstairs. A drink, a sandwich, an hour watching the news. During all that time Samantha lying tied to the bed upstairs was a vision behind his eyes and a sense of pleasurable anticipation for the future.

When Harold went back upstairs Samantha was asleep. Rather than wake her he drew the duvet over her and went to bed in the spare room. She had earned her rest, he thought. It would have been too awkward to untie her so that they could share the bed. Anyway, he knew that she would appreciate being left tied up all night. His thoughts troubled him, his reawakened pleasure in inflicting pain making for a restless night.

He untied Samantha in the morning and let her make her usual run for the toilet. She came down as he was making breakfast, looking refreshed but a bit haunted. Yes, she had slept well. The session with the whip had taken a lot out of her, she confessed. 'I can't recall ever coming like that, not even after the first time you used the whip. Then, I was wearing the leather pants and you couldn't lash me between the legs. This time I felt as if I was going to explode. The pain and the pleasure got all mixed up, and between them I nearly passed out. Do you think I'm turning into a masochist?' She sounded worried.

'Do you mean you only want me – or someone – to beat you?'

Samantha shook her head. 'No, I enjoy the rest of it – being tied up and being aroused and penetrated, and being fucked stupid. It's all great. But now there's this new thing.'

'If you enjoy all that other stuff as well, then a little masochism isn't all that much to worry about. What worries me is that I'm beginning to enjoy it too. I found it hard to stop the first time, and even harder yesterday.'

Samantha brightened at his admission. 'I'm glad you enjoyed it. I often feel selfish making you do things to me while I do nothing for you. Don't you feel that I'm getting the best of it?'

'Sometimes. But nothing's perfect. I like what we do.' In the light of day, Harold found his resentment of the night before childish. Samantha was generous and loving and, most importantly, interested – in both him and in sex. He told her so. That was a hard combination to beat, he added.

189

Samantha smiled at the pun. She hugged him from behind as he stood over the frying pan. 'Do you want to start catching up now?' she asked. 'I'm available.'

'When aren't you?' He served up the omelettes. 'But it can wait. I had planned a shopping expedition this morning that I think you'll enjoy too. Then we can spend the rest of the afternoon doing what we do best. And there's still Sunday to come.'

Harold felt happy when Samantha was around. That was more important than making everything come out even. Besides, he knew he would never be able to keep up with her in the orgasm stakes.

'Don't you want to know where we're going?' he continued. 'I thought most women were more interested in shopping than in sex.'

'I'm not most women – as we both know,' Samantha replied. 'But of course I'm interested in shopping. What did you have in mind?'

'We're going to the DIY store on the industrial estate.'

'Well, it's not what most women would classify as shopping.'

'But, as you're not most women . . .?'

'It still sounds sort of bloke-ish. Dull. All that paint and timber and stuff.'

'I think I can make it more enjoyable to you. And we can go anywhere you prefer after that.'

'Even to the Burger King?' Samantha asked with a grin.

'Don't you ever think of anything besides eating and sex?'

Harold helped Samantha to dress for their outing. She had begun to keep a few things at his house, among them her stockings and suspenders. Their games were not conducive to longevity in stockings. Harold fetched a jar of petroleum jelly from the bathroom while she

190

took off the ones she was wearing and put on some fresh ones. Samantha's expression was composed of equal parts excitement and worry as he helped her into the leather pants. The birthday gift had been a success: Samantha took pleasure in it every time she wore it, but going out in public with her dildoes locked in place still caused her some anxiety. Her short fuse often led to explosions in inappropriate places.

Harold slid the lubricated anal dildo into her. She needed no lubrication for the other one; she never did. He closed the zip and locked it at the small of her back with the padlock they kept for the purpose. Almost at once, Samantha became as skittish as a young horse. She trembled and twitched as the dildoes moved inside her. She wore a faintly distracted look, as if she felt tremors in the earth undetectable by anyone else.

Luckily, she had good dress sense. Her choice of clothing pleased Harold too, for she usually dressed younger than her thirty-eight years. Normally she wore skirts and dresses – when she was wearing clothes at all. Trousers were for workaday things like gardening or moving house.

Samantha fidgeted all the way to the industrial estate. When Harold grinned at her discomfiture, she tartly reminded him that she was the one with the extra fittings. 'It's too bad you're a man and can't be made to hold yourself back as I have to.'

Harold did not tell Samantha that there were similar articles made for men, with only one dildo that went into a place it would not take a genius to figure out. He wasn't sure he liked the idea. He did not know if Samantha would enjoy making him wear the male version of her dildo-pants. She always seemed to prefer being on the receiving end. She had never sought revenge upon him for the things she had (mostly) asked him to do to her. His mild streak of sadism matched her somewhat more robust streak of masochism. A match made in Weybridge, if not in heaven.

At the DIY store Harold went to the electrical section first. Samantha watched in growing excitement as he chose two rolls of duct tape. As they passed the display of cable ties Samantha touched his arm. 'Isn't that what the police use to subdue rioters quickly?' There was a catch in her voice as she stared at the tough nylon straps with the locking devices.

'Yes. Do you feel riotous?'

'Not just now, but I might do later on. Right now I just feel like coming.'

'Don't you always? But I've got some of them already,' Harold told her. 'I'll subdue you when we get home if you want me to.'

Samantha nodded shakily. 'Oh, yes, please.'

At the rope display Samantha held onto Harold's arm. He could feel her trembling as he bought a new supply of the thin braided nylon cord she preferred. He could read her thoughts as if she had spoken them aloud. Often he had to cut her loose after she had tightened the knots by struggling. He saw some of the light chain he had considered on the occasion of his first encounter with Samantha and her bizarre tastes. It was chrome-plated and so would not rust. The links each had a half-twist in them to make them lie flat against one another. This time he bought a long length of it, together with a supply of chain repair links. 'You never know when you might meet a woman who enjoys long-range bondage,' he murmured to her.

As they passed the picture hooks, Samantha stopped Harold. She pointed to the small coils of thin brass wire used for hanging pictures. 'Could you tie me with *that*?' she asked shakily. 'I think I'd . . . like that. It's much thinner than the cord. More . . . brutal, too – like a real abduction.'

192

Harold imagined Samantha bound with the thin wire, liking the idea. But common sense came to his (and her) rescue. 'I could do it, but it would be too dangerous. The wire would cut you as you struggled. There would be scars as well. I like your skin unblemished. Besides which, it would ruin your stockings,' he said lightly. 'You'd have to spend a fortune buying new ones.'

Samantha looked wistful, but nodded thoughtfully in agreement. Clearly the idea held strong appeal for her, because she caught his arm tightly, leaning against him. 'I'm going to come!' she whispered harshly into his ear. She was shaking. A young couple nearby looked at her in alarm and moved hurriedly away. The idea of a woman having an orgasm in a DIY shop must have shocked them. The young woman, of course, had none of Samantha's hidden advantages to help her enjoy shopping. Samantha held onto Harold and shook as silently as she could manage. It was at least a semi-controlled explosion, or a series of them.

Just then a member of staff hurried up and asked if everything was all right. Samantha could not reply, but Harold told him that his wife was not feeling well, and that they would go home. He went away with several backward glances, looking relieved.

'Do you think he knew what was happening?' Samantha asked as she gasped for breath. She was red as the proverbial beetroot. 'It's so embarrassing!'

'But fun too?' Harold asked.

Samantha nodded slowly and gave him the ghost of a smile in return. 'But get me out of here. Seeing all the things you can use for tying people up is too much for me.'

Harold paid for his choices and together they hurried to her car. 'Oh, god, I'll never be able to go through a DIY store again without getting excited.'

'I thought DIY stores were bloke-ish places,' he teased her as she sat gingerly in her seat.

'Not if you're equipped as I am,' she retorted.

'Where to now?' he asked. 'Food? More shopping? A bumpy ride through country lanes to remind you of your . . . equipment?'

'Shopping,' Samantha said, surprising him. He thought she would have chosen to go home. 'I'm practising self-control,' she told him. 'And not doing too well,' she added, as she trembled beside him.

Since Samantha had never been that interested in self-control, Harold guessed that she was actually trying to hold off as long as possible so that the final surrender would be that much more intense. He found that idea both satisfying and exciting. They went to several more conventional shops where Samantha bought some conventional clothing. She also bought several pairs of the stockings they both liked her to wear, and a new suspender belt in red. 'Black's too conventional,' she said with irony.

Harold found himself mildly excited as she shopped for the things they liked, but more deeply excited as he watched Samantha struggle against the internal secrets she harboured. Several times she grasped his arm and shuddered as she lost control. There was no doubt about her enjoyment of those moments when she could not hold back any longer. He was glad his gift gave her so much pleasure. As the instigator of those abandoned moments, he felt a sense of power. He enjoyed dominating his lover.

The shopping done, they drove past Samantha's flat so that Harold could collect his cable ties and side-cutting pliers from his van. Samantha eyed the plastic bag full of nylon straps as Harold put it into the back seat of her car. She sighed as she settled back into the seat, squirming slightly as she did so. 'Want to drive?' he asked with a grin. Samantha shook her head.

At his house they carried their purchases inside. While Harold put the food away Samantha snipped open the bag of cable ties and examined the contents with growing interest. She slipped the free end through the locking device and tested the grip. The strap did not slip. She saw why they were so popular with the police. Even easier than handcuffs, she thought excitedly, wishing she had discovered them sooner.

But it would not be fair to Harold if she demanded to plunge straight into another solo bondage session. She had been thoroughly done the night before, then left tied up, and this morning she had been simmering in her dildo-pants. Give him a chance, she thought. He must be more than ready. And besides, she needed the toilet. The pants would have to come off, however much she was enjoying them. She went into the kitchen and raised her dress so that he could reach the lock behind her back. 'The toilet calls. Duty before pleasure,' she said.

Unlocked and unplugged, she went to the bathroom, picking up several of the cable ties as she returned. Silently she handed them to him and turned around, bringing her hands behind her. She shivered as she felt the nylon strap close around her wrists, pinioning them. Harold planted a quick kiss on the side of her throat, smelling her perfume and causing Samantha to lean back against him like a cat being stroked the right way. He slid his hands under her dress and stroked her naked belly and crotch. They held that pose for long minutes, each becoming more excited.

At last Harold broke away to fasten her elbows together with the remainder of the cable ties. He admired the way her breasts jutted out. He led Samantha into the front room, where he got undressed and lay on the floor on his back while she straddled him and knelt slowly. When she was on her knees, Harold lifted her skirt out of the way and guided her down onto his cock. Samantha sighed deeply as she felt him slide into her. He decided that it had been worth the wait.

Samantha came to the same conclusion as she felt him begin to thrust into her. She bore down with pleasure, squeezing him inside her as she shuddered with her first orgasm. The day's activity had excited Harold without allowing him any release, so that he was on a short fuse. Sooner than usual he felt the first signs of his own orgasm. Samantha too felt his tension, and she squeezed down on his cock. Harold came violently, and Samantha joined him.

They lay for nearly an hour, joined, taking pleasure in the closeness while the weariness wore off. Then, with his help, she got up and sat on the sofa. Samantha with her dress up around her waist and her legs on display was a fine sight. He kissed her. 'Thank you for a lovely time,' she said. He smiled and kissed her again.

'Hungry?' he asked.

'Mmmmm,' she replied. 'But could you spare the time to tie my feet too?' She glanced at the bag of cable ties.

Harold crossed her ankles and looped the strap around them, pulling it tight.

'Tighter,' she commanded. When the strap bit into the flesh of her ankles, she said, 'That's better. Now do my knees before you go make us something nice to eat.' Samantha lifted her legs and lay down on the sofa, her bound hands against the rear cushion and her face to the room. She sighed as she settled herself comfortably.

Harold went back to the kitchen, pleased again that she was pleased. Pleased that she was waiting for him to come back, and glad that she was going to be around until Monday morning.

When they went to bed, he had to cut the cable ties away from her wrists and ankles so that she could undress – which she did, down to her stockings and suspenders. She lay on her back and held her arms up to him. When Harold got in beside her, Samantha helped him first to get on top of her, and then into her.

She crossed her ankles behind his back, pulling him firmly into her. 'That feels so good,' she murmured into his ear as they began the old rhythm.

Afterwards, still joined, Samantha spoke of the earlier whipping. Her voice sounded tremulous as she described how it had been for her. 'It was incredible,' she confessed. 'I thought I'd never stop coming. The pain and the pleasure were indistinguishable from one another. One led to the other.'

'Heterodyning, it's called,' said Harold, who had been doing a little extra-curricular research of his own.

'I don't care what it's called. I want to do it again. Soon.'

'Will tomorrow be soon enough? I don't feel like getting the whip out just now.'

'Tomorrow will be soon enough. But I'm still worried. What if I turn into a complete masochist? It was a pretty extreme form of being handled, treated as an object – what I told you about the first time we made love. This time I couldn't stop you from whipping my cunt – and then I didn't want to stop you. I just wanted you to go on and on.'

'And that worries you?'

'What if I only come when there's pain to start me off?'

'Worry about that if it happens. What worries *me* is that I enjoyed it too. Seeing you in pain and knowing that I caused it was . . . exciting. So do you think that I'm becoming a complete sadist?'

'A marriage made in heaven, you mean – the perfect match of sadist and masochist?' Samantha spoke lightly, but the idea clearly held immense attraction for her. 'You really did like it?'

'Yes,' Harold admitted.

'I'm so glad. I always worry that I'm getting the best of the bargain, and that you will begin feeling left out.'

197

'When you begin to feel like that, just remember what it's like when I'm not "left out", as you put it. Like how it felt just before I whipped you. You are an exciting bundle when you're all bundled up.'

Samantha kissed him abruptly. 'Go on liking it – and go on telling me so. I'm so glad you like it.'

'So am I.'

They slept that night as conventional people do. 'Vanilla sex is sometimes as good as the other sort,' Samantha said sleepily at the end. 'But only sometimes. Tomorrow it's back to the other variety, thank heaven! You will whip me again in the morning, won't you?'

And, in the morning, he did, Samantha once more tied to the bed with everything exposed to the pussy whip. Tightly gagged, she squealed and moaned as he lashed her breasts and belly and cunt. Harold felt once more the sense of power as Samantha's cries gradually shifted from protest to pleasure. Watching her jerk at her bonds and writhe on the bed, he couldn't decide which he liked most, making his lover scream in pain or moan in ecstasy. Later, released, Samantha confessed to the same mixed feelings: 'The pain was as exquisite as the orgasm. I came like a bomb!'

'I noticed,' Harold said. 'I'm glad you liked it.'

'And how was it for you?' Samantha smiled as she asked the question, but she was concerned that she had had all the fun while he had done the work.

'Sadists love to hear a woman scream in pain and pleasure,' he replied. 'And that's right out of the sadist's field manual.'

10

A Walk in the Woods

Samantha became bolder as the visits to Harold at the country house became an established routine. She seemed to think of it as their own, forgetting that the owners would return and they would have to find a new venue for their games. Harold tried to counter this tendency, but with little success. She took to arriving unannounced again, as she did one windy day toward the end of April. The wind masked the sound of her arrival, so that Harold was still at work somewhere upstairs when she entered the house. Her hair, which she had begun to grow longer since the New Year, was fetchingly disarranged by the strong wind. She combed a few strands back with her hand as she walked through the ground floor rooms, glancing through the windows over the surrounding fields and copses. She watched through the sitting-room window as the wind rushed through the trees of the distant wood. The new buds made a green mist as the trees tossed and swayed their branches. Cloud shadows chased one another across the fields of ripening corn. The windy day, and the onset of spring, exhilarated her. She felt the blood course through her veins with a new energy.

Samantha turned from the window and went toward the stairs. She was about to climb, but she paused with one hand on the newel post, struck by a sudden idea. Changing direction, she went into the kitchen. There she removed her light coat and laid it on the table. As on an earlier visit, she wore nothing beneath it except for stockings and suspenders. The catheter was in place, trailing down from her crotch. It was clamped shut. From her handbag Samantha produced her handcuffs and leg-irons. Variety, she thought as she laid the shackles beside her coat and took a heavy collar from the handbag. It was made of polished steel, gun-metal grey, with an integral lock and three welded rings, one at each side and one at the front. It had the look of a serious restraint, as did the leading chain which went with it. She couldn't wait to see Harold's expression when she showed him her new accoutrement.

Samantha fitted the collar around her throat. She turned it so that the lock was behind her neck, and then closed it with a decisive click. It fitted snugly, and she liked the effect. She left the key on the table as she sat on one of the kitchen chairs to put on the leg-irons, adding their key to the one on the table. Samantha spread her legs to the extent the chain allowed, admiring the contrast between the irons and her stockings. She knew Harold would appreciate it too. Her nipples grew erect as she continued to shackle herself. She could hear Harold moving about upstairs, and hoped he would not come down until she was ready.

Samantha closed one of the cuffs around her wrist and was about to close the other, when she had another idea. She opened the cuff and turned it so that her hands would be held with the palms outward when she cuffed her other wrist. She then gathered the three keys and rose from the chair. She searched the kitchen cupboards and drawers until she found a ball of string. Cutting off a short piece, she strung the keys on it, tied the ends together and hung them on one of the hooks over the

200

Aga. With her hands locked behind her back, as she intended, the keys would be out of her reach there, even if she managed to manoeuvre the chair over to them. Satisfied that she would be unable to escape without help, she returned to the chair. Seated once more, Samantha attached one end of the dog lead to the chain between her ankles. She led it over the front rung of the legs and under the seat of the chair. She pulled it up behind the chair, pulling her legs back and together so that she could clip it to the handcuff chain. Lastly, Samantha closed the cuff around her free wrist. It was a struggle with her hands held back to back behind her, but she managed in the end. The click as the cuff locked behind her made her shiver with the familiar mixture of anticipation and dread – one of the enduring pleasures of bondage that never diminished for her.

Thus fastened, there was nothing she could do but wait for Harold to find her. What they would do then caused another shiver of excitement. Samantha sat on quietly as the day turned to afternoon. She could hear Harold upstairs hammering and sawing and moving about. The passage of time was measured by the increasing pressure on her bladder. But with the catheter clamped off she could do nothing about that. To keep her mind off the increasing discomfort Samantha concentrated on what Harold would do to her when he came down. She even managed to turn the increasing pressure into excitement too, imagining that she would be left in torment, at the mercy of her captor, who would make her wait forever for relief. Like the torture of being whipped, the pain from her full bladder aroused her. She was by now an expert at transmuting pain into sexual arousal. Her helplessness, though self-imposed, was nevertheless total. She liked that.

Samantha squirmed once or twice, increasing the urge to pee. As an experiment, she tried to force the catheter from her urethra, even though success would release the flood into her lap and down her legs. Her effort, though unsuccessful, brought an acute discomfort. She relished that too. Samantha moved restlessly on the chair as she imagined Harold going home and leaving her there all night, unrelieved. She knew that would not happen because he would eventually come down from his work and see her car. Then he would search for her. But suppose his growing relish for inflicting pain took control . . . Samantha both delighted and tortured herself with 'what if's.

Eventually, Samantha heard Harold's tread on the stair. He found Samantha squirming on the chair; spotting the catheter, he guessed her predicament. Slowly, teasingly, while Samantha wriggled and whimpered and pressed her legs together, he selected a large saucepan and dropped her catheter into it.

'Should I or shouldn't I?' he asked her teasingly, toying with the clamp and tugging gently on the tube emerging from between her thighs.

Samantha moaned. 'Please,' she begged.

Harold stood up without releasing the clamp and looked at her torment for a long minute. Samantha begged him again to let her relieve herself. He smiled and did nothing. When finally he released the clamp Samantha was frantic, twisting her hips on the chair and tugging at her chains. Pleasure flooded through her as she emptied her full bladder, moaning aloud at the relief. It was like a mini-orgasm, she had once said. Harold wondered how close it was to the real thing.

'How was it for you?' he asked as she squeezed out the last drops.

'Heavenly, you beast,' she gasped. 'But you arrived only just in time.'

'Suppose I hadn't?'

Samantha flushed again at the idea of being left indefinitely helpless and with a full bladder. 'In fantasies it sounds wonderful. I don't think I'd like to try it out for real.'

'I guess you're not a real masochist then. Aren't you relieved?' The question hung in the air.

'I'll just keep on pushing the boundaries,' Samantha said.

Harold was pleased. 'But what shall I do with you now? Do you fancy a trip up the stairs?'

Samantha's reply surprised him: 'That's up to you, but since you've asked, I'd like you to put the lead on my collar and take me for a walk in the woods. When we get there I'm sure you'll think of something pleasant to do to me.'

Harold noticed the collar for the first time. He knelt beside the chair to examine it. He looked at the lock and tried unsuccessfully to slide his fingers under the tight steel band on her throat. 'Pretty,' he said. 'Where did you get it?'

'The Internet, source of all delights. I ordered it about six weeks ago; they're made individually to fit. Do you really like it?'

Harold nodded. 'Do you?'

'So much I plan to wear it forever. I want you to have the key. I hope you don't find it necessary to use it.'

It sounded like a pledge, almost like wearing a wedding ring.

'Won't it be a bit conspicuous?'

'That's my problem,' Samantha replied. She seemed serious. The idea of Samantha wearing the collar excited him too. Not many men, he reflected, had a collared female around the house.

Harold unclipped the lead from her handcuffs and leg-irons. Samantha stood waiting for him to snap it to her collar, lifting her chin to make it easier for him. She shuddered as the lead clicked into place. Harold held it short, pulling her to him. He kissed her on the lips. The kiss grew almost violent as Samantha responded. When they finally broke, she was gasping for breath. Harold's breath was coming short too, but more important, he was erect.

'Take me outside,' Samantha gasped, 'and do whatever you want to me. Only go quickly!'

Harold let the lead slide through his hand until he grasped the leather loop at the end. He picked up Samantha's coat and laid it across her shoulders.

'No, no coat. I want to be naked.'

He folded the coat and threw it over his own shoulder. The woods were a long way away, across the open fields. She might change her mind once she was out there. With a sharp tug Harold led his lover out of the house. Samantha came willingly, her face flushed and her nipples erect as he led her away from shelter and into the field. In her handcuffs and leg-irons she looked magnificent, and she seemed to know it. Harold admired the play of her muscles under the sheer nylon stockings, and the way the suspenders moved on her thighs as she took the shortened steps that were all the ankle chains allowed. Her high heels sank into the soft ground as they walked, making the going difficult. But Samantha didn't complain as she struggled on. The strong wind stirred her hair, spilling some of it across her face. Handcuffed, Samantha could only shake her head to clear it from her eyes.

They walked slowly toward the distant wood. Harold hoped for both their sakes that there was no one to witness Samantha being led naked and in chains toward the cover of the trees. Unlike her captor, Samantha did not seem worried by the prospect of being seen. She was breathing deeply, excited by her predicament, and no doubt looking forward to a good fucking once they reached the wood. Harold wondered once more if he were strictly necessary for her pleasure. Samantha seemed, as she often did, excited enough merely by her predicament.

It seemed like forever to him before they were among the trees. The going would have been impossible had there not been a bridle path leading into the woods. There was more likelihood of being seen on the path, but the undergrowth would have made it impossible to go in any other direction.

Harold led his captive along the path, and gradually the trees closed in and hid the open fields from view. Only then did he stop in a small clearing and spread Samantha's coat on the ground. He helped her to sit on it and unclipped the lead from her collar. With it, he joined her leg-irons to her handcuffs. The chain was much too short to allow her to stand, much less walk. Harold clamped the catheter and walked away, leaving Samantha sitting with her knees drawn up and her back to a tree trunk. She looked apprehensively at him, but did not ask him not to go. He felt a growing excitement as he left her and walked deeper into the woods. He knew that Samantha felt the same way. She would probably be quivering with the familiar mixture of excitement and apprehension when he returned.

Harold continued up the path for some way. Looking back, he could no longer see Samantha. The path led him westward, toward the setting sun. There were long shadows under the trees. He wondered what Samantha was thinking as he walked away from her. The silence closed in, broken only by the sound of the wind in the trees. He had no idea how far he had walked when he saw a building ahead. It appeared to be a barn, and he thought at once about Samantha's fantasy. When the owners of the house returned, that venue would be closed to them. Harold decided to take a look.

The building appeared sound, though weathered. There was no one about. Harold circled around to the front and found a rutted track leading up to the door. It was locked. The windows were too high off the ground to allow him to see inside, and there was nothing for him to stand on. He would have liked to discover if it was indeed deserted, but that would have to wait. Samantha was waiting back along the track, and dusk was falling. Another time, he told himself as he retraced his steps.

It took less time to find Samantha than he thought it would. She appeared through the trees as an indistinct lighter patch. Her body took on form and detail as he approached silently. She was as he had left her, but she was searching the woods for any signs of life. The creaking of the trees and the hissing of the wind must have unnerved her. She tugged at her handcuffs and tried to stand, giving that up after struggling to her knees, falling back and rolling onto her side. Harold watched her as she struggled to sit up. He stooped to pick up a stone, and flung it so that it landed behind her. Samantha heard the sound and struggled all the harder to rise and look around her.

Harold crept up behind her and touched her breast. Samantha gave a gasp of fear that turned to obvious relief when she saw him.

'I'm so glad you're back,' she said. 'It's getting dark, and I don't think I have the courage to spend the night in the woods like this,' indicating her chains and her nudity with a single jerk of her head. 'Not yet, anyway.' This with a tentative smile.

'Well, maybe one day,' Harold replied. 'After you've had more practice.' He unclipped the chain joining her handcuffs and leg-irons. 'But now that I'm here, how do you feel about a bit of al fresco sex?'

'Yes, please,' Samantha said, moving to allow him to lie beside her. 'I've been hoping for that ever since we came here. Take your clothes off. Hurry!'

206

Harold hurried. He lay on his back and helped Samantha to roll on top of him, lifting his legs so that the chain between Samantha's ankles could slide under, and helping her to rise straddling his hips. He guided his cock into her as she lowered herself to receive it. He slid into her and looked up at Samantha impaled astride him, her firm breasts standing out, as the handcuffs pulled her shoulders back. Samantha sighed as he slid home, and began to rise and fall above him, using her knees and hips to ride him.

Being abandoned had aroused Samantha, despite her fear. After only a minute she shuddered, moaning as a small orgasm rippled through her. Harold could feel the first clenching of her internal muscles as she came. Her next orgasm was not small, and neither was her vocal appreciation. Soon Samantha was rising and falling frantically and screaming with pleasure in the growing darkness under the trees. She went wild when he unclamped the catheter. She peed and came, each release prompting the other. Samantha shouted her pleasure to the skies. The chains creaked as she pulled at them in her frenzy.

When Harold came, she collapsed on top of him, her breasts against his chest as she shuddered and whimpered in release. They lay for a long time, until night enfolded them and Samantha shivered in the wind. Then Harold helped her to stand. He draped the light coat over her, buttoning it over her arms and upper body. She would have to wait until they got back to the house before he could remove her handcuffs and leg-irons. He clamped the catheter again and snapped the chain to her collar before getting dressed himself.

The return to the house took forever in the darkness, but eventually they got there. Harold unlocked the handcuffs and Samantha rolled her shoulders and moved her arms to relieve the cramp. He knelt to release her ankles, but Samantha said no. 'Leave them on me. I'll drive home in leg-irons. The collar stays too,' she added.

And so she put on her coat properly, buttoning it up and raising the collar to conceal the steel band on her throat from casual observers. She waited while Harold locked up the house, before they drove in convoy back to her flat. Harold was excited by the thought of Samantha driving in chains and with the catheter dangling from her crotch. It appeared that he was catching her spirit of adventure, because the outdoor aspect of bondage was becoming more attractive. However, he still possessed enough native caution to hope that there were no inquisitive policemen about.

At her flat Samantha parked as close as she could to the door before getting out of the car in her chains. Safely inside, she removed her coat once again and set about preparing dinner for them. 'Submissive and domesticated, that's me,' she remarked when Harold came up behind her to kiss the back of her neck.

'Sexy too,' he added.

Samantha smiled at that, the smile returning repeatedly throughout dinner. They spent a quiet evening in front of the television. Domestic bliss, Harold told himself sardonically, as practiced by the more perverted. He wondered what Samantha meant when she vowed to wear the collar 'forever'. Was it her idea of a binding promise, a commitment to him, a marriage, in effect? Perhaps it was. If so, he didn't find the idea too worrying. The prospect of losing Samantha, and of having to search for another like her, was much more dismaying. Was this why people got married, or decided to live together? He supposed so, but added that he and Samantha never seemed to argue. He remembered the arguments with his ex. They had been a daily occurrence.

* * *

On the following day, Harold stopped work early to check out the building in the woods. He drove toward where he knew the faint road must be, but found no sign of it. He could not see the building from the road. That made it more suitable for his plan, but at the moment it was just a nuisance. Returning to the house, he retraced yesterday's route via the fields and bridle path. He smiled as he passed the place where he had left Samantha the day before. This time he carried tools with which to open the locked door, something which would prove fairly simple. When he got to the building he had only to knock the pins from the hinges and take the door away. Replacement would not take long.

The building proved to be a stable, with several loose boxes on the ground floor and a hayloft above. The floor was wood, echoing to his footsteps. Wooden stairs led to the hayloft. A room in the loft with a door and two windows overlooked the ground floor. Judging by the amount of dust lying around, the building had been deserted for some time. Harold climbed the stairs and found the loft bare. There were scurrying noises as he moved around – most likely mice, but they soon died away. If the owner had left hay lying around, there would have been more of them.

Harold tried the door to the small room and found it open. Inside there was a desk and chair but little else. A signboard propped against the wall said, 'J. & M. Simms, Livery and Riding School. Horses Boarded.' Beneath that was a telephone number. Hanging on a nail he found a ring with two keys. One of them fitted the office door. The other probably fitted the main door. That would simplify things.

Returning to the ground floor, Harold looked into the loose boxes. They were bare and dusty as well. In the roof space the exposed beams would make a fine place to string Samantha up and beat her. He could even suspend her by her wrists or ankles. Samantha had said that she could stand that in moderation. She would be accessible from all sides.

He would need to bring in some straw when he left Samantha here. The decision to go ahead with the plan had made itself. This was almost the perfect place to let Samantha live out her fantasy. He felt a stirring of excitement as he imagined leading her bound and gagged into the stable. Someone might come while they were *in flagrante delicto*, but that was unlikely. They would just have to take the chance, and to Samantha that would add more spice to the adventure.

Harold replaced the door as he had found it, taking the keys with him. He made his way back to the house and searched once more for the faint track leading to the stable. He drove down several farm tracks and saw some promising by-roads, but it was getting dark by now. Tomorrow he would explore further, and only tell Samantha about the place when he had made his preparations. He thought it might be a good idea to make certain there were no visitors to what he was already thinking of as 'their' stable.

Samantha was on the telephone when he arrived at her place. Hearing him enter, she turned to the door and mouthed 'Amanda' to him, pointing to the phone. He nodded and made his way to the bathroom to shower. He heard snatches of the conversation as he dried off, and then a final 'goodbye' as Samantha hung up. Amanda, she reported, was doing reasonably well at university, and enjoying the new experience.

'She sent you her regards. As a rule, nothing impresses her, but you've managed to do so.' Samantha's voice sounded strained as she made this announcement. 'Have you been seeing her while I've been . . . tied up?' The question came suddenly. Samantha tried to turn it into a joke with a small smile, but she could not wholly conceal the underlying tension.

210

Harold shrugged. 'She's been in Reading while your hands were tied. She seems to have been there forever, if you count the hours you've prevailed on me to tie you up. Are you fishing for a compliment? Do you want me to say that I've never looked at another woman since you fell into my clutches?'

Samantha brightened a bit but still looked uneasy. 'I've been away several nights on business,' she said.

'That's true, but I haven't. Besides, it's true enough. I haven't looked around, except to notice that there are very few women with enough character to wear stockings instead of tights and trousers. Make sure you don't catch the habit. You have been rather a handful ever since you seduced me, you know – not that I mind. On the whole, I'm glad we found one another.'

This pronouncement seemed to allay some of Samantha's worry. 'But what about Christmas? You left me tied up for a long time and went out.'

Harold hoped that the memory of Amanda wearing her mother's dildo-pants and handcuffs did not show in his face. 'I brought back food for my slave, if you remember.'

Samantha remembered. 'And I ate it. Does that make me your slave?' The idea did not displease her. She touched the steel collar at her throat, trying to get her fingers under it. 'It itches,' she explained.

'Let me look,' Harold said. He noticed a slight rash and a reddish mark under the collar. It fit tightly to her neck and doubtless she was having trouble washing the area well. 'You're rusting,' he told her. 'I'll unlock you for a few days and see if it clears up.'

'Oh,' Samantha said in a disappointed tone of voice. 'I vowed to wear it forever just a few days ago.'

'But you didn't think about rust and sweat when you said that. Never mind. You can put it back on again, if you're that serious about it, but it will have to come off now and again to let you wash.'

'Well, I'll wear the collar always in my heart, and openly whenever you want to lock it on me. Will that be all right?'

'Just fine with me,' Harold said as he unlocked the steel band and laid it on the coffee table.

Samantha touched her throat where the collar had lain. 'I suppose it's just as well,' she said. 'Amanda will be home over the Easter weekend. It might be hard to explain a collar to her. You're sure you don't mind?'

'Mind what? Amanda coming home, or you not wearing the collar?

'Both, I suppose.'

Harold held her tightly and kissed her thoroughly. Samantha sighed in contentment. 'You're good to me.'

In the following days he discovered that there was a rutted track that led to the stables. It branched off a farmer's own track from house to fields, and that made access much easier. He bought several bales of straw and carted them one by one to the stables. No one seemed to notice, and there was no evidence that anyone had come to look at the place. Better and better, he thought. He rigged a hoist from one of the rafters to get the bales to the loft, swept the floors and the hayloft, and spread the straw. He could not bring in a great mass of it, so he arranged it in a corner of the loft. It might attract more mice, but he could not leave Samantha lying on the bare boards. When he was done, there did not seem to be that many scurrying noises from dark corners. It seemed that they retreated from the tramp of footsteps. It would have to do.

The weekend after Amanda's visit was when Harold planned to bring Samantha to the stables. He decided to visit the stable every day until then, to see if anyone came to look around, and to keep the rodents figurat ively on their toes.

Amanda breezed into town on Easter Saturday. 'See,' she said to Harold and Samantha, 'I can *so* travel on my own. But the train is seriously expensive.'

She took over Samantha's car, which put a stop to the unexpected arrivals at Harold's work site. He got a good bit more done, but missed the visits. Amanda did not evict her mother as she had on her last visit. Nevertheless, Samantha took to spending every other night at Harold's house. 'She's got her friends round at odd times,' she said in explanation. 'I only get to see her in between their visits.'

On the Tuesday after Easter Harold made his way to the stables with another bale of straw. There would be about enough, he judged, so long as Samantha did not thrash about too much, or work herself over to the edge of the nest he was preparing for her. He was hoisting the bale into the loft when Amanda arrived.

'Hello,' she said. 'I was coming to see you at the house when I saw you turn off here. So I followed.'

Harold was surprised and a bit worried by her presence. Samantha's half-joke about seeing Amanda behind her back came to mind.

Amanda was wearing the long, light coat Samantha had worn on her last visit to the house. Below its hem, Amanda wore knee-high boots. He could see that she had on dark stockings or tights as well, but nothing else of her costume. It was an attractive outfit for an attractive girl. Woman, he corrected himself. She looked so much like her mother.

Before he could ask her why she was here, Amanda asked, in typical forthright style, 'Is this where you're going to leave mum?'

The direct question was disconcerting. There was a long silence that Amanda finally broke.

213

'All right, you needn't tell me. I know about it anyway from her side. Mum has begun to keep a diary. She didn't use to, but she does now. She loves you, you know. She thinks you're the greatest thing since sliced bread – or so her diary says. You know how older women can run on. She also says quite a lot about what you've been doing while I was safely at uni. Spicy stuff. She really is a pervert. Well, I suppose you are too. But you suit one another. Did you always like to tie your women up?'

'No,' Harold replied. 'Your mum is the first woman I've ever done that with.' He went silent, not wanting to give away their secrets.

'So mum seduced you and made you tie her up!' Amanda seemed to relish the thought of her mother's strength of purpose. 'This place looks secluded and deserted enough to satisfy her,' she observed.

It was another of her show-stoppers. Harold did not know what to say.

'Don't look too surprised,' Amanda went on. 'I've read nearly all of mum's diary. She has a lot to say about you, most of it very nice.' With the abruptness he had come to associate with her, Amanda changed the subject. 'She says that this is one of her strongest fantasies.' Amanda jerked her head to indicate the building and the area in general. 'She'll love being left here.'

Harold remained silent. It would not do to reprimand Amanda for snooping when he had done the same. A reprimand would mean nothing to her. In any case, the secret was out.

'I know all her secrets now. Yours too, come to that. I could blackmail you both.' With another abrupt mental swerve, Amanda asked, 'Does she really get off when she's all tied up?'

'You know the answer to that,' Harold said at last. There was no great danger of blackmail; anything

Amanda did would hurt her mother as much as him. He was more irritated than worried by the know-it-all tone of this young woman, but did not want her to know it.

'You're cute when you're angry,' she said, laughing. 'Or is it embarrassment?'

Harold said nothing.

'Don't be so square. I told you I thought you were good for mum. I still do. The diary only tells me she feels the same about you. She's even used the L-word. You should be flattered – not many men are so lucky.' Changing the subject rapidly again, Amanda asked if he too kept a diary. 'What do you say about mum?'

Harold was glad that he had not committed his thoughts to a diary. He had no doubt that Amanda would find it if he had done so. Nothing was safe from her, and nor was anything sacred. 'I wish you hadn't told me about the diary,' he finally said.

'Why? Are you going to read it now? To see just what she says? I couldn't resist if I were you.'

'You didn't resist, even though you're not me,' Harold said uncomfortably. The knowledge that he had already snooped made him uneasy with Amanda. He put on a scowl, hoping she could not read his thoughts from his face.

'Don't be cross with me,' Amanda said. 'I didn't know you were so sensitive. Still,' she went on, 'I'm glad you two are getting on so well. As I said, mum's a lucky woman. Not many men, I guess, would go to all this trouble,' indicating again the stables and his work, 'to give their partner such a nice surprise.'

There was another uncomfortable silence. Amanda broke it.

'Listen, I'm just glad you're getting on so well. She's happy most of the time now. She didn't use to be. I remember when she split up with dad. She was lonely – I could see that straight away. The other men she saw didn't help. But all that changed when you showed up.'

215

Amanda made that sound like a compliment. Harold was curious about the 'other men,' but forbore to ask. If Samantha wanted him to know, she would tell him. It wouldn't make any difference, he told himself.

'It'll be cold, you know,' Amanda reminded him. He nodded and shrugged. 'She's very determined. I suppose she'll manage to endure the hardship. Thinking of the reward will keep her occupied. It would me. Anyway, why am I here today, I hear you ask.' She took a pair of handcuffs from her coat pocket. 'Ta-da! I thought it would be nice if you locked me up and molested me a bit in your spare moments. Sort of a trial run for you and mum. Besides, I find the idea of being molested rather intriguing.'

'Where did you get the handcuffs?' he temporised. This was dangerous ground. It was harder to deny his interest this time. This opportunity was so much more . . . opportune. He might have to resort to words like 'trust' and 'love' and 'regard for others', always an embarrassment. He mentioned instead the difficulties of such an arrangement, with the three of them living so closely together.

Amanda retorted that she was away most of the time.

'All right, ask your mother what she thinks of a threesome – before you get us all into trouble.' Harold half-hoped that Samantha would agree. Amanda was a very interesting young woman.

'One day I will,' Amanda said darkly. 'It might be fun! But what am I going to do in the meantime?'

Harold shrugged. 'What every other young woman does, I suppose – look for Mr Right. Try the Internet. I ran across a woman in Reading who advertises herself as a submissive. She might have some ideas you could use. She's local. Look her up, maybe meet her. She must have some idea about finding willing partners. She might be more open with another woman. And there are many others like her.'

Amanda sighed, and held up her handcuffs again. 'At least show me how to get loose by myself so I won't have to summon the fire brigade.'

'They would enjoy that,' he commented.

'I wouldn't,' she retorted.

Harold examined the handcuffs. They were of the same type as Samantha's. Like mother, like daughter, he thought. 'Don't lose the key, or put it where you can't get at when you're alone. Otherwise you *will* be needing the fire brigade. Remember Christmas.'

Amanda nodded. She stood and turned her back to Harold. 'Put them on me,' she commanded, bringing her hands behind her back.

He did, knowing where this might lead. Trying to avoid the inevitable, though with decreasing willpower, he asked Amanda where she got her interest from.

'It might come from mum, if such things are genetic. But I can remember my first outright exposure to sex with bondage. While I was at the pony club stage, I had a woman instructor who liked to be beaten with birch twigs and riding crops. She was about mum's age, and I had always wondered why she spent so much of her time around the stables. She was a horsy type, but she looked so much more satisfied, or happy – I don't know – when she was there. Then one day I arrived early for my lesson – Mum was running late for an appointment or something. She dropped me off and there was no one around. I was about to go into the stables when I heard strange noises, something like strangled grunting. Instead of going to the door I went around to peek in the window. There was Miss Harman, strung up by her wrists, gagged, having a fine time of it as the owner of the stables – another woman – lashed her with a riding crop.

'My first impulse was to dash in and put a stop to it. It looked painful. To this day, I don't know what made

217

me wait to see what happened, but I'm glad I did. I remember thinking it would have been terribly embarrassing for everyone. Anyway, I watched – and learned a few things I hadn't suspected. At some point in the performance, I became aware that Miss Harman was indeed enjoying the beating. When the owner dropped the crop and went down on her, I knew that for Miss Harman the real fun had started. Oh, she struggled a bit, pulling at the ropes and making loud moans through the gag, but it was her facial expression that gave it away. She had her eyes closed and was concentrating on what was happening between her legs. She shuddered several times and then went sort of limp, at which point the other woman let her down and helped her across to a pile of hay. Even a child could see that it was great fun.

'Of course, I knew about lesbians and such,' Amanda said, trying to sound grown up, 'but this was the first time I had seen any in action – and the first time I saw that pain could lead to pleasure. Later, when Miss Harman came out for my session, she looked happy and relaxed. If she felt that way, then it couldn't be all that terrible. So the seed was planted, I suppose.'

Amanda took her coat off and looked very appealing in her short tight dress, boots, dark tights and handcuffs. She turned around and looked directly at him. 'Last chance,' she said, thrusting her breasts out invitingly. 'Go on, touch them.'

Harold put the key into Amanda's hand and told her to try to fit it into the lock. She dropped it and swore. Harold handed it to her again. This time she managed to get it into the keyhole. The cuff opened in the end, and Amanda looked both satisfied and frustrated. Harold wished that she had not been able to free herself. The sight of a woman in bondage was having its usual effect on him. The sight of this particular woman in bondage inflamed him even more, as the forbidden-fruit aspect of all temptations always does.

Amanda noticed. She smiled at his obvious discomfiture. 'I'll take that as a compliment,' she said, pointing to his erection.

'That's what your mother always says.'

'Is it?'

'You're . . . very like her.'

'Another compliment, I think. Keep on like that and I'll begin to think you fancy me. You do, don't you?' she demanded suddenly. It came out like a challenge.

Weakly, Harold nodded.

'Well, what are you waiting for?'

'I'm thinking of your mother and her reaction to this.'

'She'll never know if you don't tell her.'

'*I'll* know.'

'Well, they can't say you're not a real Boy Scout,' Amanda replied, managing to sound both scornful and wistful. 'If that's your last word on the subject, I'd best be getting on. Mum is very lucky. But don't think you're completely off the hook. There'll be other days, other apples.' Amanda kissed him firmly on the lips this time. She got back into Samantha's car and drove off, waving airily out of the open window.

11

Surprise

Harold did not tell Samantha about the stables just then; she was certain to want to go there at once, and Amanda's presence would make things difficult for her. The secret anticipation gave him pleasure. Each time he visited the stables he imagined Samantha's pleasure when he finally brought her there. He left the hoist rigged, and imagined hoisting her to the loft, bound and gagged and twisting helplessly.

Samantha, meanwhile, worked on her manuscripts by day, wearing her leg-irons and the stockings and suspenders. Most evenings she spent bound and gagged as they watched television, or spread-eagled on the bed screaming as they made violent love. All in all, a pleasantly untedious lifestyle.

On one of the days when she was not in chains, Samantha engaged in some retail therapy. When Harold came over she was waiting with the results of her expedition. A half-dozen coils of picture-hanging wire lay on the coffee table, and Samantha was obviously excited by the scenario she had planned for the evening. She had prepared herself carefully for Harold's visual enjoyment, since she knew how much he liked to look at her. She wore stockings and suspenders as usual, but she had taken some pains with them this time. The dark grey stockings were extra long, reaching nearly to her crotch, and they shone with subdued highlights that accented her long legs. They were attached to the shortest of suspenders, held up by a peach silk suspender belt, one Harold had never seen before. Samantha wore her laced knee-length boots with the high heels, and a pair of long leather gloves that reached nearly to her armpits. She looked incredibly sexy.

Samantha had pinned up her growing hair in a French twist. Her makeup was carefully applied, and she had used eyeshadow to alter the shape of her eyes.

'I wanted to look different tonight,' she explained. 'I feel as if I'm about to cross another boundary and enter a new land. You can help me to make it familiar territory by being there – and loving me.' She had bought the wire, the stockings and suspenders that day, she explained, and was eager to try it all out.

Harold heard the L-word with surprise but not much alarm. He knew about her diary, and Amanda had reminded him of her mother's feelings as well. He had already expressed his misgivings about using the wire to bind her, but Samantha clearly wanted him to do it. He hugged her tightly, and she clung to him with a fierceness that was new to them both.

When she tore herself away, Samantha said, 'Tonight I want you to tie me with the wire as if it were the usual cord. It will be a test for me to see how long I can endure.'

Harold nodded, thinking that if the prospect of being bound with that thin wire fascinated her so much, the least he could do was to let her have the experience. Not that he would be totally unmoved by it, he reflected. He was not that unselfish.

The air was electric with anticipation as they ate their evening meal. Samantha did not eat much. Harold, likewise, found the food not as appetising as usual.

There was a knot of excitement in his stomach. Samantha appeared even more excited. She looked at him abruptly and said, 'Do me now!' in a fierce whisper. They left the dishes on the table.

In the front room Samantha trembled with excitement as he opened the packets of wire she had bought. When he stepped behind her she brought her gloved hands together behind her back and stood shivering as he wrapped the thin wire around her wrists and pulled it tight. He had to twist the ends instead of tying knots, but he was able to cinch the wire between her wrists, out of her fingers' reach. Samantha gasped as the wire bit into her through the thin leather.

She held still while he pulled her elbows together and twisted the wires tight around them. He gagged her, expertly now. Remembering her fondness for being handled roughly, Harold pushed Samantha suddenly to the sofa. She stumbled and fell half on and half off, her knees on the floor and her upper body on the cushions. She cried out in surprise but made no further protest. A few strands of her hair had come loose and strayed across her face. Harold thought her breathtakingly beautiful. He began to undress hurriedly. Samantha twisted her head and watched silently, her breath ragged and uneven, as his erect cock appeared.

He roughly arranged her with her upper body on the sofa and her hips in the air over the arm rest. Her legs were unsupported, only the toes of the black leather boots touching the floor. Samantha, her head turned to one side on the sofa, looked wildly at him as he approached her.

Harold kicked her feet apart and rapidly entered her from behind. Samantha cried out as he slid into her. She was wet and parted, ready for him, even though there had been no foreplay save the tying of her hands and arms. It was more than enough for Samantha. For

Harold too. He reached around her parted thighs to tease and pinch her clitoris. Samantha's moan of release was bitten off as she struggled beneath him. She came almost at once, heaving and bucking. Harold, behind her, could see the wires at wrists and elbows biting into the leather gloves. She came again, still struggling and gasping for breath. Samantha was wildly excited by this helplessness, and Harold felt new excitement as well. He plunged into her roughly, quickly, and Samantha came yet again. She moaned continuously as he rode her to another climax, and then came himself, pumping hotly into her. Samantha screamed again as she felt him come, and then slumped exhausted on the sofa. Her knees, held straight until now, sagged toward the floor. She was covered in a light sheen of perspiration, and her breath was rapid and uneven. Nevertheless, her internal muscles clenched him tightly, as if reluctant to let him go.

Not that Harold had any intention of going any-where. He lay on top of her as the aftershocks of their coupling rippled through her body. He knew why he had chosen Samantha over her daughter, and would every time – even if he could not tell her that the offer had been made twice, and might be renewed. Her maturity and sense of adventure were fully developed. It was a challenge to keep up with her. He felt his cock growing erect again.

Samantha felt his growing hardness, and began to thrust with her hips, encouraging him to fuck her again. He did, taking longer this time and savouring her responses. Samantha moaned instead of screaming, but seemed satisfied nonetheless. She fought the wire bind-ing her wrists and arms, finding new pleasure in the thin, tight strands that bound her. Helpless herself, Samantha nevertheless did all she could to let Harold know that she appreciated his efforts. This time, he used both hands to caress her breasts and tease her nipples erect. Samantha moaned as his hands aroused her. She closed down on his cock as he came inside her.

This time Harold pulled out and sat on the floor. Samantha remained as he had left her, hips raised and legs spread invitingly. She looked lovely, he decided, sweaty and disarranged, her hair escaping from the French twist and straying over her face. He looked at her for a long time, and Samantha regarded him just as earnestly in the mirror across the room. Finally she squirmed backwards and lowered her knees to the floor, kneeling beside the couch. On her knees she made her way to the front of the sofa and with a struggle she sat down. Harold reached to stroke her legs through the sheer grey stockings. They felt smooth and silky under his touch, and slightly damp from Samantha's perspiration. So erotic, he thought.

'Tie my legs,' Samantha commanded. 'I want to feel the wires bite in.'

Harold did as she asked, tying her ankles together and pulling the wire tight over her leather boots. He looked doubtfully at her knees and thighs, bare save for the sheer nylon stockings, but Samantha encouraged him to bind her there as well. When he had finished, she sighed in satisfaction, wriggling in the tight thin bonds and finding no slack. 'Do my breasts too,' she commanded. 'And gag me.'

When had done so, Harold looked at the thin wires constricting the flesh of her full breasts for a long time, absorbed by the way they protruded and by her erect nipples. He knelt before her and took a nipple in his mouth, licking and nipping it gently.

'Oh god', Samantha moaned. 'Gag me quickly,' she pleaded.

Harold felt that something special was needed, rather than the usual duct tape. He wished he had bought one

224

of the leather hoods with internal gags he had seen on the Internet. Too late now. Samantha told him to use the tape, and to hurry. He stuffed a pair of her panties into her mouth and taped it shut. Silenced, Samantha closed her eyes and lay back on the sofa. There was nothing for Harold to do save look at her. He guessed that she wanted to sleep in her bondage, and he would have to stay alert in case she had to get loose. He didn't expect her to ask for release, but this was something new for them both. He settled down to stare at his helpless lover as she struggled silently against the wire.

Eventually, Samantha drowsed off. Harold marvelled anew at her ability to sleep while tied so thoroughly and tightly. He guessed that the thin wires were very uncomfortable, but she gave no sign. He got dressed and went outside to his van. There he gathered some insulating tape and a pair of wire-cutting pliers. When Samantha woke again, he would be ready for her. He left the materials inside and went out again, locking the front door. If she awoke while he was away, Samantha would enjoy knowing that she had been left helpless in a locked flat. If she did not wake, then he planned a surprise for her. Harold went to the Pakistani shop around the corner for some emergency supplies.

Ranee, the daughter, was on duty. She smiled when she saw him. There had been a time when he had considered asking her out, but her parents' certain objections to a Westerner courting their daughter had made him hesitate. And then Samantha had come along.

Ranee was still glad to see him. They chatted easily as he bought sliced ham, bread and butter. She managed to hint that she would like to see him again. Harold thought her a nice woman, and certainly a beautiful one, but Samantha awaited him at home. He found himself relieved not to have to charm anyone else.

Samantha was awake when he returned. She lifted her head and turned to see who had come for her. Though it could hardly be anyone else, she still entertained the fantasy that a stranger would find her helpless. That was why she clung to the deserted barn fantasy. She smiled at him with her eyes and lay back down. Harold went into the kitchen to put away his purchases.

When he returned, he bent to kiss Samantha over her gag. Then he helped her to stand by the sofa. Despite her boots, the wires must have bitten painfully into her legs as her muscles tensed up, but Samantha gave no sign of it. Harold leaned down to grasp her around the thighs and lift her onto his shoulder. He carried her bent over on her stomach, with her head and torso down his back and her bound legs dangling in front, into her bedroom. He laid her on her bed and went for the insulating tape and the pliers. With the tape he covered the ends of the wires that bound her, blunting the metal so that it would not cut her when she struggled. He was sure she would. Harold taped her eyes with duct tape and left her to her own devices. He knew that Samantha would use the time to work herself to a climax before he returned.

There was nothing for him to do while he waited, and the time passed slowly in the silent flat. He heard the bed creaking, and there were muffled grunts and moans from the bedroom. In order to take his attention away from his own excitement, Harold switched on the computer and went prying into Samantha's diary. There he found what Amanda had seen, and was humbled by the way she regarded him. Even as he read of her growing dependence on and affection for him, he still felt reluctant to think of Samantha in terms of the L-word. She had no such inhibitions. When he thought of life without her and the endless variety she brought to sex, the future seemed empty and dreary. He would

226

soon have to decide what to do. But not today. He closed down the computer and went to check on his captive.

Samantha lay as he had left her, on her side, the thin wires tight at wrists and elbows, at ankles, knees and thighs. She was covered in a thin sheen of sweat, and her breathing was still rapid and ragged, her nostrils flaring as she drew in great ragged draughts of air. There was the strong scent of her rut in the air as he drew close to the bed. Harold could see that she had used her time alone to bring herself to orgasm-one of her most exciting abilities. He regarded her silently, this exciting older woman who had transformed his life. Her naked helplessness aroused him strongly, but he was loth to break the tableau. Finally he reached out to touch her.

Samantha jerked convulsively when he caressed the tight flesh of her bound breasts and began to tease her nipples. With her legs bound tightly together her cunt was inaccessible, but Samantha reacted well enough to the stimulation of her other erogenous zones. He fondled her, nuzzling her neck and throat and her ear lobes. Samantha became aroused by slow degrees. Her earlier exercise had been strenuous, and now he aroused her slowly and thoroughly once again. She began to moan softly, twisting slowly in her bonds. She came suddenly, surprising Harold by the strength of her reaction. Later he concluded that the wires had aroused her more strongly than he had imagined. Novelty, he concluded, was the key to Samantha's orgasms. Life with her was never going to be dull.

Harold used one hand to caress her face and neck, enjoying the arousal of his helpless lover. Samantha moaned more loudly as his hands brought her to another climax. She thrashed on the bed as she came. When he sensed another climax coming, Harold waited

227

for Samantha's gasping exhalation. Then, before she could fill her lungs again, he kissed her roughly over the gag. Harold felt her whole body heave with heightened excitement. Samantha, he knew, liked being kissed while gagged. Her breath came loudly in his ear as the kiss drew out. She thrashed convulsively, moaning loudly as she came.

Samantha's orgasm went on even after Harold stood up to fetch the whip from the bureau. The first blow, to her bottom, went almost unnoticed. Samantha was lost to external reality. As he continued to strike her, Harold noticed that she was struggling to present a different part of her body to the whip, thrashing around on the bed and moaning through her gag. He marveled at her ability to derive pleasure from the pain of the whipping – and he continued to give it to her. When Samantha managed to roll onto her back, Harold lashed her breasts. The nipples were erect and crinkly. The flesh of her breasts was shiny and tight, stretched tautly by the wires binding them.

Harold felt a strong urge to lash her to exhaustion – either his or hers. More likely, he thought later, it would have been his. Samantha in rut seemed tireless.

She decided the issue by rolling away from him and landing on the floor on the opposite side of the bed. As he stood to go to her, Harold heard the drumming of her booted heels on the floor. Samantha writhed wildly, rolling over and over as she struggled and came. Suddenly her body went rigid, her back arched, her muscles straining against the thin wires that bound her, and then she went limp.

Her breasts heaved as she took air into her starved lungs. She moaned loudly and continued to breathe through widely flaring nostrils. Harold began to remove her gag to allow her to draw deeper breaths, afraid that he had gone too far, had crossed a forbidden boundary.

Nevertheless, he was terribly excited by the sense of his power over her.

The sense of relief that had swept over him when Samantha showed signs of revival was so great that he knew he would not do that again. Unless Samantha asks, a part of him said. He removed the tape from her eyes. She was conscious, he saw, but weak. He rolled Samantha onto her stomach and began to cut away the wire with the pliers. When she was free he laid her on the bed and waited in trepidation for her to recover fully. Instead she rolled onto her side and fell asleep. Exhaustion, he guessed. He climbed in beside her, and Samantha, though apparently asleep, fitted herself spoon fashion to his back and put an arm around him. There might be recriminations later, but he was glad that she wanted to be near him.

In the morning, there were still angry red marks on her legs where the wires had been. Slightly less angry marks showed when she took off the boots and gloves. She was thoughtful rather than angry. 'I'm so glad we did that. When you kissed me I was so excited. I couldn't get enough air. But I came like a bomb,' she said.

'So you enjoyed it?' he asked with relief.

Samantha nodded. 'Immensely. I just let go and enjoyed the pain and the orgasm. It was a great turn-on for me. Thank you.' Samantha kissed him. 'We'll have to do it again sometime,' she said. 'I really liked the wire too. It's too bad you had to cut me free. I'll have to get some more,' she said, looking closely at the marks the wires had left on her body.

Harold considered the marks left on his psyche. He had been excited by Samantha's struggles in a way that frightened him. No more of this, he vowed. Well, not for some time anyway, another part of him said. The trouble with sadism was its addictive nature. And with

229

Samantha so willing to play the victim it was hard to avoid giving in.

Harold threw himself into finishing the last jobs at the house in order to avoid the temptation to repeat the performance. At home, he trawled the Internet as he made plans to leave Samantha in the stable. He needed something that would surprise and arouse her without harming her. He decided to buy the leather helmet and gag he had seen earlier. He liked the idea of putting it on her as a change from the tape they always used. He also bought a dog-training collar and a set of electrified dildoes to go with it. A leather 'punishment' bra with electrodes in the cups looked good. Like her dildo-pants, it locked on. He imagined she would appreciate a bit of external stimulus as she lay in the straw. He guessed he would tell Samantha about the stable when the new items came. The problem was how to get Samantha wired up without spoiling the surprise.

The solution came to him as he did a last tidying job at the stable. He decided to transport her there bound, gagged and blindfolded in the back of his van. He would not let her see the place beforehand. That would heighten the sense of mystery for her. Samantha would know that something strange was going on, but she would have no way to guess what it was. The surprise would be complete.

In the meantime, Samantha bought a fresh supply of picture-hanging wire and left it conspicuously on the kitchen counter.

12

To the Stables

Because he had a garage attached to his house, Harold and Samantha started from there. It was the best way to get a bound and gagged woman into his van without causing the neighbours to gossip. He asked her to wear her usual stockings and suspenders, and to add the high-heeled lace-up boots. He liked the effect.

'You're becoming a real fetishist,' she told him jokingly.

'And you're not?' he retorted.

Samantha asked him if he wanted her to bring the wire along. Not this time, he replied. Samantha was disappointed, but went along with his wishes. Was there anything else, she asked. Harold told her to include the dildo-pants, the long leather gloves and her steel collar. And the catheter. Kinky, she commented, but did as he asked. She had no idea where Harold was taking her, but she was intrigued.

Harold put her things into his holdall and tied her wrists and arms behind her back. This time Samantha's elbows touched fully. 'You've been practising,' he said as he tied the last knot. Samantha smiled.

'Sit on the sofa while I fit the catheter.' he said. He knelt between her spread legs and found her urethra after two tries, Samantha wincing slightly as the end went in. Harold pushed it firmly in until he felt her sphincter give way before the invading tube. He clamped it shut and gestured for Samantha to stand.

She struggled to her feet, teetering a little in her high-heeled boots. The plastic tube hung just below the hem of her skirt. Harold led her through the kitchen and into the garage, where his van stood with the rear doors open. He had cleared a space inside and covered the steel floor with a duvet. 'Your nest,' he told her.

Samantha could not get inside without help. Harold had her sit on the duvet just inside the doors with her legs hanging to the ground. Then he tied her at ankles, knees and thighs, pulling the cords tight as she liked them. With a pair of her pants he stuffed her mouth, taping her lips shut with duct tape. From the hold-all, he took her steel collar. Samantha lifted her chin when she felt its touch, making a satisfied noise when it closed around her throat and neck. He taped her eyes shut.

Harold lifted Samantha's bound legs and tipped her into the van on her back. Getting inside, Harold pulled his helpless lover further inside and arranged her on her side on the duvet. Using more of the cord, he hog-tied her.

'Comfy?' he asked.

'Mmmm,' said Samantha, with a nod.

Harold put the holdall on the floor beside her and closed the doors. He opened the garage door and got into the van. Driving it outside, he parked it at the curb and switched off the engine. 'Won't be long,' he told his live cargo as he locked the doors and walked away. 'Mmmm-mmm!' Samantha said protestingly. But Harold walked away and she was alone in the van. She shifted position as much as her bonds allowed, wriggling on the duvet beneath her. There was nothing she could do.

In the quiet street she could occasionally hear people passing by on the pavement, and the sound of distant traffic. No one paid any attention to the van, but there was always the chance that they might. There was nothing Samantha could do about that – except get excited by the prospect of being discovered by a stranger. But even that satisfaction was denied her. If she squirmed and heaved and moaned as she normally did when Harold left her tied up, the van would rock on its suspension, and someone was certain to investigate. Being actually found by a stranger was not on. Harold had left her in a situation she dared not enjoy, and could not escape from. And he was taking a long time about returning. Perforce, Samantha lay quietly, becoming more frustrated as time passed.

In time, despite her enforced immobility, Samantha felt herself growing excited. She told herself it was nothing. She commanded her body to cease and desist from reminding her that she was tied up as she liked, and to stop making her grow warm and wet between her thighs. Despite her efforts to stay calm her mind grew increasingly active. Suppose, it suggested, that Harold had really abandoned her. Silly, she told herself. He wouldn't do that. Wouldn't he? And wouldn't that be just what you wanted? Well, yes, but not just here.

Her excitement grew, and Samantha caught herself squirming on the duvet, her body doing its best to arouse itself while a part of her mind tried to rein in the rest of her. She willed her rebellious body to be still. It refused. She squirmed harder, pulling at the cords that bound her. Samantha tautened her muscles, trying to remain still. They grew tired with the enforced rigidity, and she found herself squirming and heaving once more. She moaned softly, glad that she was gagged, trying to keep as silent as possible as the familiar waves of desire threatened to sweep her away. Suddenly, she heard footsteps on the pavement outside. Were they slowing, and stopping to examine the van? Samantha bit back a moan as she shuddered with the first orgasm. Go away! she silently told the feet outside. She could hear a couple talking not three feet from where she lay bound and trying to hold back another climax. They were talking about that most English of subjects, the weather. As they exchanged clichés Samantha bit back a moan as another wave of pleasure swept through her, spreading from her belly to her stomach and down her legs. She tugged mightily at the hog-tie rope, trying to straighten her legs and roll onto her front. Her hips thrust backwards and forwards as she came.

Outside the couple were still talking, now about the new head teacher at the local secondary school and the rising tide of indiscipline evident there – and everywhere else. Inside the van Samantha was once more losing the battle to exert some discipline over her own body. It became a quivering bow, her back arched and her legs pulling down against her bound wrists and elbows. The delicious sense of her own helplessness and arousal drove her to yet another orgasm. Somehow she managed not to cry out, and perversely that self-restraint made her come even harder. She wanted to thrash about and moan but forced herself to remain still, her body straining against the cords as her release shook her.

When Samantha grew quiet, she was aware of a silence outside. The couple had gone while she was coming. She ached with relief. Her body ached, too, from the effort to remain still when the occasion called for screams of pleasure and wild thrashings. The rest of the world went on about its business outside her prison, oblivious to her plight.

The knowledge of her own helplessness in what was virtually a public place dawned on Samantha once more, and swept her over into another series of orgasms. Oh god, she thought, this is too good to be true.

When she stopped coming she felt exhausted, and would have gone to sleep if two more voices on the pavement had not jerked her wide awake. Two men, she realised. One seemed to be Irish. The other had a Geordie accent. A bolt of fear shot through her as she realised they were talking about stealing the van. Terrified, Samantha listened intently to the sound of someone trying to open the doors.

'Locked, of course,' said the Geordie.

Saved, Samantha thought.

'Nivir you mind. Oi'll have her open in a jiffy,' the Irish voice replied.

Samantha froze. Now that her fantasy of being found by a stranger looked like coming true, she was petrified. She knew what they would do to her when they discovered their helpless passenger. Oh god, where was Harold?

The door opened. Samantha felt the springs sag as someone got into the front seat. The Geordie voice said, 'Let me in the other side.' A moment later the other door opened, and the van shifted on its suspension. Oh god, Samantha thought frantically. There were muffled curses and movements from the front seat, and after a few minutes the engine started.

'Told yah it'd be easy,' said the Irish voice as the van pulled out into the road and moved away. 'It looks like a chippie's van,' the other voice put in. 'Take a look in the back, see if there's anything worth selling.'

Samantha tried to make herself small. The van hit a bump and she stifled a squeal of surprise. She need not have bothered.

'Jasus, Mary an' Joseph!' exclaimed the Irishman. 'Dere's a woman back dere, all tied up an' all. Maybe we've stumbled onto a kidnap plot. Should we tell the polis?'

'Don't be dafter than ye need be, Patrick. What d'ye think they'd do with us if we drove into the cop shop and told them we'd found her like that – an us just outa nick?'

In the silence following that announcement, Samantha thought she would black out. Her greatest fantasy had turned into her worst nightmare.

The Geordie addressed both her and his companion. 'If it wasn't a kidnap, it is now. Let's take her to a quiet place I know about and see what's under all them nice clothes. She's blindfolded, so she can't identify us.' To Samantha he continued, 'That's a bit of luck for you, duckie. We might just let you live after we're through with you.'

Samantha moaned through her gag in what she hoped was a supplicatory fashion.

'I like it when they're scared,' said the Geordie. After that there was silence.

Samantha felt the van turn away from the house and out onto a highway. She had no idea where they were taking her, though she had a pretty clear one of what they would do. Her fear nearly choked her, but there was a definite thrill of pleasure as well. She was surprised to find herself relishing her own kidnap, even though she expected to be raped. Might there be a little torture thrown in, the dark side of her asked with some eagerness. The real thing, not the kind she and Harold played at, with rules and safe words. Samantha shocked herself with her eagerness. She wriggled on the floor as she felt the warmth growing between her thighs.

'I think she's working herself up to come,' said the Geordie. 'D'you think she's one of them, what d'you call 'em . . . *masochists*? One of them women who likes to be hurt?' To Samantha he said, 'Don't worry, duckie, we'll hurt you to your heart's content.'

His voice sounded menacing to Samantha, but her excitement refused to go away. She squirmed ever harder in her bonds. A low moan got past her gag. She was on the verge of another orgasm. Samantha just had time to wonder what she was doing when it struck like a hammer-blow. She bucked and heaved as she came, straining against the cords and delighting in the way they bit into her as she struggled. Silence was no longer necessary. Samantha made as much noise as she could, not caring who heard her.

'Looks like we have a live one on our hands,' the Geordie said. 'Not much farther to the place.'

Samantha struggled and came, her fear warring with her desire. She had no idea how far they had taken her when the van finally stopped. This is it! she told herself, her fears returning.

She heard them open the doors to get out. Footsteps came around to the back of the van. Samantha grew still. The back door opened, letting in a gust of wind that felt wonderfully cool on her fevered skin. Hands pulled her roughly to the back of the van. A knife cut her hog-tie rope, and the cords binding her legs.

'Come outta dere,' said the Irishman, pulling Samantha to the rear of the van and setting her onto her feet. Her knees refused to hold her up. She slumped back to a sitting position on the tail board of the van.

'Look dere!' exclaimed the Irishman, 'she's wearin' a collar around her neck.

'Where else would she wear it, Patrick?' the Geordie asked scornfully.

Hands tugged at the collar as they examined it. They discovered the lock. Harold had the key. Oh god, where is he? Samantha asked herself. Not here, evidently.

One of them threaded a lead through the ring on the front of her collar and jerked her to her feet. This time Samantha managed to stand, and they led her stumbling from the van.

'No one comes to these stables any more,' said the Geordie. 'No one knows we have her, and no one knows about this place either. We can keep her here for a long time, even if someone's looking for her.'

Samantha's heart sank as the truth of her captor's words sank in. Even she did not know where she was. She knew they were in a building of some sort because she heard a door opening, and felt the coolness as they led her inside. The door closed again, and she was alone with her captors, out of sight and helpless. Yet perversely, her body was intent on its own agenda, despite the danger that surrounded her. 'Ohhhhh!' she moaned, shuddering as another climax took her.

'I do believe she's comin',' said the Irishman. 'She's a quare one an' all, an' all. Let's cut her clothes off. She'll not be needin' 'em again.'

Samantha heard the menace in his voice, but she could not believe they meant to kill her.

'Take the gag away first,' said the Geordie. 'There's no one around to hear her no matter how loud she gets, and I like to hear them scream and beg.'

Samantha moaned as they peeled the tape from her mouth, jerking it roughly. She spat out the pants. Flushing hotly, she swallowed her pride and begged them to let her go. 'I haven't seen your faces,' she said. 'I can't identify you, and I promise not to call the police if you'll only not hurt me.' The rebellious part of her was telling her to shut up, but she wasn't listening to it. This was her fear speaking. It was humiliating, but better than letting them believe she was ready to die.

'Dat's right,' said the Irishman. 'She hasn't seen our faces.'

'So let's take the blindfold off,' said the Geordie.

Samantha tried to pull away as the hands began to pull the tape from her eyes. They were stripping away her only defence. Now they would have to kill her. 'No!' she shouted. 'Please, I don't want to see your faces!'

But it was too late. Light flooded her eyes, blinding her after the long dark. She saw nothing but a vague shadow before her. She trembled and turned her head away, refusing to look at her captors.

A hand turned her face back forcibly, and she saw Harold. Her knees gave way. He caught her before she reached the floor, and propped her trembling body against the wall. Samantha sobbed with relief and anger.

'Oh god, you're a terrible beast. I was terrified. Why did you do this to me?'

'Surely it wasn't all that bad. I thought I heard some Samantha-orgasms as we drove along, and I'd know your smell anywhere.'

'It was still a beastly trick,' she said.

'Really? I thought you liked the idea of being found and abducted by a stranger. Isn't that what the deserted-barn fantasy was all about?'

Samantha was in the quandary familiar to everyone who comes too close to realising a favourite fantasy: frightened by reality but unwilling to let the fantasy go.

'Don't tell me I've gone to all the trouble of finding this place and making it habitable only to have you decide not to go through with it,' Harold said.

Samantha felt a flash of guilt. He had done all this for her, and now she was having second thoughts. She shook off the fear and concentrated on the fantasy. She saw that they were in a stable. It had an air of abandonment. It was obviously remote. Her 'captors' had led her from the van to the stable in broad daylight and no one had remarked on it. She saw that the floors had been swept, and the straw in the loose box across across from her looked new. There was a trail of straw leading to the loft, and she guessed that Harold had gone to the trouble to provide a bed for her to lie in. Samantha looked at her lover and told him that she still wanted to go ahead with the plan. 'It's just that your method was a bit off-putting.'

'You mean you didn't want the Mick and the Geordie to have their way with you?'

239

Samantha blushed. 'I came during the trip.'

'Several times,' Harold interjected.

Samantha blushed again. 'How can you be so sure?'

Harold merely looked at her.

'Oh, all right,' she admitted. 'I was excited. I couldn't help myself. It all seemed so real. I was all tied up and two strangers were taking me away. It only got frightening when I got here. I didn't know you were so good at accents. You certainly fooled me. Scared me, too. Did you intend to do that? To put me off?'

'Not really to put you off. I doubt that anything would do that, and you've just proved me right. I just wanted to lend a touch of realism to the affair, to see how strong your fantasy is. Damned strong, it turns out. And,' he continued sheepishly, 'I enjoyed your reaction when you thought you were being kidnapped.'

'Well, now that that's settled, what are you waiting for?' Samantha asked.

Harold lifted her to her feet, took her in his arms and kissed her thoroughly.

'Would you really like to cut my clothes off?' Samantha asked shyly.

'Well, maybe some time. But that's a nice dress – too nice to ruin.'

'Then I'll find something at the charity shop next time I'm in town.'

Harold kissed her again. Then he led her into the loose box and tethered her collar to one of the rings in the wall. 'Wait here,' he told her. 'I want to get some things from the van.'

Samantha looked worriedly at him. 'This isn't another trick, is it? You're not going to leave me here?'

'Well, isn't that the whole idea?'

'Yes,' she agreed, 'but not . . . just like that?'

'No, not just like that. Back in a minute.'

Tethered in the loose-box, Samantha examined the stable. There was nothing else to do. A good deal of time passed. Samantha had time to imagine being abandoned there. Her excitement rose in spite of the fears her practical side conjured up. She was feeling the familiar warmth between her legs. When Harold came back with the hold-all, she was well on the way to orgasm.

'We're going to do things a bit differently,' he announced. 'You'll remember this for a long time. Since you're wearing such a nice dress, though, we'll pause to get it off before we begin.'

'Are you sure you don't just want to see me naked?' Samantha seemed to have recovered from her fright remarkably well.

'That too,' Harold remarked as he unhitched her from the ring. He turned her about and set about untying her wrists and elbows. 'You must have strained a bit. I may have to cut these knots.' He finally freed her, and Samantha swung her arms in circles to get rid of the cramp. Harold stood and watched. It was still a marvel to him that she wanted to be tied for so long.

When she had finished her exercises, Samantha looked questioningly at him. 'What now?'

Harold produced the newly-purchased leather helmet from the holdall, watching for Samantha's reaction to it. Her breasts rose and fell as her breathing quickened, and he was pleased that she was pleased. 'Samantha, Samantha, let down your hair,' he paraphrased, 'otherwise this will never go over your head.'

Samantha's hair was in a French twist, slightly loosened by her earlier struggles. She removed the pins and let it down. It nearly reached her shoulders, and Harold wondered how long she intended to let it grow.

He retrieved her pants from the floor and stuffed them into her mouth before fitting the leather helmet

241

over her head. It covered her face completely. He set about fastening the buckles behind her head, pulling them tight and buckling them. He locked the straps with small padlocks that passed through eyes in the tongues of the buckles. The tight mask covered her mouth, so that she could not spit out the panties. Her eyes were covered as well. There were only two small holes for her to breathe through in the nose-piece. Except for that, the helmet rendered her featureless. Samantha shuddered as she touched her new mask with exploratory hands. She nodded in satisfaction and stood waiting for him to get to the next step.

The next step was to undress her right down to her stockings, suspenders and the high-heeled boots. Harold unlocked the steel collar and replaced it with the new leather dog-training collar, making sure that the two metal studs on the inside were in firm contact with the back of her neck. Samantha made a questioning noise from beneath her helmet as she felt the studs press into her.

'Not to worry,' Harold soothed. 'Trust me, you're going to enjoy this.'

Samantha's arms dropped to her sides.

Next he fitted the bra around her and fastened it at the back. Then her breasts went into the leather cups and her arms through the straps. Samantha remained silent, even though he guessed she was wondering about the bra. 'Hands behind your back,' he commanded when he had finished with the bra.

Obediently, as on so many past occasions, Samantha brought her hands behind her and he tied her wrists tightly, palm to palm as she had directed on their first meeting. To Harold that seemed like an age ago. Next he tied her elbows, making them touch as he had before. Harold stepped back for a moment to admire her. Even with the helmet on and her hands tied behind her back

242

Samantha looked beautiful, he thought. The stockings and suspenders, the boots and bra, added an extra *frisson*. The leather collar had a ring in front, and to this he attached a short length of cord, forming a lead. He tugged on it, and Samantha followed as he led her to the stairs and then up to the loft. He made her go first, climbing behind her in case she slipped. She stepped carefully, and their progress was slow, but eventually they were up. Aware that she was on level ground, Samantha walked more confidently as he led her into the office. There he left her while he went down again to fetch the holdall.

He produced the two new dildoes from the bag and attached the electrical connections to them, making them firm enough to resist Samantha's struggles. He screwed them into the sockets of the dildo-pants and worked the whole thing up her nylon-sheathed legs. He enjoyed the touch of the smooth stockings, and Samantha enjoyed the touch of his hands as he prepared her for her big adventure. She shivered when he inserted the dildoes. The wires dangled down beside her catheter.

Harold led the catheter and the wires out through one leg of the pants before he fitted them to her body, closed and locked the zipper. A similar lock secured the leather bra. Samantha stood docilely as he did all this to her, trusting him to care for her and to give her pleasure. Harold had never enjoyed this degree of trust, nor felt so determined to give any woman what he wanted to give this one.

He made the last connection to the leather bra, which had two terminals protruding from the undersides of the cups. The terminals were connected to wires inside the cups, designed to give the wearer the same shock as the twin dildoes in her anus and vagina. Samantha was now wired for pleasure, although she did not yet know it, and despite the fact that most people would have called it torture.

Harold led Samantha into the rudimentary bathroom at the back of the office. There he aimed the catheter at the toilet bowl and unclamped it. Judging from the enthusiasm with which Samantha peed, she must have had a very full bladder. When the stream ceased, he clamped the catheter once more. Good job they forgot to turn off the water, he thought as he flushed the toilet.

Outside the stable the sun was setting. The long shadows of trees lay across the floor as Harold led Samantha to the pile of straw he had brought for the purpose. He left her standing once again while he fetched the chair and seated her once more in the centre of the pile. There he tied her legs once more at ankles, knees and thighs. She trembled with anticipation as he finished binding her. Helpless once more, Samantha made a small sound of satisfaction. Once again he stepped back to admire the finished result.

Yes, he told himself, she was beautiful. He leaned close to her ear and told her the same thing. 'Mmm,' Samantha said. He took her featureless head in both hands and kissed her on the mouth, through the leather helmet. The thick leather allowed only the faintest sign that Samantha returned the kiss. Harold stood with both hands on the chair back. Abruptly he tipped it forward, and Samantha was catapulted onto the straw. She landed face-down, winded and surprised. Giving her no time to recover, Harold tethered her by the ankles to an upright, making sure that Samantha could not tumble from her eyrie, no matter how much she struggled. He left her to her own devices as he descended the stairs, crossed the floor of the darkening building, and closed the door. He locked it behind him and drove away in the van, trying not to think too hard about Samantha lying helpless in the abandoned stable. As before, he was not wholly successful.

Unlike the last time he had left Samantha alone all night, Harold managed to sleep. Nevertheless, he was

244

up with the lark – and with an erection. This time he did not dawdle about the house. He got straight into the van and drove back to the stable.

From outside, everything looked as it had the evening before, so he judged that Samantha was lying undisturbed on her straw pile. He took the remote control box from his pocket and thumbed the switch to the first position. That would wake Samantha with a gently pulsing current from her twin dildoes and the leather bra, if she was not yet awake. Harold imagined that her sleep had been a bit more disturbed than his had been. He opened the door and entered the building. From aloft there were animal noises and muffled thumps as Samantha woke up to the magic of electro-sex, as the advertisement had called it.

He mounted the stairs silently in order to look at Samantha without her knowledge. She must have guessed he was somewhere about, if only because her hitherto passive dildoes had become disturbingly active, and the bra was sending its disturbing signals to her breasts and nipples. Samantha lay on her side with her back to the stairs. From there, Harold could see her wrists and arms working against the cords that bound her. There were deep red marks on her skin where she had pulled against the cords during the night. Samantha's hips were thrusting gently backward and forward as she savoured the new sensations. She straightened her bound legs and rolled over onto her stomach, her hips still moving as she ground them against the floor. She moaned as she drove the dildo deeper into her cunt. Harold had to admire her instant adaptation to the electric stimuli. She seemed to have wasted no time trying to guess how it was being done, but concentrated instead on the pleasure she was getting. Her breasts pressed against the floor as well, holding her nipples in contact with the electrodes in the cups of her leather bra. Samantha wriggled and squirmed and drove herself toward orgasm. She gave a loud cry through her gag as she reached the goal, but once there she didn't stop. Her cries grew more urgent as she came repeatedly. Harold could see the pauses between climaxes, and he watched in growing excitement as Samantha rose to the next spike of pleasure.

Her moans were nearly continuous, and her heaving and bucking grew more frenzied rather than less. Obviously the night's exercises had not exhausted her. Harold turned the current up another notch. Samantha cried out, and her body did its dance to a faster tempo. She rolled from side to side, jerking herself along the floor as if trying to escape the things inside her. When her tethered ankles brought her up short she flung herself into the most remarkable gymnastics, moaning loudly, her hips pumping wildly. Her muffled cry ended abruptly as she slumped in the straw, twitching in the aftermath of her pleasure. She moaned softly with each laboured breath.

Harold's erection was getting to be a problem. He switched Samantha off and got undressed. But he didn't want to untie Samantha just yet. He went and lay beside her, holding her in his arms as she recovered. He nuzzled her and kissed her neck above the leather collar. Samantha pressed herself against him, sighing now in contentment.

They lay for a long time, Harold dividing his attention between the shadows moving across the floor and Samantha lying bound and gagged beside him. He stroked her nylon-sheathed legs, liking the contrast between the sheer stockings and the tight cords that held her legs together. Samantha wriggled to his touch. He rubbed the fronts of her thighs, moving his hand from her stockings to the leather pants holding the dildoes inside her. When he began to rub her over her cunt

Samantha moaned with renewed excitement. She began to make small thrusting movements with her hips as her excitement rose.

Harold continued to arouse her until her breathing was ragged and her movements continuous. Then he stood up and switched the control to the shock position. The batteries were still fresh, and Samantha cried out as the low voltage current shot through her cunt and anus and flowed all over her breasts and nipples. It would have been a full-throated scream but for the gag. It seemed as if every muscle in her body went into spasm as the current flowed between her cunt and anus and tortured her breasts. She rolled violently away from him and onto her back, her spine arching like a bow. She relaxed momentarily and beat a rapid tattoo on the floor with her booted heels as the agony went on and on. Harold watched, his excitement growing. The ragged, muffled scream stopped each time she had to draw breath, resuming immediately she had filled her lungs. Samantha was becoming breathless as the torture went on, the screams lower yet more desperate. Suddenly her hips began to pump up and down as the pain became the most exquisite pleasure. 'Oh!' she said, and then 'Ohhhh!' again as she came. Then she became silent, her body arched and rigid.

Harold turned off the current and Samantha's muscles relaxed, but still she made no sound other than her rapid and ragged breathing. Her breasts heaved as she drew breath and then sighed it out again. Harold called her name, and Samantha moaned feebly. He looked her over but there was nothing visibly wrong with her. Her carotid pulse beat strongly below the leather collar. She was conscious, he concluded, rolling her over onto her side but leaving her tied and gagged. The straight-sexers would have a fit, but he knew Samantha – and he knew she would not want to get loose yet.

It took a long time for Samantha to recover from the encounter with the electric shock. Harold pulled the chair over and sat watching her twitch in the straw. He admitted to himself that he had enjoyed torturing her almost as much as she had enjoyed the pain. It seemed that his growing sadism matched Samantha's growing desire for pain and humiliation. He admired his handiwork in tying his lover and wiring her up for pleasure. He didn't want to spoil the tableau either, but his cock was aching to plunge into something warm and welcoming.

When he could wait no longer, Harold went to Samantha and began to loosen the cords holding her legs together. She stirred at his touch and moaned softly. Finally her legs were free and parted. 'Can you stand?' he asked her.

Samantha shook her head. He dragged the chair over and sat her down in it. Leaving her wrists and elbows tied, Harold unlocked the leather pants, bra and helmet. He got those off her as fast as he could. Samantha blinked in the light and worked her jaws to ease the ache from being gagged for so long.

'Toilet!' she said in a hoarse croak.

She must be desperate after the night in bondage. He carried Samantha into the office and sat her on the toilet. He aimed the end of the catheter into the bowl between her thighs and unclamped it. The resulting flood would have pleased Noah.

'Take the plug out of my arse,' Samantha said. 'I have to shit as well.'

He did; she did. Then he found there was no toilet paper. He flushed the toilet and wet his hand in clean water. Reaching between her spread legs, he wiped her arse, dipping more water from the toilet until she was clean. Samantha watched him perform this intimate service with a doubtful expression.

'No one else I know would do that for a woman.'

'Of course they would,' he replied, 'if the need arose.'

Samantha shook her head. 'Why are you so good to me?'

'Because I want to be. And because you're beautiful.'

After a short silence Samantha changed the subject. 'Do you think Amanda looks like me? A younger me, I mean? Is she beautiful?'

Harold replied at once. 'Very much. And when she gets to be your age she'll be even more beautiful than she is now.' He changed the subject in his turn, feeling uncomfortable with the turn the conversation had taken. 'And speaking of age, start thinking about November, and begin leaving hints about what you'd like to get.'

Samantha looked worriedly at him. She said softly, 'Another year. Next year I'll be one year older.'

'Yes. So will I – and the rest of the world.'

'Will you still be here next year, and the one after that, when I am older still?'

Harold knelt before her as she squatted on the toilet and put his arms around her shoulders. Samantha looked steadily at him. He looked steadily back. This sounded serious. Samantha had never before asked him about the future. He remembered telling Amanda that they took each day as it came. Now, apparently, that was about to change. Harold was not sure he liked the idea of growing up, but he liked the idea of searching for another Samantha even less. 'Yes, and the ones after that, if you still want me as much as I want you.' There. The words were out. But he felt better instead of worse, free rather than trapped. It was a paradox – like the increased sense of freedom Samantha spoke of when she was bound and helpless. At least, he told himself, he hadn't actually used the L-word.

He pulled her tightly to him, her head on his shoulder. Harold was conscious of tears running down

249

his back. His lover – this beautiful older woman who had taught him about passion and tenderness and joyful sex – was crying, because he had promised to stay with her. He hoped the tears were happy ones, but did not ask just then. His earlier experience reminded him that women sometimes acted strangely. He wondered how being married again would feel. He would have to tell his mates, and his parents. His mother would be happy.

Samantha had more to say. 'I was so afraid that you might prefer Amanda to me. She's nearly twenty, just about the right age for you. I'll be thirty-nine in November. We both know what comes after that. Amanda really likes you. Do you . . . like her?'

Harold was in a corner now. No way out. 'Yes, I do,' he said. 'But I love her mother.'

Samantha began to cry again, but these seemed more like happy tears. Harold felt himself relax as the crisis passed. He had got the word out after trying for so long not to say it. Samantha seemed happy. He knew he was.

'Take me back to the straw pile and fuck me stupid,' Samantha commanded.

The leading publisher of fetish and adult fiction

TELL US WHAT YOU THINK!

Readers' ideas and opinions matter to us. Take a few minutes to fill in the questionnaire below and you'll be entered into a prize draw to win a year's worth of Nexus books (36 titles)

Terms and conditions apply – see end of questionnaire.

1. Sex: Are you male ☐ female ☐ a couple ☐?

2. Age: Under 21 ☐ 21–30 ☐ 31–40 ☐ 41–50 ☐ 51–60 ☐ over 60 ☐

3. Where do you buy your Nexus books from?

☐ A chain book shop. If so, which one(s)?

_____

☐ An independent book shop. If so, which one(s)?

_____

☐ A used book shop/charity shop
☐ Online book store. If so, which one(s)?

_____

4. How did you find out about Nexus Books?

☐ Browsing in a book shop
☐ A review in a magazine
☐ Online
☐ Recommendation
☐ Other _____

5. In terms of settings which do you prefer? (Tick as many as you like)

☐ Down to earth and as realistic as possible
☐ Historical settings. If so, which period do you prefer?

_____

☐ Fantasy settings – barbarian worlds

- ☐ Completely escapist/surreal fantasy
- ☐ Institutional or secret academy
- ☐ Futuristic/sci fi
- ☐ Escapist but still believable
- ☐ Any settings you dislike?

_____

- ☐ Where would you like to see an adult novel set?

_____

6. In terms of storylines, would you prefer:

- ☐ Simple stories that concentrate on adult interests?
- ☐ More plot and character-driven stories with less explicit adult activity?
- ☐ We value your ideas, so give us your opinion of this book:

_____

_____

_____

7. In terms of your adult interests, what do you like to read about? (Tick as many as you like)

- ☐ Traditional corporal punishment (CP)
- ☐ Modern corporal punishment
- ☐ Spanking
- ☐ Restraint/bondage
- ☐ Rope bondage
- ☐ Latex/rubber
- ☐ Leather
- ☐ Female domination and male submission
- ☐ Female domination and female submission
- ☐ Male domination and female submission
- ☐ Willing captivity
- ☐ Uniforms
- ☐ Lingerie/underwear/hosiery/footwear (boots and high heels)
- ☐ Sex rituals
- ☐ Vanilla sex
- ☐ Swinging

☐ Cross-dressing/TV
☐ Enforced feminisation
☐ Others – tell us what you don't see enough of in adult fiction:

_____

_____

_____

8. Would you prefer books with a more specialised approach to your
   interests, i.e. a novel specifically about uniforms? If so, which
   subject(s) would you like to read a Nexus novel about?

_____

_____

_____

9. Would you like to read true stories in Nexus books? For instance, the
   true story of a submissive woman, or a male slave? Tell us which
   true revelations you would most like to read about:

_____

_____

_____

10. What do you like best about Nexus books?

_____

_____

11. What do you like least about Nexus books?

_____

_____

12. Which are your favourite titles?

_____

_____

13. Who are your favourite authors?

_____

_____

14. **Which covers do you prefer? Those featuring:**
    (tick as many as you like)

☐ Fetish outfits
☐ More nudity
☐ Two models
☐ Unusual models or settings
☐ Classic erotic photography
☐ More contemporary images and poses
☐ A blank/non-erotic cover
☐ What would your ideal cover look like?

_____

15. **Describe your ideal Nexus novel in the space provided:**

_____

_____

_____

16. **Which celebrity would feature in one of your Nexus-style fantasies?**
    We'll post the best suggestions on our website – anonymously!

_____

THANKS FOR YOUR TIME

Now simply write the title of this book in the space below and cut out the
questionnaire pages. Post to: Nexus, Marketing Dept., Thames Wharf Studios,
Rainville Rd, London W6 9HA

Book title: _____

TERMS AND CONDITIONS

NEXUS NEW BOOKS

To be published in February 2006

AQUA DOMINATION
William Doughty

Just why would Mary go back to David and his bizarre bathroom? What could be crazier than designing and equipping a luxurious bathroom for the soapy, slippery domination of women? Yet she has returned to submit to watery domination, while dressed in fetish garments of plastic and rubber. And having seen the bathroom, can her friends – Jack, Carol and Faye – resist plunging into such slippery submission?

£6.99 ISBN 0 352 34020 7

TOKYO BOUND
Sachi

James Burke's mastery of the Tao of sex made him a prince of the Excalibur, a Tokyo host club that catered to wealthy women with particular tastes. He brought intense pleasure through the universal force of chi. His world was sublime until a secret society learned of his skill and sought the dark side of his Tao, the power to inflict pain. They would have it or destroy him.

£6.99 ISBN 0 352 34019 3

PLEASING THEM
William Doughty

Robert Shawnescrosse introduces his young and beautiful wife to the peculiar delights he shares with his carefully selected servants at the most peculiar house in Victorian England. Yet he has an even darker secret which requires everyone at the manor to work harder to satisfy the strange desires of three men of dubious integrity.

Why does the puritanical Mr Blanking send young ladies into a muddy pond wearing only their hats? Can the wicked Sir Horace ever obtain the satisfaction he craves through cruelty? And why is David making such strange demands? How can Robert, Jane and their servants offer pleasures extreme enough to please them?

£6.99 ISBN 0 352 34015 0

If you would like more information about Nexus titles, please visit our website at www.nexus-books.co.uk, or send a stamped addressed envelope to:

Nexus, Thames Wharf Studios,
Rainville Road, London W6 9HA

NEXUS BACKLIST

This information is correct at time of printing. For up-to-date information, please visit our website at www.nexus-books.co.uk

All books are priced at £6.99 unless another price is given.

- - - - - - ✂ -

Please send me the books I have ticked above.

Name   ....

Address   ....

               ....

               ....

               .... Post code ....

Send to: **Virgin Books Cash Sales, Thames Wharf Studios, Rainville Road, London W6 9HA**

US customers: for prices and details of how to order books for delivery by mail, call 1-800-343-4499.

Please enclose a cheque or postal order, made payable to **Nexus Books Ltd**, to the value of the books you have ordered plus postage and packing costs as follows:

UK and BFPO – £1.00 for the first book, 50p for each subsequent book.

Overseas (including Republic of Ireland) – £2.00 for the first book, £1.00 for each subsequent book.

If you would prefer to pay by VISA, ACCESS/MASTERCARD, AMEX, DINERS CLUB or SWITCH, please write your card number and expiry date here:

....

Please allow up to 28 days for delivery.

Signature ....

Our privacy policy

We will not disclose information you supply us to any other parties. We will not disclose any information which identifies you personally to any person without your express consent.

From time to time we may send out information about Nexus books and special offers. Please tick here if you do *not* wish to receive Nexus information. ☐

- - - - - - ✂ -